T

GREEN FOREST
SERIES

LIGHTFOOT THE DEER
BLACKY THE CROW
WHITEFOOT THE WOOD MOUSE
BUSTER BEAR'S TWINS

By
THORNTON W. BURGESS

With Illustrations by
HARRISON CADY

Contents

List of Illustrations

Introduction

   Since Thornton W. Burgess debuted his first book in 1910, his bedtime stories have captivated many readers in many generations. One can truly say that his stories have stood the test of time.

   Published first in 1921-1923, the four classic books of Burgess' Green Forest series (***Lightfoot the Deer, Blacky the Crow, Whitefoot the Wood Mouse,*** and ***Buster Bear's Twins***) feature the adventures of the courageous Lightfoot, the mischievous Blacky, the timid but wise Whitefoot, and the playful Buster Bear's twins (Boxer and Woof-Woof). Through Burgess' compelling and engaging storytelling way, these creatures come alive in the way they feel, think, and talk. Readers will find out how these creatures live in the Green Forest, what their characteristics and habits are, how they interact with each other, and how they react to their enemies.

   The charming fables in these books are perfect for young readers to explore the natural world and at the same time, nurture their imagination. These stories also offer invaluable lessons about friendship, teamwork, family relations, and love.

   So, enjoy the stories and have a fun reading time!

LIGHTFOOT THE DEER

Dedication

Chapter I
PETER RABBIT MEETS LIGHTFOOT

PETER RABBIT was on his way back from the pond of Paddy the Beaver deep in the Green Forest. He had just seen Mr. and Mrs. Quack start toward the Big River for a brief visit before leaving on their long, difficult journey to the far-away Southland. Farewells are always rather sad, and this particular farewell had left Peter with a lump in his throat, — a queer, choky feeling.

"If I were sure that they would return next spring, it wouldn't be so bad," he muttered. "It's those terrible guns. I know what it is to have to watch out for them. Farmer Brown's boy used to hunt me with one of them, but he doesn't anymore. But even when he did hunt me, it wasn't anything like what the Ducks have to go through. If I kept my eyes and ears open, I could tell when a hunter was coming and could hide in a hole if I wanted to. I never had to worry about my meals. But with the Ducks, it is a thousand times worse. They've got to eat while making that long journey, and they can eat only where there is the right kind of food. Hunters with terrible guns know where those places are and hide there until the Ducks come, and the Ducks have no way of knowing whether the hunters are waiting for them or not. That isn't hunting. It's— it's—"

"Well, what is it? What are you talking to yourself about, Peter Rabbit?"

Peter looked up with a start to find the soft, beautiful eyes of Lightfoot the Deer gazing down at him over the top of a little hemlock tree.

"It's awful," declared Peter. "It's worse than unfair. It doesn't give them any chance at all."

"I suppose it must be so if you say so," replied Lightfoot, "but you might tell me what all this awfulness is about."

Peter grinned. Then he began at the beginning and told Lightfoot all about Mr. and Mrs. Quack and the many dangers they must face on their long journey to the far-away Southland and back again in the spring, all because of the heartless hunters with terrible guns. Lightfoot listened and his great soft eyes were filled with pity for the Quack family.

"I hope they will get through all right," said he, "and I hope they will get back in the spring. It is bad enough to be hunted by men at one time of the year, as no one knows better than I do, but to be hunted in the spring as well as in the fall is more than twice as bad. Men are strange creatures. I do not understand them at all. None of the people of the Green Forest would think of doing such terrible things. I suppose it is quite right to hunt others in order to get enough to eat, though I am thankful to say that I never have had to do that, but to hunt others just for the fun of hunting is something I cannot understand at all. And yet that is what men seem to do it for. I guess the trouble is they never have been hunted themselves and don't know how it feels. Sometimes I think I'll hunt one someday just to teach him a lesson. What are you laughing at, Peter?"

"At the idea of you hunting a man," replied Peter. "Your heart is all right, Lightfoot, but you are too timid and gentle to frighten anyone. Big as you are I wouldn't fear you."

With a single swift bound, Lightfoot sprang out in front of Peter. He stamped his sharp hoofs, lowered his handsome head until the sharp points of his antlers, which people call horns, pointed straight at Peter, lifted the hair along the back of his neck, and made a motion as if to plunge at him. His eyes, which Peter had always thought so soft and gentle, seemed to flash fire.

"Oh!" cried Peter in a faint, frightened-sounding voice and leaped to one side before it entered his foolish little head that Lightfoot was just pretending.

Lightfoot chuckled. "Did you say I couldn't frighten anyone?" he demanded.

"I—I didn't know you could look so terribly fierce," stammered Peter. "Those antlers look really dangerous when you point them that way. Why—why—what is that hanging to them? It looks like bits of old fur. Have you been tearing somebody's coat, Lightfoot?" Peter's eyes were wide with wonder and suspicion.

Chapter II
LIGHTFOOT'S NEW ANTLERS

PETER RABBIT was puzzled. He stared at Lightfoot the Deer a wee bit suspiciously. "Have you been tearing somebody's coat?" he asked again. He didn't like to think it of Lightfoot, whom he always had believed quite as gentle, harmless, and timid as himself. But what else could he think?

Lightfoot slowly shook his head. "No," said he, "I haven't torn anybody's coat."

"Then what are those rags hanging on your antlers?" demanded Peter.

Lightfoot chuckled. "They are what is left of the coverings of my new antlers," he explained.

"What's that? What do you mean by new antlers?" Peter was sitting up very straight, with his eyes fixed on Lightfoot's antlers as though he never had seen them before.

"Just what I said," retorted Lightfoot. "What do you think of them? I think they are the finest antlers I've ever had. When I get the rest of those rags off, they will be as handsome a set as ever was grown in the Green Forest."

Lightfoot rubbed his antlers against the trunk of a tree till some of the rags hanging to them dropped off.

Peter blinked very hard. He was trying to understand, and he couldn't. Finally, he said so.

"What kind of a story are you trying to fill me up with?" he demanded indignantly. "Do you mean to tell me that those are not the antlers that you have had as long as I've known you? How can anything hard like those antlers grow? And if those are new ones, where are the old ones? Show me the old ones, and perhaps I'll believe that these are new ones. The idea of trying to make me believe that antlers grow just like plants! I've seen Bossy the Cow all summer and I know she has got the same horns she had last summer. New antlers indeed!"

"You are quite right, Peter, quite right about Bossy the Cow. She never has new horns, but that isn't any reason why I shouldn't have new antlers, is it?" replied Lightfoot patiently. "Her horns are quite different from my antlers. I have a new pair every year. You haven't seen me all summer, have you, Peter?"

"No, I don't remember that I have," replied Peter, trying very hard to remember when he had last seen Lightfoot.

"I *know* you haven't," retorted Lightfoot. "I know it because I have been hiding in a place you never visit."

"What have you been hiding for?" demanded Peter.

"For my new antlers to grow," replied Lightfoot. "When my new antlers are growing, I want to be away by myself. I don't like to be seen without them or with half-grown ones. Besides, I am very uncomfortable while the new antlers are growing, and I want to be alone."

Lightfoot spoke as if he really meant every word he said, but still Peter couldn't, he just *couldn't* believe that those wonderful great antlers had grown out of Lightfoot's head in a single summer. "Where did you leave your old ones and when did they come off?" he asked, and there was doubt in the very tone of his voice.

"They dropped off last spring, but I don't remember just where," replied Lightfoot. "I was too glad to be rid of them to notice where they dropped. You see, they were loose and uncomfortable, and I hadn't any more use for them because I knew that my new ones would be bigger and better. I've got one more point on each than I had last year." Lightfoot began once more to rub his antlers against the tree to get off the queer rags hanging to them and to polish the points. Peter watched in silence for a few minutes. Then, all his suspicions returning, he said:

"But you haven't told me anything about those rags hanging to your antlers."

"And you haven't believed what I have already told you," retorted Lightfoot. "I don't like telling things to people who won't believe me."

Chapter III
LIGHTFOOT TELLS HOW HIS ANTLERS GREW

IT is hard to believe what seems impossible. And yet what seems impossible to you may be a very commonplace matter to someone else. So, it does not do to say that a thing cannot be possible just because you cannot understand how it can be. Peter Rabbit wanted to believe what Lightfoot the Deer had just told him, but somehow he couldn't. If he had seen those antlers growing, it would have been another matter. But he hadn't seen Lightfoot since the very last of winter, and then Lightfoot had worn just such handsome antlers as he now had. So, Peter really couldn't be blamed for not being able to believe that those old ones had been lost and, in their place, new ones had grown in just the few months of spring and summer.

But Peter didn't blame Lightfoot in the least, because he had told Peter that he didn't like to tell things to people who wouldn't believe what he told them when Peter had asked him about the rags hanging to his antlers. "I'm trying to believe it," he said, quite humbly.

"It's all true," broke in another voice.

Peter jumped and turned to find his big cousin, Jumper the Hare. Unseen and unheard, he had stolen up and had overheard what Peter and Lightfoot had said.

"How do you know it is true?" snapped Peter a little crossly, for Jumper had startled him.

"Because I saw Lightfoot's old antlers after they had fallen off, and I often saw Lightfoot while his new ones were growing," retorted Jumper.

"All right! I'll believe anything that Lightfoot tells me if you say it is true," declared Peter, who greatly admires his cousin, Jumper. "Now tell me about those rags, Lightfoot. Please do."

Lightfoot couldn't resist that "please." "Those rags are what is left of a kind of covering which protected the antlers while they were growing, as I told you before," said he. "Very soon after my old ones dropped off the new ones began to grow. They were not hard, not at all like they are now. They were soft and very tender, and the blood ran through them just as it does through our bodies. They were covered with a sort of skin with hairs on it like thin fur. The ends were not sharply pointed they now are, but were big and rounded, like knobs. They were not like antlers at all, and they made my head hot and were very uncomfortable. That is why I hid away. They grew very fast, so fast that every day I could see by looking at my reflection in water that they were a little longer. It seemed to me sometimes as if all my strength went into those new antlers. And I had to be very careful not to hit them against anything. In the first place, it would have hurt, and in the second place it might have spoiled the shape of them.

"When they had grown to the length you now see, they began to shrink and grow hard. The knobs on the ends shrank until they became pointed. As soon as they stopped growing, the blood stopped flowing up in them, and as they became hard, they were no longer tender. The skin which had covered them grew dry and split, and I rubbed it off on trees and bushes. The little rags you see are what is left, but I will soon be rid of those. Then I shall be ready to fight if need be and will fear no one save man, and will fear him only when he has a terrible gun with him."

Lightfoot tossed his head proudly and rattled his wonderful antlers against the nearest tree. "Isn't he handsome," whispered Peter to Jumper the Hare; "and did you ever hear of anything so wonderful as the growing of those new antlers in such a short time? It is hard to believe, but I suppose it must be true."

"It is," replied Jumper, "and I tell you, Peter, I would hate to have Lightfoot try those antlers on me, even though I were big as a man. You've always thought of Lightfoot as timid and afraid, but you should see him when he is angry. Few people care to face him then."

Chapter IV
THE SPIRIT OF FEAR

When the days grow cold and the nights are clear,
There stalks abroad the spirit of fear.
Lightfoot the Deer.

IT is sad but true. Autumn is often called the sad time of the year, and it *is* the sad time. But it shouldn't be. Old Mother Nature never intended that it should be. She meant it to be the *glad* time. It is the time when all the little people of the Green Forest and the Green Meadows have got over the cares and worries of bringing up families and teaching their children how to look out for themselves. It is the season when food is plentiful, and everyone is fat and is, or ought to be, carefree. It is the season when Old Mother Nature intended all her little people to be happy, to have nothing to worry them for the little time before the coming of cold weather and the hard times which cold weather always brings.

But instead of this, a grim, dark figure goes stalking over the Green Meadows and through the Green Forest, and it is called the Spirit of Fear. It peers into every hiding-place and wherever it finds one of the little people, it sends little cold chills over him, little chills which jolly, round, bright Mr. Sun cannot chase away, though he shine his brightest. All night as well as all day the Spirit of Fear searches out the little people of the Green Meadows and the Green Forest. It will not let them sleep. It will not let them eat in peace. It drives them to seek new hiding-places and then drives them out of those. It keeps them ever ready to fly or run at the slightest sound.

Peter Rabbit was thinking of this as he sat at the edge of the dear Old Briar-patch, looking over to the Green Forest. The Green Forest was no longer just green; it was of many colors, for Old Mother Nature had set Jack Frost to painting the leaves of the maple-trees and the beech-trees, and the birch-trees and the poplar-trees and the chestnut-trees, and he had done his work well. Very, very lovely were the reds and yellows and browns against the dark green of the pines and the spruces and the hemlocks. The Purple Hills were more softly purple than at any other season of the year. It was all very, very beautiful.

But Peter had no thought for the beauty of it all, for the Spirit of Fear had visited even the dear Old Briar-patch, and Peter was afraid. It wasn't fear of Reddy Fox, or Redtail the Hawk, or Hooty the Owl, or Old Man Coyote. They were forever trying to catch him, but they did not strike terror to his heart because he felt quite smart enough to keep out of their clutches. To be sure, they gave him sudden frights sometimes, when they happened to surprise him, but these frights lasted only until he reached the nearest bramble-tangle or hollow log where they could not get at him. But the fear that chilled his heart now never left him even for a moment.

And Peter knew that this same fear was clutching at the hearts of Bob White, hiding in the brown stubble; of Mrs. Grouse, squatting in the thickest bramble-tangle in the Green Forest; of Uncle Billy Possum and Bobby Coon in their hollow trees; of Jerry Muskrat in the Smiling Pool; of Happy Jack Squirrel, hiding in the treetops; of Lightfoot the Deer, lying in the closest thicket he could find. It was even clutching at the hearts of Granny and Reddy Fox and of great, big Buster Bear. It seemed to Peter that no one was so big or so small that this terrible Spirit of Fear had not searched him out.

Far in the distance sounded a sudden bang. Peter jumped and shivered. He knew that everyone else who had heard that bang had jumped and shivered just as he had. It was the season of hunters with terrible guns. It was man who had sent this terrible Spirit of Fear to chill the hearts of the little meadow and forest people at this very time when Old Mother Nature had made all things so beautiful and had intended that they should be happiest and most free from care and worry. It was man who had made the autumn a sad time instead of a glad time, the very saddest time of all the year, when Old Mother Nature had done her best to make it the most beautiful.

"I don't understand these men creatures," said Peter to little Mrs. Peter,

"I DON'T UNDERSTAND THESE MEN CREATURES," SAID PETER TO LITTLE MRS. PETER.

as they stared fearfully out from the dear Old Briar-patch. "They seem to find pleasure, actually find pleasure, in trying to kill us. I don't understand them at all. They haven't any hearts. That must be the reason; they haven't any hearts."

Chapter V
SAMMY JAY BRINGS LIGHTFOOT WORD

SAMMY JAY is one of those who believe in the wisdom of the old saying, "Early to bed and early to rise." Sammy needs no alarm clock to get up early in the morning. He is awake as soon as it is light enough to see and wastes no time wishing he could sleep a little longer. His stomach wouldn't let him if he wanted to. Sammy always wakes up hungry. In this he is no different from all his feathered neighbors.

So, the minute Sammy gets his eyes open, he makes his toilet, for Sammy is very neat, and starts out to hunt for his breakfast. Long ago Sammy discovered that there is no safer time of day to visit the dooryards of those two-legged creatures called men than very early in the morning. On this particular morning, he had planned to fly over to Farmer Brown's dooryard, but at the last minute, he changed his mind. Instead, he flew over to the dooryard of another farm. It was so very early in the morning that Sammy didn't expect to find anybody stirring, so you can guess how surprised he was when, just as he came in sight of that dooryard, he saw the door of the house open, and a man step out.

Sammy stopped on the top of the nearest tree. "Now what is that man doing up as early as this?" muttered Sammy. Then he caught sight of something under the man's arm. He didn't have to look twice to know what it was. It was a gun! Yes, sir, it was a gun, a terrible gun.

"Ha!" exclaimed Sammy, and quite forgot that his stomach was empty. "Now who can that fellow be after so early in the morning? I wonder if he is going to the dear Old Briar-patch to look for Peter Rabbit, or if he is going to the Old Pasture in search of Reddy Fox, or if it is Mr. and Mrs. Grouse he hopes to kill. I think I'll sit right here and watch."

So, Sammy sat in the top of the tree and watched the hunter with the terrible gun. He saw him head straight for the Green Forest. "It's Mr. and Mrs. Grouse after all, I guess," thought Sammy. "If I knew just where they were, I'd go over and warn them." But Sammy didn't know just where they were and he knew that it might take him a long time to find them, so he once more began to think of breakfast and then, right then, another thought popped into his head. He thought of Lightfoot the Deer.

Sammy watched the hunter enter the Green Forest, then he silently followed him. From the way the hunter moved, Sammy decided that he wasn't thinking of Mr. and Mrs. Grouse. "It's Lightfoot the Deer, sure as I live," muttered Sammy. "He ought to be warned. He certainly ought to be warned. I know right where he is. I believe I'll warn him myself."

Sammy found Lightfoot right where he had expected to. "He's coming!" cried Sammy. "A hunter with a terrible gun is coming!"

Chapter VI
A GAME OF HIDE AND SEEK

THERE was a game of hide and seek that Danny Meadow Mouse once played with Buster Bear. It was a very dreadful game for Danny. But hard as it was for Danny, it didn't begin to be as hard as the game Lightfoot the Deer was playing with the hunter in the Green Forest.

In the case of Buster Bear and Danny, the latter had simply to keep out of reach of Buster. As long as Buster didn't get his great paws on Danny, the latter was safe. Then, too, Danny is a very small person. He is so small that he can hide under two or three leaves. Wherever he is, he is pretty sure to find a hiding-place of some sort. His small size gives him advantages in a game of hide and seek. It certainly does. But Lightfoot the Deer is big. He is one of the largest of the people who live in the Green Forest. Being so big, it is not easy to hide.

Moreover, a hunter with a terrible gun does not have to get close in order to kill. Lightfoot knew all this as he waited for the coming of the hunter of whom Sammy Jay had warned him. He had learned many lessons in the hunting season of the year before and he remembered every one of them. He knew that to forget even one of them might cost him his life. So, standing motionless behind a tangle of fallen trees, Lightfoot listened and watched.

Presently over in the distance he heard Sammy Jay screaming, "Thief, thief, thief!" A little sigh of relief escaped Lightfoot. He knew that that screaming of Sammy Jay's was a warning to tell him where the hunter was. Knowing just where the hunter was made it easier for Lightfoot to know what to do.

A Merry Little Breeze came stealing through the Green Forest. It came from behind Lightfoot and danced on towards the hunter with the terrible gun. Instantly Lightfoot began to steal softly away through the Green Forest. He took the greatest care to make no sound. He went in a half-circle, stopping every few steps to listen and test the air with his wonderful nose. Can you guess what Lightfoot was trying to do? He was trying to get behind the hunter so that the Merry Little Breezes would bring to him the dreaded man-scent. So long as Lightfoot could get that scent, he would know where the hunter was, though he could neither see nor hear him. If he had remained where Sammy Jay had found him, the hunter might have come within shooting distance before Lightfoot could have located him.

So, the hunter with the terrible gun walked noiselessly through the Green Forest, stepping with the greatest care to avoid snapping a stick underfoot, searching with keen eye every thicket and likely hiding-place for a glimpse of Lightfoot, and studying the ground for traces to show that Lightfoot had been there.

Chapter VII
THE MERRY LITTLE BREEZES HELP LIGHTFOOT

COULD you have seen the hunter with the terrible gun and Lightfoot the Deer that morning on which the hunting season opened, you might have thought that Lightfoot was hunting the hunter instead of the hunter hunting Lightfoot. You see, Lightfoot was behind the hunter instead of in front of him. He was following the hunter, so as to keep track of him. As long as he knew just where the hunter was, he felt reasonably safe.

The Merry Little Breezes are Lightfoot's best friends. They always bring to him all the different scents they find as they wander through the Green Forest. And Lightfoot's delicate nose is so wonderful that he can take these scents, even though they be very faint, and tell just who or what has made them. So, though he makes the best possible use of his big ears and his beautiful eyes, he trusts more to his nose to warn him of danger. For this reason, during the hunting season when he moves about, he moves in the direction from which the Merry Little Breezes may be blowing. He knows that they will bring to him warning of any danger which may lie in that direction.

Now the hunter with the terrible gun who was looking for Lightfoot knew all this, for he was wise in the ways of Lightfoot and of the other little people of the Green Forest. When he had entered the Green Forest that morning, he had first of all made sure of the direction from which the Merry Little Breezes were coming. Then he had begun to hunt in that direction, knowing that thus his scent would be carried behind him. It is more than likely that he would have reached the hiding-place of Lightfoot the Deer before the latter would have known that he was in the Green Forest, had it not been for Sammy Jay's warning.

When he reached the tangle of fallen trees behind which Lightfoot had been hiding, he worked around it slowly and with the greatest care, holding his terrible gun ready to use instantly should Lightfoot leap out.

Presently he found Lightfoot's footprints in the soft ground and studying them he knew that Lightfoot had known of his coming.

"It was that confounded Jay," muttered the hunter. "Lightfoot heard him and knew what it meant. I know what he has done; he has circled round so as to get behind me and get my scent. It is a clever trick, a very clever trick, but two can play at that game. I'll just try that little trick myself."

So, the hunter in his turn made a wide circle back, and presently there was none of the dreaded man-smell among the scents which the Merry Little Breezes brought to Lightfoot. Lightfoot had lost track of the hunter.

Chapter VIII
WIT AGAINST WIT

IT was a dreadful game the hunter with the terrible gun and Lightfoot the Deer were playing in the Green Forest. It was a matching of wit against wit, the hunter seeking to take Lightfoot's life, and Lightfoot seeking to save it. The experience of other years had taught Lightfoot much of the ways of hunters and not one of the things he had learned about them was forgotten. But the hunter in his turn knew much of the ways of Deer. So, it was that each was trying his best to outguess the other.

When the hunter found the hiding-place Lightfoot had left at the warning of Sammy Jay, he followed Lightfoot's tracks for a short distance. It was slow work, and only one whose eyes had been trained to notice little things could have done it. You see, there was no snow, and only now and then, when he had stepped on a bit of soft ground, had Lightfoot left a footprint. But there were other signs which the hunter knew how to read, — a freshly upturned leaf here, and here, a bit of moss lightly crushed. These things told the hunter which way Lightfoot had gone.

Slowly, patiently, watchfully, the hunter followed. After a while, he stopped with a satisfied grin. "I thought as much," he muttered. "He heard that pesky Jay and circled around so as to get my scent. I'll just cut across to my old trail and unless I am greatly mistaken, I'll find his tracks there."

So, swiftly but silently, the hunter cut across to his old trail, and in a few moments, he found just what he expected, — one of Lightfoot's footprints. Once more he grinned.

"Well, old fellow, I've outguessed you this time," said he to himself. "I am behind you and the wind is from you to me, so that you cannot get my scent. I wouldn't be a bit surprised if you're back right where you started from, behind that old windfall." He at once began to move forward silently and cautiously, with eyes and ears alert and his terrible gun ready for instant use.

Now when Lightfoot, following behind the hunter, had lost the scent of the latter, he guessed right away that the latter had found his tracks and had started to follow them. Lightfoot stood still and listened with all his might for some little sound to tell him where the hunter was. But there was no sound and after a little Lightfoot began to move on. He didn't dare remain still, lest the hunter should creep up within shooting distance. There was only one direction in which it was safe for Lightfoot to move, and that was the direction from which the Merry Little Breezes were blowing. So long as they brought him none of the dreaded man-smell, he knew that he was safe. The hunter might be behind him — probably he was — but ahead of him, so long as the Merry Little Breezes were blowing in his face and brought no man-smell, was safety.

Chapter IX
LIGHTFOOT BECOMES UNCERTAIN

L IGHTFOOT the Deer traveled on through the Green Forest, straight ahead in the direction from which the Merry Little Breezes were blowing. Every few steps he would raise his delicate nose and test all the scents that the Merry Little Breezes were bringing. So long as he kept the Merry Little Breezes blowing in his face, he could be sure whether or not there was danger ahead of him.

Lightfoot uses his nose very much as you and I use our eyes. It tells him the things he wants to know. He knew that Reddy Fox had been along ahead of him, although he didn't get so much as a glimpse of Reddy's red coat. Once he caught just the faintest of scents which caused him to stop abruptly and test the air more carefully than ever. It was the scent of Buster Bear. But it was so very faint that Lightfoot knew Buster was not near, so he went ahead again, but even more carefully than before. After a little he couldn't smell Buster at all, so he knew then that Buster had merely passed that way when he was going to some other part of the Green Forest.

Lightfoot knew that he had nothing to fear in that direction so long as the Merry Little Breezes brought him none of the dreaded man-scent, and he knew that he could trust the Merry Little Breezes to bring him that scent if there should be a man anywhere in front of him. You know the Merry Little Breezes are Lightfoot's best friends. But Lightfoot didn't want to keep going in that direction all day.

It would take him far away from that part of the Green Forest with which he was familiar and which he called home. It might in time take him out of the Green Forest and that wouldn't do at all. So, after a while, Lightfoot became uncertain. He didn't know just what to do. You see, he couldn't tell whether or not that hunter with the terrible gun was still following him.

Every once in a while he would stop in a thicket of young trees or behind a tangle of fallen trees uprooted by the wind. There he would stand, facing the direction from which he had come, and watch and listen for some sign that the hunter was still following. But after a few minutes of this, he would grow uneasy and then bound away in the direction from which the Merry Little Breezes were blowing, so as to be sure of not running into danger.

"If only I could know if that hunter is still following, I would know better what to do," thought Lightfoot. "I've got to find out."

Chapter X
LIGHTFOOT'S CLEVER TRICK

LIGHTFOOT the Deer is smart. Yes, Sir, Lightfoot the Deer is smart. He has to be, especially in the hunting season, to save his life. If he were not smart, he would have been killed long ago. He never makes the foolish mistake of thinking that other people are not smart. He knew that the hunter who had started out to follow him early that morning was not one to be easily discouraged or to be fooled by simple tricks. He had a very great respect for the smartness of that hunter. He knew that he couldn't afford to be careless for one little minute.

The certainty of danger is sometimes easier to bear than the uncertainty of not knowing whether or not there really is any danger. Lightfoot felt that if he could know just where the hunter was, he himself would know better what to do. The hunter might have become discouraged and given up following him. In that case he could rest and stop worrying. It would be better to know that he was being followed than not to know. But how was he to find out? Lightfoot kept turning this over and over in his mind as he traveled through the Green Forest. Then an idea came to him.

"I know what I'll do. I know just what I'll do," said Lightfoot to himself. "I'll find out whether or not that hunter is still following me, and I'll get a little rest. Goodness knows, I need a rest."

Lightfoot bounded away swiftly and ran for some distance, then he turned and quickly, but very, very quietly, returned in the direction from which he had just come but a little to one side of his old trail. After a while, he saw what he was looking for, a pile of branches which woodchoppers had left when they had trimmed the trees they had cut down. This was near the top of a little hill. Lightfoot went up the hill and stopped behind the pile of brush. For a few moments he stood there perfectly still, looking and listening. Then, with a little sigh of relief, he lay down, where, without being in any danger of being seen himself, he could watch his old trail through the hollow at the bottom of the hill. If the hunter were still following him, he would pass through that hollow in plain sight.

For a long time Lightfoot rested comfortably behind the pile of brush. There was not a suspicious movement or a suspicious sound to show that danger was abroad in the Green Forest. He saw Mr. and Mrs. Grouse fly down across the hollow and disappear among the trees on the other side. He saw Unc' Billy Possum looking over a hollow tree and guessed that Unc' Billy was getting ready to go into winter quarters. He saw Jumper the Hare squat down under a low-hanging branch of a hemlock-tree and prepare to take a nap. He heard Drummer the Woodpecker at work drilling after worms in a tree not far away. Little by little Lightfoot grew easy in his mind. It must be that that hunter had become discouraged and was no longer following him.

Chapter XI
THE HUNTED WATCHES THE HUNTER

IT was so quiet and peaceful and altogether lovely there in the Green Forest, where Lightfoot the Deer lay resting behind a pile of brush near the top of a little hill, that it didn't seem possible such a thing as sudden death could be anywhere near. It didn't seem possible that there could be any need for watchfulness. But Lightfoot long ago had learned that often danger is nearest when it seems least to be expected. So, though he would have liked very much to have taken a nap, Lightfoot was too wise to do anything so foolish. He kept his beautiful, great, soft eyes fixed in the direction from which the hunter with the terrible gun would come if he were still following that trail. He kept his great ears gently moving to catch every little sound.

Lightfoot had about decided that the hunter had given up hunting for that day, but he didn't let this keep him from being any the less watchful. It was better to be over watchful than the least bit careless. By and by Lightfoot's keen ears caught the sound of the snapping of a little stick in the distance. It was so faint a sound that you or I would have missed it altogether. But Lightfoot heard it and instantly he was doubly alert, watching in the direction from which that faint sound had come. After what seemed a long, long time, he saw something moving, and a moment later a man came into view. It was the hunter and across one arm he carried the terrible gun.

Lightfoot knew now that this hunter had patience and perseverance and had not yet given up hope of getting near enough to shoot Lightfoot. He moved forward slowly, setting each foot down with the greatest care, so as not to snap a stick or rustle the leaves. He was watching sharply ahead, ready to shoot should he catch a glimpse of Lightfoot within range.

Right along through the hollow at the foot of the little hill below Lightfoot, the hunter passed. He was no longer studying the ground for Lightfoot's tracks, because the ground was so hard and dry down there that Lightfoot had left no tracks. He was simply hunting in the direction from which the Merry Little Breezes were blowing because he knew that Lightfoot had gone in that direction, and he also knew that if Lightfoot were still ahead of him, his scent could not be carried to Lightfoot. He was doing what is called "hunting up-wind."

Lightfoot kept perfectly still and watched the hunter disappear among the trees. Then he silently got to his feet, shook himself lightly, and noiselessly stole away over the hilltop towards another part of the Green Forest. He felt sure that that hunter would not find him again that day.

Chapter XII
LIGHTFOOT VISITS PADDY THE BEAVER

DEEP in the Green Forest is the pond where lives Paddy the Beaver. It is Paddy's own pond, for he made it himself. He made it by building a dam across the Laughing Brook.

When Lightfoot bounded away through the Green Forest, after watching the hunter pass through the hollow below him, he remembered

Paddy's pond. "That's where I'll go," thought Lightfoot. "It is such a lonesome part of the Green Forest that I do not believe that hunter will come there. I'll just run over and make Paddy a friendly call."

So, Lightfoot bounded along deeper and deeper into the Green Forest. Presently through the trees he caught the gleam of water. It was Paddy's pond. Lightfoot approached it cautiously. He felt sure he was rid of the hunter who had followed him so far that day, but he knew that there might be other hunters in the Green Forest. He knew that he couldn't afford to be careless for even one little minute. Lightfoot had lived long enough to know that most of the sad things and dreadful things that happen in the Green Forest and on the Green Meadows are due to carelessness. No one who is hunted, be he big or little, can afford ever to be careless.

Now Lightfoot had known of hunters hiding near water, hoping to shoot him when he came to drink. That always seemed to Lightfoot a dreadful thing, an unfair thing. But hunters had done it before, and they might do it again. So, Lightfoot was careful to approach Paddy's pond upwind. That is, he approached the side of the pond from which the Merry Little Breezes were blowing toward him, and all the time he kept his nose working. He knew that if any hunters were hidden there, the Merry Little Breezes would bring him their scent and thus warn him.

He had almost reached the edge of Paddy's pond when from the farther shore there came a sudden crash. It startled Lightfoot terribly for just an instant. Then he guessed what it meant. That crash was the falling of a tree. There wasn't enough wind to blow over even the shakiest dead tree. There had been no sound of axes, so he knew it could not have been chopped down by men. It must be that Paddy the Beaver had cut it, and if Paddy had been working in daylight, it was certain that no one had been around that pond for a long time.

So, Lightfoot hurried forward eagerly, cautiously. When he reached the bank, he looked across towards where the sound of that falling tree had come from; a branch of a tree was moving along in the water and half hidden by it was a brown head. It was Paddy the Beaver taking the branch to his food pile.

Chapter XIII
LIGHTFOOT AND PADDY BECOME PARTNERS

THE instant Lightfoot saw Paddy the Beaver he knew that for the time being, at least, there was no danger. He knew that Paddy is one of the shyest of all the little people of the Green Forest and that when he is found working in the daytime it means that he has been undisturbed for a long time; otherwise, he would work only at night.

Paddy saw Lightfoot almost as soon as he stepped out on the bank. He kept right on swimming with the branch of a poplar-tree until he reached his food pile, which, you know, is in the water. There he forced the branch down until it was held by other branches already sunken in the pond. This done, he swam over to where Lightfoot was watching. "Hello, Lightfoot!" he exclaimed. "You are looking handsomer than ever. How are you feeling these fine autumn days?"

"Anxious," replied Lightfoot. "I am feeling terribly anxious. Do you know what day this is?"

"No," replied Paddy, "I don't know what day it is, and I don't particularly care. It is enough for me that it is one of the finest days we've had for a long time."

"I wish I could feel that way," said Lightfoot wistfully. "I wish I could feel that way, Paddy, but I can't. No, Sir, I can't. You see, this is the first of the most dreadful days in all the year for me. The hunters started looking for me before Mr. Sun was really out of bed. At least one hunter did, and I don't doubt there are others. I fooled that one, but from now to the end of the hunting season, there will not be a single moment of daylight when I will feel absolutely safe."

Paddy crept out on the bank and chewed a little twig of poplar thoughtfully. Paddy says he can always think better if he is chewing something. "That's bad news, Lightfoot. I'm sorry to hear it. I certainly am sorry to hear it," said Paddy. "Why anybody wants to hunt such a handsome fellow as you are, I cannot understand. My, but that's a beautiful set of antlers you have!"

"MY, BUT THAT'S A BEAUTIFUL SET OF ANTLERS YOU HAVE!"

"They are the best I've ever had; but do you know, Paddy, I suspect that they may be one of the reasons I am hunted so," replied Lightfoot a little sadly. "Good looks are not always to be desired. Have you seen any hunters around here lately?"

Paddy shook his head. "Not a single hunter," he replied. "I tell you what it is, Lightfoot, let's be partners for a while. You stay right around my pond. If I see or hear or smell anything suspicious, I'll warn you. You do the same for me. Two sets of eyes, ears and noses are better than one. What do you say, Lightfoot?"

"I'll do it," replied Lightfoot.

Chapter XIV
How Paddy Warned Lightfoot

IT was a queer partnership, that partnership between Lightfoot and Paddy, but it was a good partnership. They had been the best of friends for a long time. Paddy had always been glad to have Lightfoot visit his pond. To tell the truth, he was rather fond of handsome Lightfoot. You know Paddy is himself not at all handsome. On land he is a rather clumsy-looking fellow and really homely. So, he admired Lightfoot greatly. That is one reason why he proposed that they be partners.

Lightfoot himself thought the idea a splendid one. He spent that night browsing not far from Paddy's pond. With the coming of daylight, he lay down in a thicket of young hemlock-trees near the upper end of the pond. It was a quiet, peaceful day. It was so quiet and peaceful and beautiful; it was hard to believe that hunters with terrible guns were searching the Green Forest for beautiful Lightfoot. But they were, and Lightfoot knew that sooner or later one of them would be sure to visit Paddy's pond. So, though he rested and took short naps all through that beautiful day, he was anxious. He couldn't help but be.

The next morning found Lightfoot back in the same place. But this morning he took no naps. He rested, but all the time he was watchful and alert. A feeling of uneasiness possessed him. He felt in his bones that danger in the shape of a hunter with a terrible gun was not far distant.

But the hours slipped away, and little by little he grew less uneasy. He began to hope that that day would prove as peaceful as the previous day had been. Then suddenly there was a sharp report from the farther end of Paddy's pond. It was almost like a pistol shot. However, it wasn't a pistol shot. It wasn't a shot at all. It was the slap of Paddy's broad tail on the surface of the water. Instantly Lightfoot was on his feet. He knew just what that meant. He knew that Paddy had seen or heard or smelled a hunter.

It was even so. Paddy had heard a dry stick snap. It was a very tiny snap, but it was enough to warn Paddy. With only his head above water, he had watched in the direction from which that sound had come. Presently, stealing quietly along towards the pond, a hunter had come in view. Instantly Paddy had brought his broad tail down on the water with all his force. He knew that Lightfoot would know that that meant danger. Then Paddy had dived, and swimming under water, had sought the safety of his house. He had done his part, and there was nothing more he could do.

Chapter XV
THE THREE WATCHERS

WHEN Paddy the Beaver slapped the water with his broad tail, making a noise like a pistol shot, Lightfoot understood that this was meant as a warning of danger. He was on his feet instantly, with eyes, ears and nose seeking the cause of Paddy's warning. After a moment or two, he stole softly up to the top of a little ridge some distance back from Paddy's pond, but from the top of which he could see the whole of the pond. There he hid among some close-growing young hemlock-trees. It wasn't long before he saw a hunter with a terrible gun come down to the shore of the pond.

Now the hunter had heard Paddy slap the water with his broad tail. Of course. There would have been something very wrong with his ears had he failed to hear it.

"Confound that Beaver!" muttered the hunter crossly. "If there was a Deer anywhere around this pond, he probably is on his way now. I'll have a look around and see if there are any signs."

So, the hunter went on to the edge of Paddy's pond and then began to walk around it, studying the ground as he walked. Presently he found the footprints of Lightfoot in the mud where Lightfoot had gone down to the pond to drink.

"I thought as much," muttered the hunter. "Those tracks were made last night. That Deer probably was lying down somewhere near here, and I might have had a shot but for that pesky Beaver. I'll just look the land over, and then I think I'll wait here awhile. If that Deer isn't too badly scared, he may come back."

So, the hunter went quite around the pond, looking into all likely hiding-places. He found where Lightfoot had been lying, and he knew that in all probability Lightfoot had been there when Paddy gave the danger signal.

"It's of no use for me to try to follow him," thought the hunter. "It is too dry for me to track him. He may not be so badly scared, after all. I'll just find a good place and wait."

So, the hunter found an old log behind some small trees and there sat down. He could see all around Paddy's pond. He sat perfectly still. He was a clever hunter, and he knew that so long as he did not move, he was not likely to be noticed by any sharp eyes that might come that way. What he didn't know was that Lightfoot had been watching him all the time and was even then standing where he could see him. And another thing he didn't know was that Paddy the Beaver had come out of his house and, swimming under water, had reached a hiding-place on the opposite shore from which he too had seen the hunter sit down on the log. So, the hunter watched for Lightfoot, and Lightfoot and Paddy watched the hunter.

Chapter XVI
VISITORS TO PADDY'S POND

THAT hunter was a man of patience. Also, he was a man who understood the little people of the Green Forest and the Green Meadows. He knew that if he would not be seen he must not move. So, he didn't move. He kept as motionless as if he were a part of the very log on which he was sitting.

For some time there was no sign of any living thing. Then, from over the treetops in the direction of the Big River, came the whistle of swift wings, and Mr. and Mrs. Quack alighted with a splash in the pond. For a few moments they sat on the water, a picture of watchful suspicion. They were looking and listening to make sure that no danger was near. Satisfied at last, they began to clean their feathers. It was plain that they felt safe. Paddy the Beaver was tempted to warn them that they were not as safe as they thought, but as long as the hunter did not move Paddy decided to wait.

Now the hunter was sorely tempted to shoot these Ducks, but he knew that if he did, he would have no chance that day to get Lightfoot the Deer, and it was Lightfoot he wanted. So, Mr. and Mrs. Quack swam about within easy range of that terrible gun without once suspecting that danger was anywhere near.

By and by the hunter's keen eyes caught a movement at one end of Paddy's dam. An instant later Bobby Coon appeared. It was clear that Bobby was quite unsuspicious. He carried something, but just what the hunter could not make out. He took it down to the edge of the water and there carefully washed it. Then he climbed up on Paddy's dam and began to eat. You know Bobby Coon is very particular about his food. Whenever there is water near, Bobby washes his food before eating. Once more the hunter was tempted, but did not yield to the temptation, which was a very good thing for Bobby Coon.

All this Lightfoot saw as he stood among the little hemlock-trees at the top of the ridge behind the hunter. He saw and he understood. "It is because he wants to kill me that he doesn't shoot at Mr. and Mrs. Quack or Bobby Coon," thought Lightfoot a little bitterly. "What have I ever done that he should be so anxious to kill me?"

Still the hunter sat without moving. Mr. and Mrs. Quack contentedly hunted for food in the mud at the bottom of Paddy's pond. Bobby Coon finished his meal, crossed the dam and disappeared in the Green Forest. He had gone off to take a nap somewhere. Time slipped away. The hunter continued to watch patiently for Lightfoot, and Lightfoot and Paddy the Beaver watched the hunter. Finally, another visitor appeared at the upper end of the pond — a visitor in a wonderful coat of red. It was Reddy Fox.

Chapter XVII
SAMMY JAY ARRIVES

WHEN Reddy Fox arrived at the pond of Paddy the Beaver, the hunter who was hiding there saw him instantly. So did Lightfoot. But no one else did. He approached in that cautious, careful way that he always uses when he is hunting. The instant he reached a place where he could see all over Paddy's pond, he stopped as suddenly as if he had been turned to stone. He stopped with one foot lifted in the act of taking a step. He had seen Mr. and Mrs. Quack.

Now you know there is nothing Reddy Fox likes better for a dinner than a Duck. The instant he saw Mr. and Mrs. Quack, a gleam of longing crept into his eyes and his mouth began to water. He stood motionless until both Mr. and Mrs. Quack had their heads under water as they searched for food in the mud in the bottom of the pond. Then like a red flash, he bounded out of sight behind the dam of Paddy the Beaver.

Presently the hunter saw Reddy's black nose at the end of the dam as Reddy peeped around it to watch Mr. and Mrs. Quack. The latter were slowly moving along in that direction as they fed. Reddy was quick to see this. If he remained right where he was, and Mr. And Mrs. Quack kept on feeding in that direction, the chances were that he would have a dinner of fat Duck. All he need to do was to be patient and wait. So, with his eyes fixed fast on Mr. and Mrs. Quack, Reddy Fox crouched behind Paddy's dam and waited.

Watching Reddy and the Ducks, the hunter almost forgot Lightfoot the Deer. Mr. and Mrs. Quack were getting very near to where Reddy was waiting for them. The hunter was tempted to get up and frighten those Ducks. He didn't want Reddy Fox to have them, because he hoped someday to get them himself.

"I suppose," thought he, "I was foolish not to shoot them when I had the chance. They are too far away now, and it looks very much as if that red rascal will get one of them. I believe I'll spoil that red scamp's plans by frightening them away. I don't believe that Deer will be back here today anyway, so I may as well save those Ducks."

But the hunter did nothing of the kind. You see, just as he was getting ready to step out from his hiding-place, Sammy Jay arrived. He perched in a tree close to the end of Paddy's dam and at once he spied Reddy Fox. It didn't take him a second to discover what Reddy was hiding there for. "Thief, thief, thief!" screamed Sammy, and then looked down at Reddy with a mischievous look in his sharp eyes. There is nothing Sammy Jay delights in more than in upsetting the plans of Reddy Fox. At the sound of Sammy's voice, Mr. and Mrs. Quack swam hurriedly towards the middle of the pond. They knew exactly what that warning meant. Reddy Fox looked up at Sammy Jay and snarled angrily. Then, knowing it was useless to hide longer, he bounded away through the Green Forest to hunt elsewhere.

Chapter XVIII
THE HUNTER LOSES HIS TEMPER

THE hunter, hidden near the pond of Paddy the Beaver, chuckled silently. That is to say, he laughed without making any sound. The hunter thought the warning of Mr. and Mrs. Quack by Sammy Jay was a great joke on Reddy. To tell the truth, he was very much pleased. As you know, he wanted those Ducks himself. He suspected that they would stay in that little pond for some days, and he planned to return there and shoot them after he had got Lightfoot the Deer. He wanted to get Lightfoot first, and he knew that to shoot at anything else might spoil his chance of getting a shot at Lightfoot.

"Sammy Jay did me a good turn," thought the hunter, "although he doesn't know it. Reddy Fox certainly would have caught one of those Ducks had Sammy not come along just when he did. It would have been a shame to have had one of them caught by that Fox. I mean to get one, and I hope both of them, myself."

Now when you come to think of it, it would have been a far greater shame for the hunter to have killed Mr. and Mrs. Quack than for Reddy Fox to have done so. Reddy was hunting them because he was hungry. The hunter would have shot them for sport. He didn't need them. He had plenty of other food. Reddy Fox doesn't kill just for the pleasure of killing.

So, the hunter continued to sit in his hiding-place with very friendly feelings for Sammy Jay. Sammy watched Reddy Fox disappear and then flew over to that side of the pond where the hunter was. Mr. and Mrs. Quack called their thanks to Sammy, to which he replied, that he had done no more for them than he would do for anybody, or than they would have done for him.

For some time Sammy sat quietly in the top of the tree, but all the time his sharp eyes were very busy. By and by he spied the hunter sitting on the log. At first, he couldn't make out just what it was he was looking at. It didn't move, but nevertheless Sammy was suspicious. Presently he flew over to a tree where he could see better. Right away he spied the terrible gun, and he knew just what that was. Once more he began to yell, "Thief! thief! thief!" at the top of his lungs. It was then that the hunter lost his temper. He knew that now he had been discovered by Sammy Jay, and it was useless to remain there longer. He was angry clear through.

Chapter XIX
SAMMY JAY IS MODEST

AS soon as the angry hunter with the terrible gun had disappeared among the trees of the Green Forest, and Lightfoot was sure that he had gone for good, Lightfoot came out from his hiding-place on top of the ridge and walked down to the pond of Paddy the Beaver for a drink. He knew that it was quite safe to do so, for Sammy Jay had followed the hunter, all the time screaming, "Thief! thief! thief!" Everyone within hearing could tell just where that hunter was by Sammy's voice. It kept growing fainter and fainter, and by that Lightfoot knew that the hunter was getting farther and farther away.

Paddy the Beaver swam out from his hiding-place and climbed out on the bank near Lightfoot. There was a twinkle in his eyes. "That blue-coated mischief-maker isn't such a bad fellow at heart, after all, is he?" said he.

Lightfoot lifted his beautiful head and set his ears forward to catch the sound of Sammy's voice in the distance.

"Sammy Jay may be a mischief-maker, as some people say," said he, "but you can always count on him to prove a true friend in time of danger. He brought me warning of the coming of the hunter the other morning. You saw him save Mr. and Mrs. Quack a little while ago, and then he actually drove that hunter away. I suppose Sammy Jay has saved more lives than anyone I know of. I wish he would come back here and let me thank him."

Some time later Sammy Jay did come back. "Well," said he, as he smoothed his feathers, "I chased that fellow clear to the edge of the Green Forest, so I guess there will be nothing more to fear from him today. I'm glad to see he hasn't got you yet, Lightfoot. I've been a bit worried about you."

"Sammy," said Lightfoot, "you are one of the best friends I have. I don't know how I can ever thank you for what you have done for me."

"Don't try," replied Sammy shortly. "I haven't done anything but what anybody else would have done. Old Mother Nature gave me a pair of good eyes and a strong voice. I simply make the best use of them I can. Just to see a hunter with a terrible gun makes me angry clear through. I'd rather spoil his hunting than eat."

"You want to watch out, Sammy. One of these days a hunter will lose his temper and shoot you, just to get even with you," warned Paddy the Beaver.

"Don't worry about me," replied Sammy. "I know just how far those terrible guns can shoot, and I don't take any chances. By the way, Lightfoot, the Green Forest is full of hunters looking for you. I 've seen a lot of them, and I know they are looking for you because they do not shoot at anybody else even when they have a chance."

Chapter XX
LIGHTFOOT HEARS A DREADFUL SOUND

DAY after day, Lightfoot the Deer played hide and seek for his life with the hunters who were seeking to kill him. He saw them many times, though not one of them saw him. More than once a hunter passed close to Lightfoot's hiding-place without once suspecting it.

But poor Lightfoot was feeling the strain. He was growing thin, and he was so nervous that the falling of a dead leaf from a tree would startle him. There is nothing quite so terrible as being continually hunted. It was getting so that Lightfoot half expected a hunter to step out from behind every tree. Only when the Black Shadows wrapped the Green Forest in darkness did he know a moment of peace. And those hours of safety were filled with dread of what the next day might bring.

Early one morning a terrible sound rang through the Green Forest and brought Lightfoot to his feet with a startled jump. It was the baying of hounds following a trail. At first, it did not sound so terrible. Lightfoot had often heard it before. Many times he had listened to the baying of Bowser the Hound, as he followed Reddy Fox. It had not sounded so terrible then because it meant no danger to Lightfoot.

At first, as he listened early that morning, he took it for granted that those hounds were after Reddy, and so, though startled, he was not worried. But suddenly a dreadful suspicion came to him, and he grew more and more anxious as he listened. In a few minutes there was no longer any doubt in his mind. Those hounds were following his trail. It was then that the sound of that baying became terrible. He must run for his life! Those hounds would give him no rest. And he knew that in running from them, he would no longer be able to watch so closely for the hunters with terrible guns. He would no longer be able to hide in thickets. At any time he might be driven right past one of those hunters.

Lightfoot bounded away with such leaps as only Lightfoot can make. In a little while the voices of the hounds grew fainter. Lightfoot stopped to get his breath and stood trembling as he listened. The baying of the hounds again grew louder and louder. Those wonderful noses of theirs were following his trail without the least difficulty. In a panic of fear, Lightfoot bounded away again. As he crossed an old road, the Green Forest rang with the roar of a terrible gun. Something tore a strip of bark from the trunk of a tree just above Lightfoot's back. It was a bullet and it had just missed Lightfoot. It added to his terror and this in turn added to his speed.

So, Lightfoot ran and ran, and behind him the voices of the hounds continued to ring through the Green Forest.

Chapter XXI
HOW LIGHTFOOT GOT RID OF THE HOUNDS

POOR Lightfoot! It seemed to him that there were no such things as justice and fair play. Had it been just one hunter at a time against whom he had to match his wits, it would not have been so bad. But there were many hunters with terrible guns looking for him, and in dodging one he was likely at any time to meet another. This in itself seemed terribly unfair and unjust. But now, added to this was the greater unfairness of being trailed by hounds.

Do you wonder that Lightfoot thought of men as utterly heartless? You see, he could not know that those hounds had not been put on his trail but had left home to hunt for their own pleasure. He could not know that it was against the law to hunt him with dogs. But though none of those hunters looking for him were guilty of having put the hounds on his trail, each one of them was willing and eager to take advantage of the fact that the hounds were on his trail. Already he had been shot at once and he knew that he would be shot at again if he should be driven where a hunter was hidden.

The ground was damp, and scent always lies best on damp ground. This made it easy for the hounds to follow him with their wonderful noses. Lightfoot tried every trick he could think of to make those hounds lose the scent.

"If only I could make them lose it long enough for me to get a little rest, it would help," panted Lightfoot, as he paused for just an instant to listen to the baying of the hounds.

But he couldn't. They allowed him no rest. He was becoming very, very tired. He could no longer bound lightly over fallen logs or brush, as he had done at first. His lungs ached as he panted for breath. He realized that even though he should escape the hunters, he would meet an even more terrible death unless he could get rid of those hounds. There would come a time when he would have to stop. Then those hounds would catch up with him and tear him to pieces.

It was then that he remembered the Big River. He turned towards it. It was his only chance, and he knew it. Straight through the Green Forest, out across the Green Meadows to the bank of the Big River, Lightfoot ran. For just a second he paused to look behind. The hounds were almost at his heels. Lightfoot hesitated no longer but plunged into the Big River and began to swim. On the banks, the hounds stopped and bayed their disappointment, for they did not dare follow Lightfoot out into the Big River.

Chapter XXII
LIGHTFOOT'S LONG SWIM

THE Big River was very wide. It would have been a long swim for Lightfoot had he been fresh and at his best. Strange as it may seem, Lightfoot is a splendid swimmer, despite his small, delicate feet. He enjoys swimming.

But now Lightfoot was terribly tired from his long run ahead of the hounds. For a time, he swam rapidly, but those weary muscles grew still more weary, and by the time he reached the middle of the Big River, it seemed to him that he was not getting ahead at all. At first, he had tried to swim towards a clump of trees he could see on the opposite bank above the point where he had entered the water, but to do this he had to swim against the current and he soon found that he hadn't the strength to do this. Then he turned and headed for a point down the Big River. This made the swimming easier, for the current helped him instead of hindering him.

Even then he could feel his strength leaving him. Had he escaped those hounds and the terrible hunters only to be drowned in the Big River? This new fear gave him more strength for a little while. But it did not last long. He was three fourths of the way across the Big River but still that other shore seemed a long distance away. Little by little hope died in the heart of Lightfoot the Deer. He would keep on just as long as he could and then, — well, it was better to drown than to be torn to pieces by dogs.

Just as Lightfoot felt that he could not take another stroke and that the end was at hand, one foot touched something. Then, all four feet touched. A second later he had found solid footing and was standing with the water only up to his knees. He had found a little sand bar out in the Big River. With a little gasp of returning hope, Lightfoot waded along until the water began to grow deeper again. He had hoped that he would be able to wade ashore, but he saw now that he would have to swim again.

So, for a long time he remained right where he was. He was so tired that he trembled all over, and he was as frightened as he was tired. He knew that standing out there in the water he could be seen for a long distance, and that made him nervous and fearful. Supposing a hunter on the shore he was trying to reach should see him. Then he would have no chance at all, for the hunter would simply wait for him and shoot him as he came out of the water.

But rest he must, and so he stood for a long time on the little sand bar in the Big River. And little by little he felt his strength returning.

Chapter XXIII
LIGHTFOOT FINDS A FRIEND

AS Lightfoot rested, trying to recover his breath, out there on the little sand bar in the Big River, his great, soft, beautiful eyes watched first one bank and then the other. On the bank he had left, he could see two black-and-white specks moving about, and across the water came the barking of dogs. Those two specks were the hounds who had driven him into the Big River. They were barking now, instead of baying. Presently a brown form joined the black-and-white specks. It was a hunter drawn there by the barking of the dogs. He was too far away to be dangerous, but the mere sight of him filled Lightfoot with terror again. He watched the hunter walk along the bank and disappear in the bushes.

Presently out of the bushes came a boat, and in it was the hunter. He headed straight towards Lightfoot, and then Lightfoot knew that his brief rest was at an end. He must once more swim or be shot by the hunter in the boat. So, Lightfoot again struck out for the shore. His rest had given him new strength, but still he was very, very tired and swimming was hard work.

Slowly, oh so slowly, he drew nearer to the bank. What new dangers might be waiting there, he did not know. He had never been on that side of the Big River. He knew nothing of the country on that side. But the uncertainty was better than the certainty behind him. He could hear the sound of the oars as the hunter in the boat did his best to get to him before he should reach the shore.

On Lightfoot struggled. At last he felt bottom beneath his feet. He staggered up through some bushes along the bank and then for an instant it seemed to him his heart stopped beating. Right in front of him stood a man. He had come out into the back yard of the home of that man. It is doubtful which was the more surprised, Lightfoot or the man. Right then and there Lightfoot gave up in despair. He couldn't run. It was all he could do to walk. The long chase by the hounds on the other side of the Big River and the long swim across the Big River had taken all his strength.

Not a spark of hope remained to Lightfoot. He simply stood still and trembled, partly with fear and partly with weariness. Then a surprising thing happened. The man spoke softly. He advanced, not threateningly but slowly, and in a friendly way. He walked around back of Lightfoot and then straight towards him. Lightfoot walked on a few steps, and the man followed, still talking softly. Little by little he urged Lightfoot on, driving him towards an open shed in which was a pile of hay. Without understanding just how, Lightfoot knew that he had found a friend. So, he entered the open shed and with a long sigh lay down in the soft hay.

Chapter XXIV
THE HUNTER IS DISAPPOINTED

HOW he knew he was safe, Lightfoot the Deer couldn't have told you. He just knew it, that was all. He couldn't understand a word said by the man in whose yard he found himself when he climbed the bank after his long swim across the Big River. But he didn't have to understand words to know that he had found a friend. So, he allowed the man to drive him gently over to an open shed where there was a pile of soft hay and there he lay down, so tired that it seemed to him he couldn't move another step.

It was only a few minutes later that the hunter who had followed Lightfoot across the River reached the bank and scrambled out of his boat. Lightfoot's friend was waiting just at the top of the bank. Of course, the hunter saw him at once.

"Hello, Friend!" cried the hunter. "Did you see a Deer pass this way a few minutes ago? He swam across the river, and if I know anything about it, he's too tired to travel far now. I've been hunting that fellow for several days, and if I have any luck at all, I ought to get him this time."

"I'm afraid you won't have any luck at all," said Lightfoot's friend. "You see, I don't allow any hunting on my land."

The hunter looked surprised, and then his surprise gave way to anger. "You mean," said he, "that you intend to get that Deer yourself."

Lightfoot's friend shook his head. "No," said he, "I don't mean anything of the kind. I mean that that Deer is not to be killed if I can prevent it, and while it is on my land, I think I can. The best thing for you to do, my friend, is to get into your boat and row back where you came from. Are those your hounds barking over there?"

"No," replied the hunter promptly. "I know the law just as well as you do, and it is against the law to hunt Deer with dogs. I don't even know who owns those two hounds over there."

"That may be true," replied Lightfoot's friend. "I don't doubt it is true. But you are willing to take advantage of the fact that the dogs of someone else have broken the law. You knew that those dogs had driven that Deer into the Big River and you promptly took advantage of the fact to try to reach that Deer before he could get across. You are not hunting for the pleasure of hunting but just to kill. You don't know the meaning of justice or fairness. Now get off my land. Get back into your boat and off my land as quick as you can. That Deer is not very far from here and so tired that he cannot move. Just as long as he will stay here, he will be safe, and I hope he will stay until this miserable hunting season is ended. Now go."

Muttering angrily, the hunter got back into his boat and pushed off, but he didn't row back across the river.

Chapter XXV
THE HUNTER LIES IN WAIT

IF ever there was an angry hunter, it was the one who had followed Lightfoot the Deer across the Big River. When he was ordered to get off the land where Lightfoot had climbed out, he got back into his boat, but he didn't row back to the other side. Instead, he rowed down the river, finally landing on the same side but on land which Lightfoot's friend did not own.

"When that Deer has become rested, he'll become uneasy," thought the hunter. "He won't stay on that man's land. He'll start for the nearest woods. I'll go up there and wait for him. I'll get that Deer if only to spite that fellow back there who drove me off. Had it not been for him, I'd have that Deer right now. He was too tired to have gone far. He's got the handsomest pair of antlers I've seen for years. I can sell that head of his for a good price."

So, the hunter tied his boat to a tree and once more climbed out. He climbed up the bank and studied the land. Across a wide meadow, he could see a brushy old pasture and back of that some thick woods. He grinned.

"That's where that Deer will head for," he decided. "There isn't any other place for him to go. All I've got to do is be patient and wait."

So, the hunter took his terrible gun and tramped across the meadow to the brush-grown pasture. There he hid among the bushes where he could peep out and watch the land of Lightfoot's friend. He was still angry because he had been prevented from shooting Lightfoot. At the same time, he chuckled, because he thought himself very smart. Lightfoot couldn't possibly reach the shelter of the woods without giving him a shot, and he hadn't the least doubt that Lightfoot would start for the woods just as soon as he felt able to travel. So, he made himself comfortable and prepared to wait the rest of the day, if necessary.

Now Lightfoot's friend who had driven the hunter off had seen him row down the river and he had guessed just what was in that hunter's mind. "We'll fool him," said he, chuckling to himself, as he walked back towards the shed where poor Lightfoot was resting.

He did not go too near Lightfoot, for he did not want to alarm him. He just kept within sight of Lightfoot, paying no attention to him but going about his work. You see, this man loved and understood the little people of the Green Forest and the Green Meadows, and he knew that there was no surer way of winning Lightfoot's confidence and trust than by appearing to take no notice of him. Lightfoot, watching him, understood. He knew that this man was a friend and would do him no harm. Little by little, the wonderful, blessed feeling of safety crept over Lightfoot. No hunter could harm him here.

Chapter XXVI
LIGHTFOOT DOES THE WISE THING

ALL the rest of that day, the hunter with the terrible gun lay hidden in the bushes of the pasture where he could watch for Lightfoot the Deer to leave the place of safety he had found. It required a lot of patience on the part of the hunter, but the hunter had plenty of patience. It sometimes seems as if hunters have more patience than any other people.

But this hunter waited in vain. Jolly, round, red Mr. Sun sank down in the west to his bed behind the Purple Hills. The Black Shadows crept out and grew blacker. One by one the stars began to twinkle. Still the hunter waited, and still there was no sign of Lightfoot. At last it became so dark that it was useless for the hunter to remain longer. Disappointed and once more becoming angry, he tramped back to the Big River, climbed into his boat and rowed across to the other side. Then he tramped home and his thoughts were very bitter. He knew that he could have shot Lightfoot had it not been for the man who had protected the Deer. He even began to suspect that this man had himself killed Lightfoot, for he had been sure that as soon as he had become rested Lightfoot would start for the woods, and Lightfoot had done nothing of the kind. In fact, the hunter had not had so much as another glimpse of Lightfoot.

The reason that the hunter had been so disappointed was that Lightfoot was smart. He was smart enough to understand that the man who was saving him from the hunter had done it because he was a true friend. All the afternoon Lightfoot had rested on a bed of soft hay in an open shed and had watched this man going about his work and taking the utmost care to do nothing to frighten Lightfoot.

"He not only will let no one else harm me, but he himself will not harm me," thought Lightfoot. "As long as he is near, I am safe. I'll stay right around here until the hunting season is over, then I'll swim back across the Big River to my home in the dear Green Forest."

So, all afternoon Lightfoot rested and did not so much as put his nose outside that open shed. That is why the hunter got no glimpse of him. When it became dark, so dark that he knew there was no longer danger, Lightfoot got up and stepped out under the stars. He was feeling quite himself again. His splendid strength had returned. He bounded lightly across the meadow and up into the brushy pasture where the hunter had been hidden. There and in the woods back of the pasture, he browsed, but at the first hint of the coming of another day, Lightfoot turned back, and when his friend, the farmer, came out early in the morning to milk the cows, there was Lightfoot back in the open shed. The farmer smiled. "You are as wise as you are handsome, old fellow," said he.

Chapter XXVII
Sammy Jay Worries

IT isn't often Sammy Jay worries about anybody but himself. Truth to tell, he doesn't worry about himself very often. You see, Sammy is smart, and he knows he is smart. Under that pointed cap of his are some of the cleverest wits in all the Green Forest. Sammy seldom worries about himself because he feels quite able to take care of himself.

But Sammy Jay was worrying now. He was worrying about Lightfoot the Deer. Yes, Sir, Sammy Jay was worrying about Lightfoot the Deer. For two days he had been unable to find Lightfoot or any trace of Lightfoot. But he did find plenty of hunters with terrible guns. It seemed to him that they were everywhere in the Green Forest. Sammy began to suspect that one of them must have succeeded in killing Lightfoot the Deer.

Sammy knew all of Lightfoot's hiding-places. He visited every one of them. Lightfoot wasn't to be found, and no one whom Sammy met had seen Lightfoot for two days.

Sammy felt badly. You see, he was very fond of Lightfoot. You remember it was Sammy who warned Lightfoot of the coming of the hunter on the morning when the dreadful hunting season began. Ever since the hunting season had opened, Sammy had done his best to make trouble for the hunters. Whenever he had found one of them, he had screamed at the top of his voice to warn everyone within hearing just where that hunter was. Once a hunter had lost his temper and shot at Sammy, but Sammy had suspected that something of the kind might happen, and he had taken care to keep just out of reach.

Sammy had known all about the chasing of Lightfoot by the hounds. Everybody in the Green Forest had known about it. You see, everybody had heard the voices of those hounds. Once, Lightfoot had passed right under the tree in which Sammy was sitting, and a few moments later the two hounds had passed with their noses to the ground as they followed Lightfoot's trail. That was the last Sammy had seen of Lightfoot. He had been able to save Lightfoot from the hunters, but he couldn't save him from the hounds.

The more Sammy thought things over, the more he worried. "I am afraid those hounds drove him out where a hunter could get a shot and kill him, or else that they tired him out and killed him themselves," thought Sammy. "If he were alive, somebody certainly would have seen him and nobody has, since the day those hounds chased him. I declare, I have quite lost my appetite worrying about him. If Lightfoot is dead, and I am almost sure he is, the Green Forest will never seem the same."

Chapter XXVIII
THE HUNTING SEASON ENDS

THE very worst things come to an end at last. No matter how bad a thing is, it cannot last forever. So, it was with the hunting season for Lightfoot the Deer. There came a day when the law protected all Deer, — a day when the hunters could no longer go searching for Lightfoot.

Usually there was great rejoicing among the little people of the Green Forest and the Green Meadows when the hunting season ended, and they knew that Lightfoot would be in no more danger until the next hunting season. But this year there was no rejoicing. You see, no one could find Lightfoot. The last seen of him was when he was running for his life with two hounds baying on his trail and the Green Forest filled with hunters watching for a chance to shoot him.

Sammy Jay had hunted everywhere through the Green Forest. Blacky the Crow, whose eyes are quite as sharp as those of Sammy Jay, had joined in the search. They had found no trace of Lightfoot. Paddy the Beaver said that for three days Lightfoot had not visited his pond for a drink. Billy Mink, who travels up and down the Laughing Brook, had looked for Lightfoot's footprints in the soft earth along the banks and had found only old ones. Jumper the Hare had visited Lightfoot's favorite eating places at night, but Lightfoot had not been in any of them.

"I tell you what it is," said Sammy Jay to Bobby Coon, "something has happened to Lightfoot. Either those hounds caught him and killed him, or he was shot by one of those hunters. The Green Forest will never be the same without him. I don't think I shall want to come over here very much. There isn't one of all the other people who live in the Green Forest who would be missed as Lightfoot will be."

Bobby Coon nodded. "That's true, Sammy," said he. "Without Lightfoot, the Green Forest will never be the same. He never harmed anybody. Why those hunters should have been so anxious to kill one so beautiful is something I can't understand. For that matter, I don't understand why they want to kill any of us. If they really needed us for

"I TELL YOU WHAT IT IS," SAID SAMMY JAY TO BOBBY COON, "SOMETHING
HAS HAPPENED TO LIGHTFOOT."

food, it would be a different matter, but they don't. Have you been up in the Old Pasture and asked Old Man Coyote if he has seen anything of Lightfoot?"

Sammy nodded. "I've been up there twice," said he. "Old Man Coyote has been lying very low during the days, but nights he has done a lot of traveling. You know Old Man Coyote has a mighty good nose, but not once since the day those hounds chased Lightfoot has he found so much as a tiny whiff of Lightfoot's scent. I thought he might have found the place where Lightfoot was killed, but he hasn't, although he has looked for it. Well, the hunting season for Lightfoot is over, but I am afraid it has ended too late."

Chapter XXIX
MR. AND MRS. QUACK ARE STARTLED

IT was the evening of the day after the closing of the hunting season for Lightfoot the Deer. Jolly, round, red Mr. Sun had gone to bed behind the Purple Hills, and the Black Shadows had crept out across the Big River. Mr. and Mrs. Quack were getting their evening meal among the brown stalks of the wild rice along the edge of the Big River. They took turns in searching for the rice grains in the mud. While Mrs. Quack tipped up and seemed to stand on her head as she searched in the mud for rice, Mr. Quack kept watch for possible danger. Then Mrs. Quack took her turn at keeping watch, while Mr. Quack stood on his head and hunted for rice.

It was wonderfully quiet and peaceful. There was not even a ripple on the Big River. It was so quiet that they could hear the barking of a dog at a farmhouse a mile away. They were far enough out from the bank to have nothing to fear from Reddy Fox or Old Man Coyote. So, they had nothing to fear from anyone save Hooty the Owl. It was for Hooty that they took turns in watching. It was just the hour when Hooty likes best to hunt.

By and by they heard Booty's hunting call. It was far away in the Green Forest, Then Mr. and Mrs. Quack felt easier, and they talked in low, contented voices. They felt that for a while, at least there was nothing to fear.

Suddenly a little splash out in the Big River caught Mr. Quack's quick ear. As Mrs. Quack brought her head up out of the water, Mr. Quack warned her to keep quiet. Noiselessly they swam among the brown stalks until they could see out across the Big River. There was another little splash out there in the middle. It wasn't the splash made by a fish; it was a splash made by something much bigger than any fish. Presently they made out a silver line moving towards them from the Black Shadows. They knew exactly what it meant. It meant that someone was out there in the Big River moving towards them. Could it be a boat containing a hunter?

With their necks stretched high, Mr. and Mrs. Quack watched. They were ready to take to their strong wings the instant they discovered danger. But they did not want to fly until they were sure that it *was* danger approaching. They were startled, very much startled.

Presently they made out what looked like the branch of a tree moving over the water towards them. That was queer, very queer. Mr. Quack said so. Mrs. Quack said so. Both were growing more and more suspicious. They couldn't understand it at all, and it is always best to be suspicious of things you cannot understand. Mr. and Mrs. Quack half lifted their wings to fly.

Chapter XXX
THE MYSTERY IS SOLVED

IT was very mysterious. Yes, Sir, it was very mysterious. Mr. Quack thought so. Mrs. Quack thought so. There, out in the Big River, in the midst of the Black Shadows, was something which looked like the branch of a tree. But instead of moving down the river, as the branch of a tree would if it were floating, this was coming straight across the river as if it were swimming. But how could the branch of a tree swim? That was too much for Mr. Quack. It was too much for Mrs. Quack.

So, they sat perfectly still among the brown stalks of the wild rice along the edge of the Big River, and not for a second did they take their eyes from that strange thing moving towards them. They were ready to spring into the air and trust to their swift wings the instant they should detect danger. But they did not want to fly unless they had to. Besides, they were curious. They were very curious indeed. They wanted to find out what that mysterious thing moving through the water towards them was.

So, Mr. and Mrs. Quack watched that thing that looked like a swimming branch draw nearer and nearer, and the nearer it drew the more they were puzzled, and the more curious they felt. If it had been the pond of Paddy the Beaver instead of the Big River, they would have thought it was Paddy swimming with a branch for his winter food pile. But Paddy the Beaver was way back in his own pond, deep in the Green Forest, and they knew it. So, this thing became more and more of a mystery. The nearer it came, the more nervous and anxious they grew, and at the same time the greater became their curiosity.

At last Mr. Quack felt that not even to gratify his curiosity would it be safe to wait longer. He prepared to spring into the air, knowing that Mrs. Quack would follow him. It was just then that a funny little sound reached him. It was half snort, half cough, as if someone had sniffed some water up his nose. There was something familiar about that sound. Mr. Quack decided to wait a few minutes longer.

"I'll wait," thought Mr. Quack, "until that thing, whatever it is, comes out of those Black Shadows into the moonlight. Somehow I have a feeling that we are in no danger."

So, Mr. and Mrs. Quack waited and watched. In a few minutes the thing that looked like the branch of a tree came out of the Black Shadows into the moonlight, and then the mystery was solved. It was a mystery no longer. They saw that they had mistaken the antlers of Lightfoot the Deer for the branch of a tree. Lightfoot was swimming across the Big River on his way back to his home in the Green Forest. At once Mr. and Mrs. Quack swam out to meet him and to tell him how glad they were that he was alive and safe.

Chapter XXXI
A Surprising Discovery

PROBABLY there was no happier Thanksgiving in all the Great World than the Thanksgiving of Lightfoot the Deer, when the dreadful hunting season ended and he was once more back in his beloved Green Forest with nothing to fear. All his neighbors called on him to tell him how glad they were that he had escaped and how the Green Forest would not have been the same if he had not returned. So, Lightfoot roamed about without fear and was happy. It seemed to him that he could not be happier. There was plenty to eat and that blessed feeling of nothing to fear. What more could anyone ask? He began to grow sleek and fat and handsomer than ever. The days were growing colder, and the frosty air made him feel good.

Just at dusk one evening he went down to his favorite drinking place at the Laughing Brook. As he put down his head to drink, he saw something which so surprised him that he quite forgot he was thirsty. What do you think it was he saw? It was a footprint in the soft mud. Yes, Sir, it was a footprint.

For a long time Lightfoot stood staring at that footprint. In his great, soft eyes was a look of wonder and surprise. You see, that footprint was exactly like one of his own, only smaller. To Lightfoot it was a very wonderful footprint. He was quite sure that never had he seen such a dainty footprint. He forgot to drink. Instead, he began to search for other footprints, and presently he found them. Each was as dainty as that first one.

Who could have made them? That is what Lightfoot wanted to know and what he meant to find out. It was clear to him that there was a stranger in the Green Forest, and somehow he didn't resent it in the least. In fact, he was glad. He couldn't have told why, but it was true.

Lightfoot put his nose to the footprints and sniffed of them. Even had he not known by looking at those prints that they had been made by a stranger, his nose would have told him this. A great longing to find the maker of those footprints took possession of him. He lifted his handsome head and listened for some slight sound which might show that the stranger was near. With his delicate nostrils, he tested the wandering little Night Breezes for a stray whiff of scent to tell him which way to go. But there was no sound and the wandering little Night Breezes told him nothing. Lightfoot followed the dainty footprints up the bank. There they disappeared, for the ground was hard. Lightfoot paused, undecided which way to go.

Chapter XXXII
LIGHTFOOT SEES THE STRANGER

LIGHTFOOT the Deer was unhappy. It was a strange unhappiness, an unhappiness such as he had never known before. You see, he had discovered that there was a stranger in the Green Forest, a stranger of his own kind, another Deer. He knew it by dainty footprints in the mud along the Laughing Brook and on the edge of the pond of Paddy the Beaver. He knew it by other signs which he ran across every now and then. But search as he would, he was unable to find that newcomer. He had searched everywhere but always he was just too late. The stranger had been and gone.

Now there was no anger in Lightfoot's desire to find that stranger. Instead, there was a great longing. For the first time in his life Lightfoot felt lonely. So, he hunted and hunted and was unhappy. He lost his appetite. He slept little. He roamed about uneasily, looking, listening, testing every Merry Little Breeze, but all in vain.

Then, one never-to-be-forgotten night, as he drank at the Laughing

Brook, a strange feeling swept over him. It was the feeling of being watched. Lightfoot lifted his beautiful head, and a slight movement caught his quick eye and drew it to a thicket not far away. The silvery light of gentle Mistress Moon fell full on that thicket and thrust out from it was the most beautiful head in all the Great World. At least, that is the way it seemed to Lightfoot, though to tell the truth it was not as beautiful as his own, for it was uncrowned by antlers. For a long minute Lightfoot stood gazing. A pair of wonderful, great, soft eyes gazed back at him. Then that beautiful head disappeared.

With a mighty bound, Lightfoot cleared the Laughing Brook and rushed over to the thicket in which that beautiful head had disappeared. He plunged in, but there was no one there. Frantically he searched, but that thicket was empty. Then he stood still and listened. Not a sound reached him. It was as still as if there were no other living things in all the Green Forest. The beautiful stranger had slipped away as silently as a shadow.

All the rest of that night Lightfoot searched through the Green Forest, but his search was in vain. The longing to find that beautiful stranger had become so great that he fairly ached with it. It seemed to him that until he found her, he could know no happiness.

Chapter XXXIII
A DIFFERENT GAME OF HIDE AND SEEK

ONCE more Lightfoot the Deer was playing hide and seek in the Green Forest. But it was a very different game from the one he had played just a short time before. You remember that then it had been for his life that he had played, and he was the one who had done all the hiding. Now, he was "it", and someone else was doing the hiding. Instead of the dreadful fear which had filled him in that other game, he was now filled with longing, — longing to find and make friends with the beautiful stranger of whom he had just once caught a glimpse, but of whom every day he found tracks.

At times Lightfoot would lose his temper. Yes, Sir, Lightfoot would lose his temper. That was a foolish thing to do, but it seemed to him that he just couldn't help it. He would stamp his feet angrily and thrash the bushes with his great spreading antlers as if they were an enemy with whom he was fighting. More than once when he did this a pair of great, soft, gentle eyes were watching him, though he didn't know it. If he could have seen them and the look of admiration in them, he would have been more eager than ever to find that beautiful stranger.

At other times Lightfoot would steal about through the Green Forest as noiselessly as a shadow. He would peer into thickets and behind tangles of fallen trees and brush piles, hoping to surprise the one he sought. He would be very, very patient. Perhaps he would come to the thicket which he knew from the signs the stranger had left only a few moments before. Then his patience would vanish in impatience, and he would dash ahead, eager to catch up with the shy stranger. But always it was in vain. He had thought himself very clever, but this stranger was proving herself cleverer.

Of course, it wasn't long before all the little people in the Green Forest knew what was going on. They knew all about that game of hide and seek just as they had known all about that other game of hide and seek with the hunters. But now, instead of trying to help Lightfoot as they did then, they gave him no help at all. The fact is, they were enjoying that game. Mischievous Sammy Jay even went so far as to warn the stranger several times when Lightfoot was approaching. Of course, Lightfoot knew when Sammy did this, and each time he lost his temper. For the time being, he quite forgot all that Sammy had done for him when he was the one that was being hunted.

Once Lightfoot almost ran smack into Buster Bear and was so provoked by his own carelessness that instead of bounding away, he actually threatened to fight Buster. But when Buster grinned good-naturedly at him, Lightfoot thought better of it and bounded away to continue his search.

Then there were times when Lightfoot would sulk and would declare over and over to himself, "I don't care anything about that stranger. I won't spend another minute looking for her." And then within five minutes he would be watching, listening and seeking some sign that she was still in the Green Forest.

Chapter XXXIV
A STARTLING NEW FOOTPRINT

THE game of hide and seek between Lightfoot the Deer and the beautiful stranger whose dainty footprints had first started Lightfoot to seeking her had been going on for several days and nights when Lightfoot found something which gave him a shock. He had stolen very softly clown to the Laughing Brook, hoping to surprise the beautiful stranger drinking there. She wasn't to be seen. Lightfoot wondered if she had been there, so looked in the mud at the edge of the Laughing Brook to see if there were any fresh prints of those dainty feet. Almost at once he discovered fresh footprints. They were not the prints he was looking for. No, Sir, they were not the dainty prints he had learned to know so well. They were prints very near the size of his own big ones, and they had been made only a short time before.

The finding of those prints was a dreadful shock to Lightfoot. He understood instantly what they meant. They meant that a second stranger had come into the Green Forest, one who had antlers like his own. Jealousy took possession of Lightfoot the Deer; jealousy that filled his heart with rage.

"He has come here to seek that beautiful stranger I have been hunting for," thought Lightfoot. "He has come here to try to steal her away from me. He has no right here in my Green Forest. He belongs back up on the Great Mountain from which he must have come, for there is no other place he could have come from. That is where that beautiful stranger must have come from, too. I want her to stay, but I must drive this fellow out. I'll make him fight. That's what I'll do; I'll make him fight! I'm not afraid of him, but I'll make him fear me."

Lightfoot stamped his feet and with his great antlers thrashed the bushes as if he felt that they were the enemy he sought. Could you have looked into his great eyes then, you would have found nothing soft and beautiful about them. They became almost red with anger. Lightfoot quivered all over with rage. The hair on the back of his neck stood up. Lightfoot the Deer looked anything but gentle.

After he had vented his spite for a few minutes on the harmless, helpless bushes, he threw his head high in the air and whistled angrily. Then he leaped over the Laughing Brook and once more began to search through the Green Forest. But this time it was not for the beautiful stranger with the dainty feet. He had no time to think of her now. He must first find this newcomer and he meant to waste no time in doing it.

Chapter XXXV
LIGHTFOOT IS RECKLESS

IN his search for the new stranger who had come to the Green Forest, Lightfoot the Deer was wholly reckless. He no longer stole like a gray shadow from thicket to thicket as he had done when searching for the beautiful stranger with the dainty feet. He bounded along, careless of how much noise he made. From time to time, he would stop to whistle a challenge and to clash his horns against the trees and stamp the ground with his feet.

After such exhibitions of anger, he would pause to listen, hoping to hear some sound which would tell him where the stranger was. Now and then he found the stranger's tracks, and from them he knew that this stranger was doing just what he had been doing, seeking to find the beautiful newcomer with the dainty feet. Each time he found these signs, Lightfoot's rage increased.

Of course, it didn't take Sammy Jay long to discover what was going on. There is little that escapes those sharp eyes of Sammy Jay. As you know, he had early discovered the game of hide and seek Lightfoot had been playing with the beautiful young visitor who had come down to the Green Forest from the Great Mountain. Then, by chance, Sammy had visited the Laughing Brook just as the big stranger had come down there to drink. For once Sammy had kept his tongue still. "There is going to be excitement here when Lightfoot discovers this fellow," thought Sammy. "If they ever meet, and I have a feeling that they will, there is going to be a fight worth seeing. I must pass the word around."

So, Sammy Jay hunted up his cousin, Blacky the Crow, and told him what he had discovered. Then he hunted up Bobby Coon and told him. He saw Unc' Billy Possum sitting in the doorway of his hollow tree and told him. He discovered Jumper the Hare sitting under a little hemlock-tree and told him. Then he flew over to the dear Old Briar-patch to tell Peter Rabbit. Of course, he told Drummer the Woodpecker, Tommy Tit the Chickadee, and Yank Yank the Nuthatch, who were over in the Old Orchard, and they at once hurried to the Green Forest, for they couldn't think of missing anything so exciting as would be the meeting between Lightfoot and the big stranger from the Great Mountain.

Sammy didn't forget to tell Paddy the Beaver, but it was no news to Paddy. Paddy had seen the big stranger on the edge of his pond early the night before.

Of course, Lightfoot knew nothing about all this. His one thought was to find that big stranger and drive him from the Green Forest, and so he continued his search tirelessly.

Chapter XXXVI
SAMMY JAY TAKES A HAND

SAMMY JAY was bubbling over with excitement as he flew about through the Green Forest, following Lightfoot the Deer. He was so excited he wanted to scream. But he didn't. He kept his tongue still. You see, he didn't want Lightfoot to know that he was being followed. Under that pointed cap of Sammy Jay's are quick wits. It didn't take him long to discover that the big stranger whom Lightfoot was seeking was doing his best to keep out of Lightfoot's way and that he was having no difficulty in doing so because of the reckless way in which Lightfoot was searching for him. Lightfoot made so much noise that it was quite easy to know just where he was and so keep out of his sight.

"That stranger is nearly as big as Lightfoot, but it is very plain that he doesn't want to fight," thought Sammy. "He must be a coward."

Now the truth is, the stranger was not a coward. He was ready and willing to fight if he had to, but if he could avoid fighting, he meant to. You see, big as he was, he wasn't quite so big as Lightfoot, and he knew it. He had seen Lightfoot's big footprints, and from their size he knew that Lightfoot must be bigger and heavier than he. Then, too, he knew that he really had no right to be there in the Green Forest. That was Lightfoot's home and so he was an intruder. He knew that Lightfoot would feel this way about it and that this would make him fight all the harder. So, the big stranger wanted to avoid a fight if possible. But he wanted still more to find that beautiful young visitor with the dainty feet for whom Lightfoot had been looking. He wanted to find her just as Lightfoot wanted to find her, and he hoped that if he did find her, he could take her away with him back to the Great Mountain. If he had to, he would fight for her, but until he had to, he would keep out of the fight. So, he dodged Lightfoot and at the same time looked for the beautiful stranger.

All this Sammy Jay guessed, and after a while, he grew tired of following Lightfoot for nothing. "I'll have to take a hand in this thing myself," muttered Sammy. "At this rate, Lightfoot never will find that big stranger!"

So, Sammy stopped following Lightfoot and began to search through the Green Forest for the big stranger. It didn't take very long to find him. He was over near the pond of Paddy the Beaver. As soon as he saw him, Sammy began to scream at the top of his lungs. At once he heard the sound of snapping twigs at the top of a little ridge back of Paddy's pond and knew that Lightfoot had heard and understood.

Chapter XXXVII
THE GREAT FIGHT

DOWN from the top of the ridge back of the pond of Paddy the Beaver plunged Lightfoot the Deer, his eyes blazing with rage. He had understood the screaming of Sammy Jay. He knew that somewhere down there was the big stranger he had been looking for.

The big stranger had understood Sammy's screaming quite as well as Lightfoot. He knew that to run away now would be to prove himself a coward and forever disgrace himself in the eyes of Miss Daintyfoot, for that was the name of the beautiful stranger he had been seeking. He *must* fight. There was no way out of it, he *must* fight. The hair on the back of his neck stood up with anger just as did the hair on the neck of Lightfoot. His eyes also blazed. He bounded out into a little open place by the pond of Paddy the Beaver and there he waited.

Meanwhile Sammy Jay was flying about in the greatest excitement, screaming at the top of his lungs, "A fight! A fight! A fight!" Blacky the Crow, over in another part of the Green Forest, heard him and took up the cry and at once hurried over to Paddy's pond. Everybody who was near enough hurried there. Bobby Coon and Unc' Billy Possum climbed trees from which they could see and at the same time be safe. Billy Mink hurried to a safe place on the dam of Paddy the Beaver. Paddy himself climbed up on the roof of his house out in the pond. Peter Rabbit and Jumper the Hare, who happened to be not far away, hurried over where they could peep out from under some young hemlock-trees. Buster Bear shuffled down the hill and watched from the other side of the pond. Reddy and Granny Fox were both there.

For what seemed like the longest time, but which was for only a minute, Lightfoot and the big stranger stood still, glaring at each other. Then, snorting with rage, they lowered their heads and plunged together. Their antlers clashed with a noise that rang through the Green Forest, and both felt to their knees. There they pushed and struggled. Then they separated and backed away, to repeat the movement over again. It was a terrible fight. Everybody said so. If they had not known before, everybody knew now what those great antlers were for. Once the big stranger managed to reach Lightfoot's right shoulder with one of the sharp points of his antlers and made a long tear in Lightfoot's gray coat. It only made Lightfoot fight harder.

Sometimes they would rear up and strike with their sharp hoofs. Back and forth they plunged, and the ground was torn up by their feet. Both were getting out of breath, and from time to time, they had to stop for a moment's rest. Then they would come together again more fiercely than ever. Never had such a fight been seen in the Green Forest.

Chapter XXXVIII
An Unseen Watcher

AS Lightfoot the Deer and the big stranger from the Great Mountain fought in the little opening near the pond of Paddy the Beaver, neither knew or cared who saw them. Each was filled fully with rage and determined to drive the other from the Green Forest. Each was fighting for the right to win the love of Miss Daintyfoot.

Neither of them knew that Miss Daintyfoot herself was watching them. But she was. She had heard the clash of their great antlers as they had come together the first time, and she had known exactly what it meant. Timidly she had stolen forward to a thicket where, safely hidden, she could watch that terrible fight. She knew that they were fighting for her. Of course. She knew it just as she had known how both had been hunting for her. What she didn't know for some time was which one she wanted to win that fight.

Both Lightfoot and the big stranger were handsome. Yes, indeed, they were very handsome. Lightfoot was just a little bit the bigger and it seemed to her just a little bit the handsomer. She almost wanted him to win. Then, when she saw how bravely the big stranger was fighting and how well he was holding his own, even though he was a little smaller than Lightfoot, she almost hoped he would win.

That great fight lasted a long time. To pretty Miss Daintyfoot, it seemed that it never would end. But after a while, Lightfoot's greater size and strength began to tell. Little by little the big stranger was forced back towards the edge of the open place. Now he would be thrown to his knees when Lightfoot wasn't. As Lightfoot saw this, he seemed to gain new strength. At last he caught the stranger in such a way that he threw him over. While the stranger struggled to get to his feet again, Lightfoot's sharp antlers made long tears in his gray coat. The stranger was beaten, and he knew it. The instant he succeeded in getting to his feet, he turned tail and plunged for the shelter of the Green Forest. With a snort of triumph, Lightfoot plunged after him.

But now that he was beaten, fear took possession of the stranger. All desire to fight left him. His one thought was to get away, and fear gave him speed. Straight back towards the Great Mountain from which he had come the stranger headed. Lightfoot followed only a short distance. He knew that that stranger was going for good and would not come back. Then Lightfoot turned back to the open place where they had fought. There he threw up his beautiful head, crowned by its great antlers, and whistled a challenge to all the Green Forest. As she looked at him, Miss Daintyfoot knew that she had wanted him to win. She knew that there simply couldn't be anybody else so handsome and strong and brave in all the Great World.

Chapter XXXIX
LIGHTFOOT DISCOVERS LOVE

WONDERFULLY handsome was Lightfoot the Deer as he stood in the little opening by the pond of Paddy the Beaver, his head thrown back proudly, as he received the congratulations of his neighbors of the Green Forest who had seen him win the great fight with the big stranger

WONDERFULLY HANDSOME WAS LIGHTFOOT THE DEER.

who had come down from the Great Mountain. To beautiful Miss Daintyfoot, peeping out from the thicket where she had hidden to watch the great fight, Lightfoot was the most wonderful person in all the Great World. She adored him, which means that she loved him just as much as it was possible for her to love.

But Lightfoot didn't know this. In fact, he didn't know that Miss Daintyfoot was there. His one thought had been to drive out of the Green Forest the big stranger who had come down from the Great Mountain. He had been jealous of that big stranger, though he hadn't known that he was jealous. The real cause of his anger and desire to fight had been the fear that the big stranger would find Miss Daintyfoot and take her away. Of course, this was nothing but jealousy.

Now that the great fight was over, and he knew that the big stranger was hurrying back to the Great Mountain, all Lightfoot's anger melted away. In its place was a great longing to find Miss Daintyfoot. His great eyes became once more soft and beautiful. In them was a look of wistfulness. Lightfoot walked down to the edge of the water and drank, for he was very, very thirsty. Then he turned, intending to take up once more his search for beautiful Miss Daintyfoot.

When he turned, he faced the thicket in which Miss Daintyfoot was hiding. His keen eyes caught a little movement of the branches. A beautiful head was slowly thrust out, and Lightfoot gazed again into a pair of soft eyes which he was sure were the most beautiful eyes in all the Great World. He wondered if she would disappear and run away as she had the last time he saw her.

He took a step or two forward. The beautiful head was withdrawn. Lightfoot's heart sank. Then he bounded forward into that thicket. He more than half expected to find no one there, but when he entered that thicket, he received the most wonderful surprise in all his life. There stood Miss Daintyfoot, timid, bashful, but with a look in her eyes which Lightfoot could not mistake. In that instant Lightfoot understood the meaning of that longing which had kept him hunting for her and of the rage which had filled him when he had discovered the presence of the big stranger from the Great Mountain. It was love. Lightfoot knew that he loved Miss Daintyfoot and, looking into her soft, gentle eyes, he knew that Miss Daintyfoot loved him.

Chapter XL
HAPPY DAYS IN THE GREEN FOREST

THESE were happy days in the Green Forest. At least, they were happy for Lightfoot the Deer. They were the happiest days he had ever known. You see, he had won beautiful, slender, young Miss Daintyfoot, and now she was no longer Miss Daintyfoot but Mrs. Lightfoot. Lightfoot was sure that there was no one anywhere so beautiful as she, and Mrs. Lightfoot knew that there was no one so handsome and brave as he.

Wherever Lightfoot went, Mrs. Lightfoot went. He showed her all his favorite hiding-places. He led her to his favorite eating-places. She did not tell him that she was already acquainted with every one of them, that she knew the Green Forest quite as well as he did. If he had stopped to think how day after day she had managed to keep out of his sight while he hunted for her, he would have realized that there was little he could show her which she did not already know. But he didn't stop to think and proudly led her from place to place. And Mrs. Lightfoot wisely expressed delight with all she saw quite as if it were all new.

Of course, all the little people of the Green Forest hurried to pay their respects to Mrs. Lightfoot and to tell Lightfoot how glad they felt for him. And they really did feel glad. You see, they all loved Lightfoot and they knew that now he would be happier than ever, and that there would be no danger of his leaving the Green Forest because of loneliness. The Green Forest would not be the same at all without Lightfoot the Deer.

Lightfoot told Mrs. Lightfoot all about the terrible days of the hunting season and how glad he was that she had not been in the Green Forest then. He told her how the hunters with terrible guns had given him no rest and how he had had to swim the Big River to get away from the hounds.

"I know," replied Mrs. Lightfoot softly. "I know all about it. You see, there were hunters on the Great Mountain. In fact, that is how I happened to come down to the Green Forest. They hunted me so up there that I did not dare stay, and I came down here thinking that there might be fewer hunters. I wouldn't have believed that I could ever be thankful to hunters for anything, but I am, truly I am."

There was a puzzled look on Lightfoot's face. "What for?" he demanded. "I can't imagine anybody being thankful to hunters for anything."

"Oh, you stupid," cried Mrs. Lightfoot. "Don't you see that if I hadn't been driven down from the Great Mountain, I never would have found *you*?"

"You mean, I never would have found *you*," retorted Lightfoot. "I guess I owe these hunters more than you do. I owe them the greatest happiness I have ever known, but I never would have thought of it myself. Isn't it queer how things which seem the very worst possible sometimes turn out to be the very best possible?"

Blacky the Crow is one of Lightfoot's friends, but sometimes even friends are envious. It is so with Blacky. He insists that he is quite as important in the Green Forest as is Lightfoot and that his doings are quite as interesting. Therefore, just to please him the next book is to be Blacky the Crow.

BLACKY THE CROW

Dedication

TO AN AMERICAN CITIZEN WHO, DESPITE
PERSECUTION AND CHANGED CONDITIONS, HAS
BY HIS ADAPTABILITY AND INTELLIGENCE
MAINTAINED HIS PLACE IN THE LAND OF HIS
FOREFATHERS — THE CROW

Chapter I
BLACKY THE CROW MAKES A DISCOVERY

B LACKY the Crow is always watching for things not intended for his sharp eyes. The result is that he gets into no end of trouble which he could avoid. In this respect, he is just like his cousin, Sammy Jay. Between them they see a great deal with which they have no business and which it would be better for them not to see.

Now Blacky the Crow finds it no easy matter to pick up a living when snow covers the Green Meadows and the Green Forest, and ice binds the Big River and the Smiling Pool. He has to use his sharp eyes for all they are worth in order to find enough to fill his stomach, and he will eat anything in the way of food that he can swallow. Often, he travels long distances looking for food, but at night he always comes back to the same place in the Green Forest, to sleep in company with others of his family.

Blacky dearly loves company, particularly at night, and about the time jolly, round, red Mr. Sun is beginning to think about his bed behind the Purple Hills, you will find Blacky heading for a certain part of the Green Forest where he knows he will have neighbors of his own kind. Peter Rabbit says that it is because Blacky's conscience troubles him so that he doesn't dare sleep alone, but Happy Jack Squirrel says that Blacky hasn't any conscience. You can believe just which you please, though I suspect that neither of them really knows.

As I have said, Blacky is quite a traveler at this time of year, and sometimes his search for food takes him to out-of-the-way places. One day toward the very last of winter, the notion entered his black head that he would have a look in a certain lonesome corner of the Green Forest where once upon a time Redtail the Hawk had lived. Blacky knew well enough that Redtail wasn't there now; he had gone south in the fall and wouldn't be back until he was sure that Mistress Spring had arrived on the Green Meadows and in the Green Forest.

Like the black imp he is, Blacky flew over the treetops, his sharp eyes watching for something interesting below. Presently he saw ahead of him the old nest of Redtail. He knew all about that nest. He had visited it before when Redtail was away. Still, it might be worth another visit. You never can tell what you may find in old houses. Now, of course, Blacky knew perfectly well that Redtail was miles and miles, hundreds of miles away, and so there was nothing to fear from him. But Blacky learned ever so long ago that there is nothing like making sure that there is no danger. So, instead of flying straight to that old nest, he first flew over the tree so that he could look down into it.

Right away he saw something that made him gasp and blink his eyes. It was quite large and white, and it looked — it looked very much indeed like an egg! Do you wonder that Blacky gasped and blinked? Here was snow on the ground, and Rough Brother North Wind and Jack Frost had given no hint that they were even thinking of going back to the Far North. The idea of anyone laying an egg at this time of year! Blacky flew over to a tall pine-tree to think it over.

"Must be it was a little lump of snow," thought he. "Yet if ever I saw an egg, that looked like one. Jumping grasshoppers, how good an egg would taste right now!" You know Blacky has a weakness for eggs. The more he thought about it, the hungrier he grew. Several times he almost made up his mind to fly straight over there and make sure, but he didn't quite dare. If it were an egg, it must belong to somebody, and perhaps it would be best to find out who. Suddenly Blacky shook himself. "I must be dreaming," said he. "There couldn't, there just couldn't be an egg at this time of year, or in that old tumble-down nest! I'll just fly away and forget it."

So, he flew away, but he couldn't forget it. He kept thinking of it all day, and when he went to sleep that night, he made up his mind to have another look at that old nest.

Chapter II
BLACKY MAKES SURE

"As true as ever I've cawed a caw
That was a new-laid egg I saw."

"WHAT are you talking about?" demanded Sammy Jay, coming up just in time to hear the last part of what Blacky the Crow was mumbling to himself.

"Oh nothing, Cousin, nothing at all," replied Blacky. "I was just talking foolishness to myself."

Sammy looked at him sharply. "You aren't feeling sick, are you, Cousin Blacky?" he asked. "Must be something the matter with you when you begin talking about new-laid eggs, when everything's covered with snow and ice. Foolishness is no name for it. Whoever heard of such a thing as a new-laid egg this time of year."

"Nobody, I guess," replied Blacky. "I told you I was just talking foolishness. You see, I'm so hungry that I just got to thinking what I'd have if I could have anything I wanted. That made me think of eggs, and I tried to think just how I would feel if I should suddenly see a great big egg right in front of me. I guess I must have said something about it."

"I guess you must have. It isn't egg time yet, and it won't be for a long time. Take my advice and just forget about impossible things. I'm going over to Farmer Brown's corncrib. Corn may not be as good as eggs, but it is very good and very filling. Better come along," said Sammy.

"Not this morning, thank you. Some other time, perhaps," replied Blacky.

He watched Sammy disappear through the trees. Then he flew to the top of the tallest pine-tree to make sure that no one was about. When he was quite sure that no one was watching him, he spread his wings and headed for the most lonesome corner of the Green Forest.

"I'm foolish. I know I'm foolish," he muttered. "But I've just got to have another look in that old nest of Redtail the Hawk. I just can't get it out of my head that that was an egg, a great, big, white egg, that I saw there yesterday. It won't do any harm to have another look, anyway."

Straight toward the tree in which was the great tumble-down nest of Redtail the Hawk he flew, and as he drew near, he flew high, for Blacky is too shrewd and smart to take any chances. Not that he thought that there could be any danger there; but you never can tell, and it is always the part of wisdom to be on the safe side. As he passed over the top of the tree, he looked down eagerly. Just imagine how he felt when instead of one, he saw *two* white things in the old nest, — two white things that looked for all the world like eggs! The day before there had been but one; now there were *two*. That settled it in Blacky's mind; they were eggs! They couldn't be anything else.

Blacky kept right on flying. Somehow he didn't dare stop just then. He was too much excited by what he had discovered to think clearly. He had got to have time to get his wits together. Whoever had laid those eggs was big and strong. He felt sure of that. It must be someone a great deal bigger than himself, and he was of no mind to get into trouble, even for a dinner of fresh eggs. He must first find out whose they were; then he would know better what to do. He felt sure that no one else knew about them, and he knew that they couldn't run away. So, he kept right on flying until he reached a certain tall pine-tree where he could sit and think without being disturbed.

"Eggs!" he muttered. "Real eggs! Now who under the sun can have moved into Redtail's old house? And what can they mean by laying eggs before Mistress Spring has even sent word that she has started? It's too much for me. It certainly is too much for me."

Chapter III
BLACKY FINDS OUT WHO OWNS THE EGGS

TWO big white eggs in a tumbledown nest, and snow and ice everywhere! Did ever anybody hear of such a thing before?

"Wouldn't believe it, if I hadn't seen it with my own eyes," muttered

Blacky the Crow. "Have to believe them. If I can't believe them, it's of no use to try to believe anything in this world. As sure as I sit here, that old nest has two eggs in it. Whoever laid them must be crazy to start housekeeping at this time of year. I must find out whose eggs they are and then—"

Blacky didn't finish, but there was a hungry look in his eyes that would have told any who saw it, had there been any to see it, that he had a use for those eggs. But there was none to see it, and he took the greatest care that there should be none to see him when he once again started for a certain lonesome corner of the Green Forest.

"First, I'll make sure that the eggs are still there," thought he, and flew high above the treetops, so that as he passed over the tree in which was the old nest of Redtail the Hawk, he might look down into it. To have seen him, you would never have guessed that he was looking for anything in particular. He seemed to be just flying over on his way to some distant place. If the eggs were still there, he meant to come back and hide in the top of a near-by pine-tree to watch until he was sure that he might safely steal those eggs, or to find out whose they were.

Blacky's heart beat fast with excitement as he drew near that old tumble-down nest. Would those two big white eggs be there? Perhaps there would be three! The very thought made him flap his wings a little faster. A few more wing strokes and he would be right over the tree. How he did hope to see those eggs! He could almost see into the nest now. One stroke! Two strokes! Three strokes! Blacky bit his tongue to keep from giving a sharp caw of disappointment and surprise.

There were no eggs to be seen. No, Sir, there wasn't a sign of eggs in that old nest. There wasn't because — why, do you think? There wasn't because Blacky looked straight down on a great mass of feathers which quite covered them from sight, and he didn't have to look twice to know that that great mass of feathers was really a great bird, the bird to whom those eggs belonged.

Blacky didn't turn to come back as he had planned. He kept right on, just as if he hadn't seen anything, and as he flew, he shivered a little. He shivered at the thought of what might have happened to him if he had tried to steal those eggs the day before and had been caught doing it.

"I'm thankful I knew enough to leave them alone," said he. "Funny I never once guessed whose eggs they are. I might have known that no one but Hooty the Horned Owl would think of nesting at this time of year. And that was Mrs. Hooty I saw on the nest just now. My, but she's big! She's bigger than Hooty himself! Yes, Sir, it's a lucky thing I didn't try to get those eggs yesterday. Probably both Hooty and Mrs. Hooty were sitting close by, only they were sitting so still that I thought they were parts of the tree they were in. Blacky, Blacky, the sooner you forget those eggs the better."

> Some things are best forgotten
> As soon as they are learned.
> Who never plays with fire
> Will surely not get burned.

Chapter IV
THE CUNNING OF BLACKY

NOW when Blacky the Crow discovered that the eggs in the old tumble-down nest of Redtail the Hawk in a lonesome corner of the Green Forest belonged to Hooty the Owl, he straightway made the best of resolutions; he would simply forget all about those eggs. He would forget that he ever had seen them, and he would stay away from that corner of the Green Forest. That was a very wise resolution. Of all the people who live in the Green Forest, none is fiercer or more savage than Hooty the Owl, unless it is Mrs. Hooty. She is bigger than Hooty and certainly quite as much to be feared by the little people.

All this Blacky knows. No one knows it better. And Blacky is not one to poke his head into trouble with his eyes open. So, he very wisely resolved to forget all about those eggs. Now it is one thing to make a resolution and quite another thing to live up to it, as you all know. It was easy enough to say that he would forget, but not at all easy to forget. It would have been different if it had been spring or early summer, when there were plenty of other eggs to be had by anyone smart enough to find them and steal them. But now, when it was still winter (such an unheard-of time for anyone to have eggs!), and it was hard work to find enough to keep a hungry Crow's stomach filled, the thought of those eggs *would* keep popping into his head. He just *couldn't* seem to forget them. After a little, he didn't try.

Now Blacky the Crow is very, very cunning. He is one of the smartest of all the little people who fly. No one can get into more mischief and still keep out of trouble than can Blacky the Crow. That is because he uses the wits in that black head of his. In fact, some people are unkind enough to say that he spends all his spare time in planning mischief. The more he thought of those eggs, the more he wanted them, and it wasn't long before he began to try to plan some way to get them without risking his own precious skin.

"I can't do it alone," thought he, "and yet if I take anyone into my secret, I'll have to share those eggs. That won't do at all, because I want them myself. I found them, and I ought to have them." He quite forgot or overlooked the fact that those eggs really belonged to Hooty and Mrs. Hooty and to no one else. "Now let me see, what can I do?"

He thought and he thought and he thought and he thought, and little by little, a plan worked out in his little black head. Then he chuckled. He chuckled right out loud, then hurriedly looked around to see if anyone had heard him. No one had, so he chuckled again. He cocked his head on one side and half closed his eyes, as if that plan was something he could see, and he was looking at it very hard. Then he cocked his head on the other side and did the same thing.

"It's all right," said he at last. "It'll give my relatives a lot of fun, and of course they will be very grateful to me for that. It won't hurt Hooty or Mrs. Hooty a bit, but it will make them very angry. They have very short tempers, and people with short tempers usually forget everything else when they are angry. We'll pay them a visit while the sun is bright, because then perhaps they cannot see well enough to catch us, and we'll tease them until they lose their tempers and forget all about keeping guard over those eggs. Then I'll slip in and get one and perhaps both of them. Without knowing that they are doing anything of the kind, my friends and relatives will help me to get a good meal. My, how good those eggs will taste!"

It was a very clever and cunning plan, for Blacky is a very clever and cunning rascal, but of course it didn't deserve success because nothing that means needless worry and trouble for others deserves to succeed.

Chapter V
BLACKY CALLS HIS FRIENDS

When Blacky cries "Caw, caw, caw, caw!"
As if he'd dislocate his jaw,
His relatives all hasten where
He waits them with a crafty air.

THEY know that there is mischief afoot, and the Crow family is always ready for mischief. So, on this particular morning when they heard Blacky cawing at the top of his lungs from the tallest pine-tree in the Green Forest, they hastened over there as fast as they could fly, calling to each other excitedly and sure that they were going to have a good time of some kind.

Blacky chuckled as he saw them coming. "Come on! Come on! Caw, caw, caw! Hurry up and flap your wings faster. I know where Hooty the Owl is, and we'll have no end of fun with him," he cried.

"Caw, caw, caw, caw, caw, caw!" shouted all his relatives in great glee. "Where is he? Lead us to him. We'll drive him out of the Green Forest!"

So, Blacky led the way over to the most lonesome corner of the Green Forest, straight to the tree in which Hooty the Owl was comfortably sleeping. Blacky had taken pains to slip over early that morning and make sure just where he was. He had discovered Hooty fast asleep, and he knew that he would remain right where he was until dark. You know Hooty's eyes are not meant for much use in bright light, and the brighter the light, the more uncomfortable his eyes feel. Blacky knows this, too, and he had chosen the very brightest part of the morning to call his relatives over to torment poor Hooty. Jolly, round, bright Mr. Sun was shining his very brightest, and the white snow on the ground made it seem brighter still. Even Blacky had to blink, and he knew that poor Hooty would find it harder still.

But one thing Blacky was very careful not to even hint of, and that was that Mrs. Hooty was right close at hand. Mrs. Hooty is bigger and even more fierce than Hooty, and Blacky didn't want to frighten any of the more timid of his relatives. What he hoped down deep in his crafty heart was that when they got to teasing and tormenting Hooty and making the great racket which he knew they would, Mrs. Hooty would lose her temper and fly over to join Hooty in trying to drive away the black tormentors. Then Blacky would slip over to the nest which she had left unguarded and steal one and perhaps both of the eggs he knew were there.

When they reached the tree where Hooty was, he was blinking his great yellow eyes and had fluffed out all his feathers, which is a way he has when he is angry, to make himself look twice as big as he really is. Of course, he had heard the noisy crew coming, and he knew well enough what to expect. As soon as they saw him, they began to scream as loud as ever they could and to call him all manner of names. The boldest of them would dart at him as if to pull out a mouthful of feathers but took the greatest care not to get too near. You see, the way Hooty hissed and snapped his great bill was very threatening, and they knew that if once he got hold of one of them with those big cruel claws of his, that would be the end.

So, they were content to simply scold and scream at him and fly around him, just out of reach, and make him generally uncomfortable, and they were so busy doing this that no one noticed that Blacky was not joining in the fun, and no one paid any attention to the old tumble-down nest of Redtail the Hawk only a few trees distant. So far Blacky's plans were working out just as he had hoped.

Chapter VI
HOOTY THE OWL DOESN'T STAY STILL

Now what's the good of being smart
When others do not do their part?

IF Blacky the Crow didn't say this to himself, he thought it. He knew that he had made a very cunning plan to get the eggs of Hooty the Owl, a plan so shrewd and cunning that no one else in the Green Forest or on the Green Meadows would have thought of it. There was only one weakness in it, and that was that it depended for success on having Hooty the Owl do as he usually did when tormented by a crowd of noisy Crows, — stay where he was until they got tired and flew away.

Now Blacky sometimes makes a mistake that smart people are very apt to make; he thinks that because he is so smart, other people are stupid. That is where he proves that smart as he is, he isn't as smart as he thinks he is. He always thought of Hooty the Owl as stupid. That is, he always thought of him that way in daytime. At night, when he was waked out of a sound sleep by the fierce hunting cry of Hooty, he wasn't so sure about Hooty being stupid, and he always took care to sit perfectly still in the darkness, lest Hooty's great ears should hear him and Hooty's great eyes, made for seeing in the dark, should find him. No, in the night Blacky was not at all sure that Hooty was stupid.

But in the daytime, he was sure. You see, he quite forgot the fact that the brightness of day is to Hooty what the blackness of night is to him. So, because Hooty would simply sit still and hiss and snap his bill, instead of trying to catch his tormentors or flying away, Blacky called him stupid. He felt sure that Hooty would stay right where he was now, and he hoped that Mrs. Hooty would lose her temper and leave the nest where she was sitting on those two eggs and join Hooty to help him try to drive away that noisy crew.

But Hooty isn't stupid. Not a bit of it. The minute he found out that Blacky and his friends had discovered him, he thought of Mrs. Hooty and the two precious eggs in the old nest of Redtail the Hawk close by.

"Mrs. Hooty mustn't be disturbed," thought he. "That will never do at all. I must lead these black rascals away where they won't discover Mrs. Hooty. I certainly must."

So, he spread his broad wings and blundered away among the trees a little way. He didn't fly far because the instant he started to fly that whole noisy crew with the exception of Blacky were after him. Because he couldn't use his claws or bill while flying, they grew bold enough to pull a few feathers out of his back. So, he flew only a little way to a thick hemlock-tree, where it wasn't easy for the Crows to get at him, and where the light didn't hurt his eyes so much. There he rested a few minutes and then did the same thing over again. He meant to lead those bothersome Crows into the darkest part of the Green Forest and there — well, he could see better there, and it might be that one of them would be careless enough to come within reach. No, Hooty wasn't stupid. Certainly not.

Blacky awoke to that fact as he sat in the top of a tall pine-tree silently watching. He could see Mrs. Hooty on the nest, and as the noise of Hooty's tormentors sounded from farther and farther away, she settled herself more comfortably and closed her eyes. Blacky could imagine that she was smiling to herself. It was clear that she had no intention of going to help Hooty. His splendid plan had failed just because stupid Hooty, who wasn't stupid at all, had flown away when he ought to have sat still. It was very provoking.

Chapter VII
BLACKY TRIES ANOTHER PLAN

When one plan fails, just try another;
Declare you'll win some way or other.

PEOPLE who succeed are those who do not give up because they fail the first time they try. They are the ones who, as soon as one plan fails, get busy right away and think of another plan and try that. If the thing they are trying to do is a good thing, sooner or later they succeed. If they are trying to do a wrong thing, very likely all their plans fail, as they should.

Now Blacky the Crow knows all about the value of trying and trying. He isn't easily discouraged. Sometimes it is a pity that he isn't, because he plans so much mischief. But the fact remains that he isn't, and he tries and tries until he cannot think of another plan and just *has* to give up. When he invited all his relatives to join him in tormenting Hooty the Owl, he thought he had a plan that just couldn't fail. He felt sure that Mrs. Hooty would leave her nest and help Hooty try to drive away his tormentors. But Mrs. Hooty didn't do anything of the kind, because Hooty was smart enough and thoughtful enough to lead his tormentors away from the nest into the darkest part of the Green Forest where their noise wouldn't bother Mrs. Hooty. So, she just settled herself more comfortably than ever on those eggs which Blacky had hoped she would give him a chance to steal, and his fine plan was quite upset.

Not one of his relatives had noticed that nest. They had been too busy teasing Hooty. This was just as Blacky had hoped. He didn't want them to know about that nest because he was selfish and wanted to get those eggs just for himself alone. But now he knew that the only way he could get Mrs. Hooty off of them would be by teasing her so that she would lose her temper and try to catch some of her tormentors. If she did that, there would be a chance that he might slip in and get at least one of those eggs. He would try it.

For a few minutes he listened to the noise of his relatives growing fainter and fainter, as Hooty led them farther and farther into the Green Forest. Then he opened his mouth.

"Caw, caw, caw, caw!" he screamed. "Caw, caw, caw, caw! Come back, everybody! Here is Mrs. Hooty on her nest! Caw, caw, caw, caw!"

Now as soon as they heard that, all Blacky's relatives stopped chasing and tormenting Hooty and started back as fast as they could fly. They didn't like the dark part of the Green Forest into which Hooty was leading them. Besides, they wanted to see that nest. So back they came, cawing at the top of their lungs, for they were very much excited. Some of them never had seen a nest of Hooty's. And anyway, it would be just as much fun to tease Mrs. Hooty as it was to tease Hooty.

"Where is the nest?" they screamed, as they came back to where Blacky was cawing and pretending to be very much excited.

"Why," exclaimed one, "that is the old nest of Redtail the Hawk. I know all about that nest." And he looked at Blacky as if he thought Blacky was playing a joke on them.

"It was Redtail's, but it is Hooty's now. If you don't believe me, just look in it," retorted Blacky.

At once they all began to fly over the top of the tree where they could look down into the nest and there, sure enough, was Mrs. Hooty, her great, round, yellow eyes glaring up at them angrily. Such a racket! Right away Hooty was forgotten, and the whole crowd at once began to torment Mrs. Hooty. Only Blacky sat watchful and silent, waiting for Mrs. Hooty to lose her temper and try to catch one of her tormentors. He had hope, a great hope, that he would get one of those eggs.

Chapter VIII
HOOTY COMES TO MRS. HOOTY'S AID

NO one can live just for self alone. A lot of people think they can, but they are very much mistaken. They are making one of the greatest mistakes in the world. Every teeny, weeny act, no matter what it is, affects somebody else. That is one of Old Mother Nature's great laws. And it is just as true among the little people of the Green Forest and the Green Meadows as with boys and girls and grown people. It is Old Mother Nature's way of making each of us responsible for the good of all and of teaching us that always we should help each other.

As you know, when Blacky the Crow called all his relatives over to the nest where Mrs. Hooty was sitting on her eggs, they at once stopped tormenting Hooty and left him alone in a thick hemlock-tree in the darkest part of the Green Forest. Of course, Hooty was very, very glad to be left in peace, and he might have spent the rest of the day there sleeping in comfort. But he didn't. No, Sir, he didn't. At first, he gave a great sigh of relief and settled himself as if he meant to stay. He listened to the voices of those noisy Crows growing fainter and fainter and was glad. But it was only for a few minutes. Presently those voices stopped growing fainter. They grew more excited-sounding than ever, and they came right from one place. Hooty knew then that his tormentors had found the nest where Mrs. Hooty was, and that they were tormenting her just as they had tormented him.

He snapped his bill angrily and then more angrily.

"I guess Mrs. Hooty is quite able to take care of herself," he grumbled, "but she ought not to be disturbed while she is sitting on those eggs. I hate to go back there in that bright sunshine. It hurts my eyes, and I don't like it, but I guess I'll have to go back there. Mrs. Hooty needs my help. I'd rather stay here, but—"

He didn't finish. Instead, he spread his broad wings and flew back towards the nest and Mrs. Hooty. His great wings made no noise, for they are made so that he can fly without making a sound. "If I once get hold of one of those Crows!" he muttered to himself. "If I once get hold of one of those Crows, I'll—" He didn't say what he would do, but if you had been near enough to hear the snap of his bill, you could have guessed the rest.

All this time the Crows were having what they called fun with Mrs. Hooty. Nothing is true fun which makes others uncomfortable, but somehow a great many people seem to forget this. So, while Blacky sat watching, his relatives made a tremendous racket around Mrs. Hooty, and the angrier she grew, the more they screamed and called her names and darted down almost in her face, as they pretended that they were going to fight her. They were so busy doing this, and Blacky was so busy watching them, hoping that Mrs. Hooty would leave her nest and give him a chance to steal the eggs he knew were under her, that no one gave Hooty a thought.

All of a sudden he was there, right in the tree close to the nest! No one had heard a sound, but there he was, and in the claws of one foot, he held

ALL OF A SUDDEN, HE WAS THERE, RIGHT IN THE TREE CLOSE TO THE NEST!

the tail feathers of one of Blacky's relatives. It was lucky, very lucky indeed for that one that the sun was in Hooty's eyes and so he had missed his aim. Otherwise, there would have been one less Crow.

Now it is one thing to tease one lone Owl and quite another to tease two together. Besides, there were those black tail feathers floating down to the snow-covered ground. Quite suddenly those Crows decided that they had had fun enough for one day, and in spite of all Blacky could do to stop them, away they flew, cawing loudly and talking it all over noisily. Blacky was the last to go, and his heart was sorrowful. However, could he get those eggs?

Chapter IX
BLACKY THINKS OF FARMER BROWN'S BOY

"SUCH luck!" grumbled Blacky, as he flew over to his favorite tree to do a little thinking. "Such luck! Now all my neighbors know about the nest of Hooty the Owl, and sooner or later one of them will find out that there are eggs in it. There is one thing about it, though, and that is that if I can't get them, nobody can. That is to say, none of my relatives can. I've tried every way I can think of, and those eggs are still there. My, my, my, how I would like one of them right now!"

Then Blacky the Crow did a thing which disappointed scamps often do, — began to blame the ones he was trying to wrong because his plans had failed. To have heard him talking to himself, you would have supposed that those eggs really belonged to him and that Hooty and Mrs. Hooty had cheated him out of them. Yes, Sir, that is what you would have thought if you could have heard him muttering to himself there in the treetop. In his disappointment over not getting those eggs, he was so sorry for himself that he actually did feel that he was the one wronged, — that Hooty and Mrs. Hooty should have let him have those eggs.

Of course, that was absolute foolishness, but he made himself believe it just the same. At least, he pretended to believe it. And the more he pretended, the angrier he grew. This is often the way with people who try to wrong others. They grow angry with the ones they have tried to wrong. When at last Blacky had to confess to himself that he could think of no other way to get those eggs, he began to wonder if there was some way to make trouble for Hooty and Mrs. Hooty. It was right then that he thought of Farmer Brown's boy.

Blacky's eyes snapped. He remembered how, once upon a time, Farmer Brown's boy had delighted to rob nests. Blacky had seen him take the eggs from the nests of Blacky's own relatives and from many other feathered people. What he did with the eggs, Blacky had no idea. Just now he didn't care. If Farmer Brown's boy would just happen to find Hooty's nest, he would be sure to take those eggs, and then he, Blacky, would feel better. He would feel that he was even with Hooty.

Right away he began to try to think of some way to bring Farmer Brown's boy over to the lonesome corner of the Green Forest where Hooty's nest was. If he could once get him there, he felt sure that Farmer Brown's boy would see the nest and climb up to it, and then of course he would take the eggs. If he couldn't have those eggs himself, the next best thing would be to see someone else get them.

Dear me, dear me, such dreadful thoughts! I am afraid that Blacky's heart was as black as his coat. And the worst of it was, he seemed to get a lot of pleasure in his wicked plans. Now right down in his heart, he knew that they were wicked plans, but he tried to make excuses to himself.

"Hooty the Owl is a robber," said he. "Everybody is afraid of him. He lives on other people, and so far as I know, he does no good in the world. He is big and fierce, and no one loves him. The Green Forest would be better off without him. If those eggs hatch, there will be little Owls to be fed, and they will grow up into big fierce Owls, like their father and mother. So, if I show Farmer Brown's boy that nest and he takes those eggs, I will be doing a kindness to my neighbors."

So, Blacky talked to himself and tried to hush the still, small voice down inside that tried to tell him that what he was planning to do was really a dreadful thing. And all the time he watched for Farmer Brown's boy.

Chapter X
FARMER BROWN'S BOY AND HOOTY

FARMER BROWN'S boy had taken it into his head to visit the Green Forest. It was partly because he hadn't anything else to do, and it was partly because now that it was very near the end of winter, he wanted to see how things were there and if there were any signs of the coming of spring. Blacky the Crow saw him coming, and Blacky chuckled to himself. He had watched every day for a week for just this thing. Now he would tell Farmer Brown's boy about that nest of Hooty the Owl.

He flew over to the lonesome corner of the Green Forest where Hooty and Mrs. Hooty had made their home and at once began to caw at the top of his voice and pretend that he was terribly excited over something.

"Caw, caw, caw, caw, caw!" shouted Blacky. At once all his relatives within hearing hurried over to join him. They knew that he was tormenting Hooty, and they wanted to join in the fun. It wasn't long before there was a great racket going on over in that lonesome corner of the Green Forest.

Of course, Farmer Brown's boy heard it. He stopped and listened. "Now I wonder what Blacky and his friends have found this time," said he. "Whenever they make a fuss like that, there is usually something to see there. I believe I'll so over and have a look."

So, he turned in the direction of the lonesome corner of the Green Forest, and as he drew near, he moved very carefully, so as to see all that he could without frightening the Crows. He knew that as soon as they saw him, they would fly away, and that might alarm the one they were tormenting, for he knew enough of Crow ways to know that when they were making such a noise as they were now making, they were plaguing someone.

Blacky was the first to see him because he was watching for him. But he didn't say anything until Farmer Brown's boy was so near that he couldn't help but see that nest and Hooty himself, sitting up very straight and snapping his bill angrily at his tormentors. Then Blacky gave the alarm, and at once all the Crows rose in the air and headed for the Green Meadows, cawing at the top of their lungs. Blacky went with them a little way. The first chance he got, he dropped out of the flock and silently flew back to a place where he could see all that might happen at the nest of Hooty the Owl.

When Farmer Brown's boy first caught sight of the nest and saw the Crows darting down toward it and acting so excited, he was puzzled.

"That's an old nest of Redtail the Hawk," thought he. "I found that last spring. Now what can there be there to excite those Crows so?"

Then he caught sight of Hooty the Owl. "Ha, so that's it!" he exclaimed. "Those scamps have discovered Hooty and have been having no end of fun tormenting him. I wonder what he's doing there."

He no longer tried to keep out of sight but walked right up to the foot of the tree, all the time looking up. Hooty saw him, but instead of flying away, he snapped his bill just as he had at the Crows and hissed.

"That's funny," thought Farmer Brown's boy. "If I didn't know that to be the old nest of Redtail the Hawk, and if it weren't still the tail-end of winter, I would think that was Hooty's nest."

He walked in a circle around the tree, looking up. Suddenly he gave a little start. Was that a tail sticking over the edge of the nest? He found a stick and threw it up. It struck the bottom of the nest, and out flew a great bird. It was Mrs. Hooty! Blacky the Crow chuckled.

Chapter XI
FARMER BROWN'S BOY IS TEMPTED

When you're tempted to do wrong
Is the time to prove you're strong.
Shut your eyes and clench each fist;
It will help you to resist.

WHEN a bird is found sitting on a nest, it is a pretty sure sign that that nest holds something worthwhile. It is a sign that that bird has set up housekeeping. So, when Farmer Brown's boy discovered Mrs.

Hooty sitting so close on the old nest of Redtail the Hawk, in the most lonesome corner of the Green Forest, he knew what it meant. Perhaps I should say that he knew what it ought to mean. It ought to mean that there were eggs in that nest.

But it was hard for Farmer Brown's boy to believe that. Why, spring had not come yet! There was still snow, and the Smiling Pool was still covered with ice. Who ever heard of birds nesting at this time of year? Certainly not Farmer Brown's boy. And yet Hooty the Owl and Mrs. Hooty were acting for all the world as feathered folks do act when they have eggs and are afraid that something is going to happen to them. It was very puzzling.

"That nest was built by Redtail the Hawk, and it hasn't even been repaired," muttered Farmer Brown's boy, as he stared up at it. "If Hooty and his wife have taken it for their home, they are mighty poor housekeepers. And if Mrs. Hooty has laid eggs this time of year, she must be crazy. I suppose the way to find out is to climb up there. It seems foolish, but I'm going to do it. Those Owls certainly act as if they are mighty anxious about something, and I'm going to find out what it is."

He looked at Hooty and Mrs. Hooty, at their hooked bills and great claws, and decided that he would take a stout stick along with him. He had no desire to feel these great claws. When he had found a stick to suit him, he began to climb the tree. Hooty and Mrs. Hooty snapped their bills and hissed fiercely. They drew nearer. Farmer Brown's boy kept a watchful eye on them. They looked so big and fierce that he was almost tempted to give up and leave them in peace. But he just *had* to find out if there was anything in that nest, so he kept on. As he drew near it, Mrs. Hooty swooped very near to him, and the snap of her bill made an ugly sound. He held his stick ready to strike and kept on.

The nest was simply a great platform of sticks. When Farmer Brown's boy reached it, he found that he could not get where he could look into it, so he reached over and felt inside. Almost at once his fingers touched something that made him tingle all over. It was an egg, a great big egg! There was no doubt about it. It was just as hard for him to believe as it had been for Blacky the Crow to believe, when he first saw those eggs. Farmer

Brown's boy's fingers closed over that egg and took it out of the nest. Mrs. Hooty swooped very close, and Farmer Brown's boy nearly dropped the egg as he struck at her with his stick. Then Mrs. Hooty and Hooty seemed to lose courage and withdrew to a tree nearby, where they snapped their bills and hissed.

Then Farmer Brown's boy looked at the prize in his hand. It was a big, dirty-white egg. His eyes shone. What a splendid prize to add to his collection of birds' eggs! It was the first egg of the Great Horned Owl, the largest of all Owls, that he ever had seen.

Once more he felt in the nest and found there was another egg there. "I'll take both of them," said he. "It's the first nest of Hooty's that I've ever found, and perhaps I'll never find another. Gee, I'm glad I came over here to find out what those Crows were making such a fuss about. I wonder if I can get these down without breaking them."

Just at that very minute he remembered something. He remembered that he had stopped collecting eggs. He remembered that he had resolved never to take another bird's egg.

"But this is different," whispered the tempter. "This isn't like taking the eggs of the little songbirds."

Chapter XII
A TREETOP BATTLE

As black is black and white is white,
So wrong is wrong and right is right.

THERE isn't any half way about it. A thing is wrong, or it is right, and that is all there is to it. But most people have hard work to see this when they want very much to do a thing that the still small voice way down inside tells them isn't right. They try to compromise. To compromise is to do neither one thing nor the other but a little of both. But you can't do that with right and wrong. It is a queer thing, but a half right never is as good as a whole right, while a half wrong often, very often, is as bad as a whole wrong.

Farmer Brown's boy, up in the tree by the nest of Hooty the Owl in the lonesome corner of the Green Forest, was fighting a battle. No, he wasn't fighting with Hooty or Mrs. Hooty. He was fighting a battle right inside himself. It was a battle between right and wrong. Once upon a time he had taken great delight in collecting the eggs of birds, in trying to see how many kinds he could get. Then as he had come to know the little forest and meadow people better, he had seen that taking the eggs of birds is very, very wrong, and he had stopped stealing them. He bad declared that never again would he steal an egg from a bird.

But never before had he found a nest of Hooty the Owl. Those two big eggs would add ever so much to his collection. "Take 'em," said a little voice inside. "Hooty is a robber. You will be doing a kindness to the other birds by taking them."

"Don't do it," said another little voice. "Hooty may be a robber, but he has a place in the Green Forest, or Old Mother Nature never would have put him here. It is just as much stealing to take his eggs as to take the eggs of any other bird. He has just as much right to them as Jenny Wren has to hers."

"Take one and leave one," said the first voice.

"That will be just as much stealing as if you took both," said the second voice. "Besides, you will be breaking your own word. You said that you never would take another egg."

"I didn't promise anybody but myself," declared Farmer Brown's boy right out loud. At the sound of his voice, Hooty and Mrs. Hooty, sitting in the next tree, snapped their bills and hissed louder than ever.

"A promise to yourself ought to be just as good as a promise to anyone else. I don't wonder Hooty hisses at you," said the good little voice.

"Think how fine those eggs will look in your collection and how proud you will be to show them to the other fellows who never have found a nest of Hooty's," said the first little voice.

"And think how mean and small and cheap you'll feel every time you look at them," added the good little voice. "You'll get a lot more fun if you leave them to hatch out and then watch the little Owls grow up and learn all about their ways. Just think what a stout, brave fellow Hooty is to start housekeeping at this time of year, and how wonderful it is that Mrs. Hooty can keep these eggs warm and when they have hatched, take care of the baby Owls before others have even begun to build their nests. Besides, wrong is wrong and right is right, always."

Slowly Farmer Brown's boy reached over the edge of the nest and put back the egg. Then he began to climb down the tree. When he reached the ground, he went off a little way and watched. Almost at once Mrs. Hooty flew to the nest and settled down on the eggs, while Hooty mounted guard close by.

"I'm glad I didn't take 'em," said Farmer Brown's boy. "Yes, Sir, I'm glad I didn't take 'em."

As he turned back toward home, he saw Blacky the Crow flying over the Green Forest and little did he guess how he had upset Blacky's plans.

Chapter XIII
BLACKY HAS A CHANGE OF HEART

BLACKY the Crow isn't all black. No, indeed. His coat is black, and sometimes it seems as if his heart is all black, but this isn't so. It certainly seemed as if his heart was all black when he tried so hard to make trouble for Hooty the Owl. It would seem as if only a black heart could have urged him to try so hard to steal the eggs of Hooty and Mrs. Hooty, but this wasn't really so. You see, it didn't seem at all wrong to try to get those eggs. Blacky was hungry, and those eggs would have given him a good meal. He knew that Hooty wouldn't hesitate to catch him and eat him if he had the chance, and so it seemed to him perfectly right and fair to steal Hooty's eggs if he was smart enough to do so. And most of the other little people of the Green Forest and the Green Meadows would have felt the same way about it. You see, it is one of the laws of Old Mother Nature that each one must learn to look out for himself.

But when Blacky showed that nest of Hooty's to Farmer Brown's boy with the hope that Farmer Brown's boy would steal those eggs, there *was* blackness in his heart. He was doing something then which was pure meanness. He was just trying to make trouble for Hooty, to get even because Hooty had been too smart for him. He had sat in the top of a tall pine-tree where he could see all that happened, and he had chuckled wickedly as he had seen Farmer Brown's boy climb to Hooty's nest and take out an egg. He felt sure that he would take both eggs. He hoped so, anyway.

When he saw Farmer Brown's boy put the eggs back and climb down the tree without any, he had to blink his eyes to make sure that he saw straight. He just couldn't believe what he saw. At first, he was dreadfully disappointed and angry. It looked very much as if he weren't going to get even with Hooty after all. He flew over to his favorite tree to think things over. Now sometimes it is a good thing to sit by oneself and think things over. It gives the little small voice deep down inside a chance to be heard. It was just that way with Blacky now.

The longer he thought, the meaner his action in calling Farmer Brown's boy looked. It was one thing to try to steal those eggs himself, but it was quite another matter to try to have them stolen by someone against whom Hooty had no protection whatever.

"If it had been anyone but Hooty, you would have done your best to have kept Farmer Brown's boy away," said the little voice inside. Blacky hung his head. He knew that it was true. More than once, in fact many times, he had warned other feathered folks when Farmer Brown's boy had been hunting for their nests and had helped to lead him away.

At last Blacky threw up his head and chuckled, and this time his chuckle was good to hear. "I'm glad that Farmer Brown's boy didn't take those eggs," said he right out loud. "Yes, sir, I'm glad. I'll never do such a thing as that again. I'm ashamed of what I did; yet I'm glad I did it. I'm glad because I've learned some things. I've learned that Farmer Brown's boy isn't as much to be feared as he used to be. I've learned that Hooty isn't as stupid as I thought he was. I've learned that while it may be all right for us people of the Green Forest to try to outwit each other, we ought to protect each other against common dangers. And I've learned something I didn't know before, and that is that Hooty the Owl is the very first of us to set up housekeeping. Now I think I'll go hunt for an honest meal." And he did.

Chapter XIV
BLACKY MAKES A CALL

Judge no one by his style of dress;
Your ignorance you thus confess.
Blacky the Crow.

"CAW, caw, caw, caw." There was no need of looking to see who that was. Peter Rabbit knew without looking. Mrs. Quack knew without looking. Just the same, both looked up. Just alighting in the top of a tall tree was Blacky the Crow. "Caw, caw, caw, caw," he repeated, looking down at Peter and Mrs. Quack and Mr. Quack and the six young Quacks. "I hope I am not interrupting any secret gossip."

"Not at all," Peter hastened to say. "Mrs. Quack was just telling me of the troubles and dangers in bringing up a young family in the Far North. How did you know the Quacks had arrived?"

Blacky chuckled hoarsely. "I didn't," said he. "I simply thought there might be something going on I didn't know about over here in the pond of Paddy the Beaver, so I came over to find out. Mr. Quack, you and Mrs. Quack are looking very fine this fall. And those handsome young Quacks, you don't mean to tell me that they are your children!"

Mrs. Quack nodded proudly. "They are," said she.

"You don't say so!" exclaimed Blacky, as if he were very much surprised, when all the time he wasn't surprised at all. "They are a credit

"I HOPE I AM NOT INTERRUPTING ANY SECRET GOSSIP."

to their parents. Yes, indeed, they are a credit to their parents. Never have I seen finer young Ducks in all my life. How glad the hunters with terrible guns will be to see them."

Mrs. Quack shivered at that, and Blacky saw it. He chuckled softly. You know he dearly loves to make others uncomfortable. "I saw three hunters over on the edge of the Big River early this very morning," said he.

Mrs. Quack looked more anxious than ever. Blacky's sharp eyes noted this.

"That is why I came over here," he added kindly. "I wanted to give you warning."

"But you didn't know the Quacks were here!" spoke up Peter.

"True enough, Peter. True enough," replied Blacky, his eyes twinkling. "But I thought they might be. I had heard a rumor that those who go south are traveling earlier than usual this fall, so I knew I might find Mr. and Mrs. Quack over here any time now. Is it true, Mrs. Quack, that we are going to have a long, hard, cold winter?"

"That is what they say up in the Far North," replied Mrs. Quack. "And it is true that Jack Frost had started down earlier than usual. That is how it happens we are here now. But about those hunters over by the Big River, do you suppose they will come over here?" There was an anxious note in Mrs. Quack's voice.

"No," replied Blacky promptly. "Farmer Brown's boy won't let them. I know. I've been watching him, and he has been watching those hunters. As long as you stay here, you will be safe. What a great world this would be if all those two-legged creatures were like Farmer Brown's boy."

"Wouldn't it!" cried Peter. Then he added, "I wish they were."

"You don't wish it half as much as I do," declared Mrs. Quack.

"Yet I can remember when he used to hunt with a terrible gun and was as bad as the worst of them," said Blacky.

"What changed him?" asked Mrs. Quack, looking interested.

"Just getting really acquainted with some of the little people of the Green Forest and the Green Meadows," replied Blacky. "He found them ready to meet him more than halfway in friendship and that some of them really are his best friends."

"And now he is their best friend," spoke up Peter.

Blacky nodded. "Right, Peter," said he. "That is why the Quacks are safe here and will be as long as they stay."

Chapter XV
BLACKY DOES A LITTLE LOOKING ABOUT

Do not take the word of others
That things are or are not so
When there is a chance that you may
Find out for yourself and *know*.
Blacky the Crow.

BLACKY the Crow is a shrewd fellow. He is one of the smartest and shrewdest of all the little people in the Green Forest and on the Green Meadows. Everybody knows it. And because of this, all his neighbors have a great deal of respect for him, despite his mischievous ways.

Of course, Blacky had noticed that Johnny Chuck had dug his house deeper than usual and had stuffed himself until he was fatter than ever before. He had noticed that Jerry Muskrat was making the walls of his house thicker than in other years, and that Paddy the Beaver was doing the same thing to his house. You know there is very little that escapes the sharp eyes of Blacky the Crow.

He had guessed what these things meant. "They think we are going to have a long, hard, cold winter," muttered Blacky to himself. "Perhaps they know, but I want to see some signs of it for myself. They may be only guessing. Anybody can do that, and one guess is as good as another."

Then he found Mr. and Mrs. Quack, the Mallard Ducks, and their children in the pond of Paddy the Beaver and remembered that they never had come down from their home in the Far North as early in the fall as

JOHNNY CHUCK HAD STUFFED HIMSELF UNTIL HE WAS FATTER THAN EVER
BEFORE.

this. Mrs. Quack explained that Jack Frost had already started south, and so they had started earlier to keep well ahead of him.

"Looks as if there may be something in this idea of a long, hard, cold winter," thought Blacky, "but perhaps the Quacks are only guessing, too. I wouldn't take their word for it any more than I would the word of Johnny Chuck or Jerry Muskrat or Paddy the Beaver. I'll look about a little."

So, after warning the Quacks to remain in the pond of Paddy the Beaver if they would be safe, Blacky bade them goodbye and flew away. He headed straight for the Green Meadows and Farmer Brown's cornfield. A little of that yellow corn would make a good breakfast.

When he reached the cornfield, Blacky perched on top of a shock of corn, for it already had been cut and put in shocks in readiness to be carted up to Farmer Brown's barn. For a few minutes he sat there silent and motionless, but all the time his sharp eyes were making sure that no enemy was hiding behind one of those brown shocks. When he was quite certain that things were as safe as they seemed, he picked out a plump ear of corn and began to tear open the husks, so as to get at the yellow grains.

"Seems to me these husks are unusually thick," muttered Blacky, as he tore at them with his stout bill. "Don't remember ever having seen them as thick as these. Wonder if it just happens to be so on this ear."

Then, as a sudden thought popped into his black head, he left that ear and went to another. The husks of this were as thick as those on the first. He flew to another shock and found the husks there just the same. He tried a third shock with the same result.

"Huh, they are all alike," said he. Then he looked thoughtful and for a few minutes sat perfectly still like a black statue. "They are right," said he at last. "Yes, Sir, they are right." Of course, he meant Johnny Chuck and Jerry Muskrat and Paddy the Beaver and the Quacks. "I don't know how they know it, but they are right; we are going to have a long, hard, cold winter. I know it myself now. I've found a sign. Old Mother Nature has wrapped this corn in extra thick husks, and of course she has done it to protect it. She doesn't do things without a reason. We are going to have a cold winter, or my name isn't Blacky the Crow."

Chapter XVI
Blacky Finds Other Signs

A single fact may fail to prove you either right or wrong;
Confirm it with another and your proof will then be strong.
Blacky the Crow.

AFTER his discovery that Old Mother Nature had wrapped all the ears of corn in extra thick husks, Blacky had no doubt in his own mind that Johnny Chuck and Jerry Muskrat and Paddy the Beaver and the Quacks were quite right in feeling that the coming winter would be long, hard and cold. But Blacky long ago learned that it isn't wise or wholly safe to depend altogether on one thing.

"Old Mother Nature never does things by halves," thought Blacky, as he sat on the fence post on the Green Meadows, thinking over his discovery of the thick husks on the corn. "She wouldn't take care to protect the corn that way and not do as much for other things. There must be other signs, if I am smart enough to find them."

He lifted one black wing and began to set in order the feathers beneath it. Suddenly he made a funny little hop straight up.

"Well, I never!" he exclaimed, as he spread his wings to regain his balance. "I never did!"

"Is that so?" piped a squeaky little voice. "If you say you never did, I suppose you never did, though I want the word of someone else before I will believe it. What is it you never did?"

Blacky looked down. Peeping up at him from the brown grass were two bright little eyes.

"Hello, Danny Meadow Mouse!" exclaimed Blacky. "I haven't seen you for a long time. I've looked for you several times lately."

"I don't doubt it. I don't doubt it at all," squeaked Danny. "You'll never see me when you are looking for me. That is, you won't if I can help it. You won't if I see you first."

Blacky chuckled. He knew what Danny meant. When Blacky goes looking for Danny Meadow Mouse, it usually is in hope of having a Meadow Mouse dinner, and he knew that Danny knew this. "I've had my breakfast," said Blacky, "and it isn't dinner time yet."

"What is it you never did?" persisted Danny, in his squeaky voice.

"That was just an exclamation," explained Blacky. "I made a discovery that surprised me, so I exclaimed right out."

"What was it?" demanded Danny.

"It was that the feathers of my coat are coming in thicker than I ever knew them to before. I hadn't noticed it until I started to set them in order a minute ago." He buried his bill in the feathers of his breast. "Yes, sir," said he in a muffled voice, "they are coming in thicker than I ever knew them to before. There is a lot of down around the roots of them. I am going to have the warmest coat I've ever had."

"Well, don't think you are the only one," retorted Danny. "My fur never was so thick at this time of year as it is now, and it is the same way with Nanny Meadow Mouse and all our children. I suppose you know what it means."

"What does it mean?" asked Blacky, just as if he didn't have the least idea, although he had guessed the instant he discovered those extra feathers.

"It means we are going to have a long, hard, cold winter, and Old Mother Nature is preparing us for it," replied Danny, quite as if he knew all about it. "You'll find that everybody who doesn't go south or sleep all winter has a thicker coat than usual. Hello! There is old Roughleg the Hawk! He has come extra early this year. I think I'll go back to warn Nanny."

Without another word, Danny disappeared in the brown grass. Again Blacky chuckled. "More signs," said he to himself. "More signs. There isn't a doubt that we are going to have a hard winter. I wonder if I can stand it or if I'd better go a little way south, where it will be warmer."

Chapter XVII
BLACKY WATCHES A QUEER PERFORMANCE

This much to me is very clear:
A thing not understood is queer.
Blacky the Crow.

BLACKY the Crow may be right. Again, he may not be. If he is right, it will account for a lot of the queer people in the world. They are not understood, and so they are queer. At least, that is what other people say, and never once think that perhaps they are the queer ones for not understanding.

But Blacky isn't like those people who are satisfied not to understand and to think other people and things queer. He does his best to understand. He waits and watches and uses those sharp eyes of his and those quick wits of his until at last usually he does understand.

The day of his discovery of Old Mother Nature's signs that the coming winter would be long, hard and cold, Blacky paid a visit to the Big River. Long ago he discovered that many things are to be seen on or beside the Big River, things not to be seen elsewhere. So, there are few clays in which he does not get over there.

As he drew near the Big River, he was very watchful and careful, was Blacky, for this was the season when hunters with terrible guns were abroad, and he had discovered that they were likely to be hiding along the Big River, hoping to shoot Mr. or Mrs. Quack or some of their relatives. So, he was very watchful as he drew near the Big River, for he had learned that it was dangerous to pass too near a hunter with a terrible gun. More than once he had been shot at. But he had learned by these experiences. Oh, yes, Blacky had learned. For one thing, he had learned to know a gun when he saw it. For another thing, he had learned just how far away one of these dreadful guns could be and still hurt the one it was pointed at, and to always keep just a little farther away. Also, he had learned that a man or boy without a terrible gun is quite harmless, and he had learned that hunters with terrible guns are tricky and sometimes hide from those they seek to kill, so that in the dreadful hunting season it is best to look sharply before approaching any place.

On this afternoon, as he drew near the Big River, he saw a man who seemed to be very busy on the shore of the Big River, at a place where wild rice and rushes grew for some distance out in the water, for just there it was shallow far out from the shore. Blacky looked sharply for a terrible gun. But the man had none with him and therefore was not to be feared. Blacky boldly drew near until he was able to see what the man was doing.

Then Blacky's eyes stretched their widest and he almost cawed right out with surprise. The man was taking yellow corn from a bag, a handful at a time, and throwing it out in the water. Yes, Sir, that is what he was doing, scattering nice yellow corn among the rushes and wild rice in the water!

"That's a queer performance," muttered Blacky, as he watched. "What is he throwing perfectly good corn out in the water for? He isn't planting it, for this isn't the planting season. Besides, it wouldn't grow in the water, anyway. It is a shame to waste nice corn like that. What is he doing it for?"

Blacky flew over to a tree some distance away and alighted in the top of it to watch the queer performance. You know Blacky has very keen eyes and he can see a long distance. For a while, the man continued to scatter corn and Blacky continued to wonder what he was doing it for. At last the man went away in a boat. Blacky watched him until he was out of sight. Then he spread his wings and slowly flew back and forth just above the rushes and wild rice, at the place where the man had been scattering the corn. He could see some of the yellow grains on the bottom. Presently he saw something else. "Ha!" exclaimed Blacky.

Chapter XVIII
BLACKY BECOMES VERY SUSPICIOUS

Of things you do not understand,
Beware!
They may be wholly harmless but—
Beware!
You'll find the older that you grow
That only things and folks you know
Are fully to be trusted, so
Beware!

Blacky the Crow.

THAT is one of Blacky's wise sayings, and he lives up to it. It is one reason why he has come to be regarded by all his neighbors as one of the smartest of all who live in the Green Forest and on the Green Meadow. He seldom gets into any real trouble because he first makes sure there is no trouble to get into. When he discovers something, he does not understand, he is at once distrustful of it.

As he watched a man scattering yellow corn in the water from the shore of the Big River, he at once became suspicious. He couldn't understand why a man should throw good corn among the rushes and wild rice in the water, and because he couldn't understand, he at once began to suspect that it was for no good purpose. When the man left in a boat, Blacky slowly flew over the rushes where the man had thrown the corn, and presently his sharp eyes made a discovery that caused him to exclaim right out.

What was it Blacky had discovered? Only a few feathers. No one with eyes less sharp than Blacky's would have noticed them. And few would have given them a thought if they had noticed them. But Blacky knew right away that those were feathers from a Duck. He knew that a Duck, or perhaps a flock of Ducks, had been resting or feeding in there among those rushes, and that in moving about they had left those two or three downy feathers.

"Ha!" exclaimed Blacky. "Mr. and Mrs. Quack or some of their relatives have been here. It is just the kind of a place Ducks like. Also, some Ducks like corn. If they should come back here and find this corn, they would have a feast, and they would be sure to come again. That man who scattered the corn here didn't have a terrible gun, but that doesn't mean that he isn't a hunter. He may come back again, and then he may have a terrible gun. I'm suspicious of that man. I am so. I believe he put that corn here for Ducks and I don't believe he did it out of the kindness of his heart. If it was Farmer Brown's boy, I would know that all is well; that he was thinking of hungry Ducks, with few places where they can feed in safety, as they make the long journey from the Far North to the Sunny South. But it wasn't Farmer Brown's boy. I don't like the looks of it. I don't indeed. I'll keep watch of this place and see what happens."

All the way to his favorite perch in a certain big hemlock-tree in the Green Forest, Blacky kept thinking about that corn and the man who had seemed to be generous with it, and the more he thought, the more suspicious he became. He didn't like the looks of it at all.

"I'll warn the Quacks to keep away from there. I'll do it the very first thing in the morning," he muttered, as he prepared to go to sleep. "If they have any sense at all, they will stay in the pond of Paddy the Beaver. But if they should go over to the Big River, they would be almost sure to find that corn, and if they should once find it, they would keep going back for more. It may be all right, but I don't like the looks of it."

And still full of suspicions, Blacky went to sleep.

Chapter XIX
Blacky Makes More Discoveries

Little things you fail to see
May important prove to be.
Blacky the Crow.

ONE of the secrets of Blacky's success in life is the fact that he never fails to take note of little things. Long ago he learned that little things which in themselves seem harmless and not worth noticing may together prove the most important things in life. So, no matter how unimportant a thing may appear, Blacky examines it closely with those sharp eyes of his and remembers it.

The very first thing Blacky did, as soon as he was awake the morning after he discovered the man scattering corn in the rushes at a certain place on the edge of the Big River, was to fly over to the pond of Paddy the Beaver and again warn Mr. and Mrs. Quack to keep away from the Big River, if they and their six children would remain safe. Then he got some breakfast. He ate it in a hurry and flew straight over to the Big River to the place where he had seen that yellow corn scattered.

Blacky wasn't wholly surprised to find Dusky the Black Duck, own cousin to Mr. and Mrs. Quack the Mallard Ducks, with a number of his relatives in among the rushes and wild rice at the very place where that corn had been scattered. They seemed quite contented and in the best of spirits. Blacky guessed why. Not a single grain of that yellow corn could Blacky see. He knew the ways of Dusky and his relatives. He knew that they must have come in there just at dusk the night before and at once had found that corn. He knew that they would remain hiding there until frightened out, and that then they would spend the day in some little pond where they would not be likely to be disturbed or where at least no danger could approach them without being seen in plenty of time. There they would rest all day, and when the Black Shadows came creeping out from the Purple Hills, they would return to that place on the Big River to feed, for that is the time when they like best to hunt for their food.

Dusky looked up as Blacky flew over him, but Blacky said nothing, and Dusky said nothing. But if Blacky didn't use his tongue, he did use his eyes. He saw just on the edge of the shore what looked like a lot of small bushes growing close together on the very edge of the water. Mixed in with them were a lot of the brown rushes. They looked very harmless and innocent. But Blacky knew every foot of that shore along the Big River, and he knew that those bushes hadn't been there during the summer. He knew that they hadn't grown there.

He flew directly over them. Just back of them were a couple of logs. Those logs hadn't been there when he passed that way a few days before.

He was sure of it.

"Ha!" exclaimed Blacky under his breath. "Those look to me as if they might be very handy, very handy indeed, for a hunter to sit on. Sitting there behind those bushes, he would be hidden from any Duck who might come in to look for nice yellow corn scattered out there among the rushes. It doesn't look right to me. No, Sir, it doesn't look right to me. I think I'll keep an eye on this place."

So, Blacky came back to the Big River several times that day. The second time back he found that Dusky the Black Duck and his relatives had left. When he returned in the afternoon, he saw the same man he had seen there the afternoon before, and he was doing the same thing, — scattering yellow corn out in the rushes. And as before, he went away in a boat.

"I don't like it," muttered Blacky, shaking his black head. "I don't like it."

Chapter XX
BLACKY DROPS A HINT

When you see another's danger
Warn him though he be a stranger.
Blacky the Crow.

EVERY day for a week a man came in a boat to scatter corn in the rushes at a certain point along the bank of the Big River, and every day Blacky the Crow watched him and shook his black head and talked to himself and told himself that he didn't like it, and that he was sure that it was for no good purpose. Sometimes Blacky watched from a distance, and sometimes he flew right over the man. But never once did the man have a gun with him.

Every morning, very early, Blacky flew over there, and every morning he found Dusky the Black Duck and his flock in the rushes and wild rice at that particular place, and he knew that they had been there all night. He knew that they had come in there just at dusk the night before, to feast on the yellow corn the man had scattered there in the afternoon.

"It is no business of mine what those Ducks do," muttered Blacky to himself, "but as surely as my tail feathers are black, something is going to happen to some of them one of these days. That man may be fooling them, but he isn't fooling me. Not a bit of it. He hasn't had a gun with him once when I have seen him, but just the same he is a hunter. I feel it in my bones. He knows those silly Ducks come in here every night for that corn he puts out. He knows that after they have been here a few times and nothing has frightened them, they will be so sure that it is a safe place that they will not be the least bit suspicious. Then he will hide behind those bushes he has placed close to the edge of the water and wait for them with his terrible gun. That is what he will do, or my name isn't Blacky."

Finally, Blacky decided to drop a hint to Dusky the Black Duck. So, the next morning he stopped for a call. "Good morning," said he, as Dusky swam in just in front of him. "I hope you are feeling as fine as you look."

"Quack, quack," replied Dusky. "When Blacky the Crow flatters, he hopes to gain something. What is it this time?"

"Not a thing," replied Blacky. "On my honor, not a thing. There is nothing for me here, though there seems to be plenty for you and your relatives, to judge by the fact that I find you in this same place every morning. What is it?"

"Corn," replied Dusky in a low voice, as if afraid someone might overhear him. "Nice yellow corn."

"Corn!" exclaimed Blacky, as if very much astonished. "How does corn happen to be way over here in the water?"

Dusky shook his head. "Don't ask me, for I can't tell you," said he. "I haven't the least idea. All I know is that every evening when we arrive, we find it here. How it gets here, I don't know, and furthermore I don't care. It is enough for me that it is here."

"I've seen a man over here every afternoon," said Blacky. "I thought he might be a hunter."

"Did he have a terrible gun?" asked Dusky suspiciously.

"No-o," replied Blacky.

"Then he isn't a hunter," declared Dusky, looking much relieved.

"But perhaps one of these days he will have one and will wait for you to come in for your dinner," suggested Blacky. "He could hide behind these bushes, you know."

"Nonsense," retorted Dusky, tossing his head. "There hasn't been a sign of danger here since we have been here. I know you, Blacky; you are jealous because we find plenty to eat here, and you find nothing. You are trying to scare us. But I'll tell you right now, you can't scare us away from such splendid eating as we have had here. So there!"

Chapter XXI
AT LAST BLACKY IS SURE

Who for another conquers fear
Is truly brave, it is most clear.
Blacky the Crow.

IT was late in the afternoon, and Blacky the Crow was on his way to the Green Forest. As usual, he went around by the Big River to see if that man was scattering corn for the Ducks. He wasn't there. No one was to be seen along the bank of the Big River.

"He hasn't come today, or else he came early and has left," thought Blacky. And then his sharp eyes caught sight of something that made him turn aside and make straight for a certain tree, from the top of which he could see all that went on for a long distance. What was it Blacky saw? It was a boat coming down the Big River.

Blacky sat still and watched. Presently the boat turned in among the rushes, and a moment later a man stepped out on the shore. It was the same man Blacky had watched scatter corn in the rushes every day for a week.

There wasn't the least doubt about it, it was the same man.

"Ha, ha!" exclaimed Blacky, and nearly lost his balance in his excitement. "Ha, ha! It is just as I thought!" You see, Blacky's sharp eyes had seen that the man was carrying something, and that something was a gun, a terrible gun. Blacky knows a terrible gun as far as he can see it.

The hunter, for of course that is what he was, tramped along the shore until he reached the bushes which Blacky had noticed close to the water and which he knew had not grown there. The hunter looked out over the Big River. Then he walked along where he had scattered corn the day before. Not a grain was to be seen. This seemed to please him. Then he went back to the bushes and sat down on a log behind them, his terrible gun across his knees.

"I was sure of it," muttered Blacky. "He is going to wait there for those Ducks to come in, and then something dreadful will happen. What terrible creatures these hunters are! They don't know what fairness is. No, Sir, they don't know what fairness is. He has put food there day after day, where Dusky the Black Duck and his flock would be sure to find it and has waited until they have become so sure there is no danger that they are no longer suspicious. He knows they will feel so sure that all is safe that they will come in without looking for danger. Then he will fire that terrible gun and kill them without giving them any chance at all.

"Reddy Fox is a sly, clever hunter, but he wouldn't do a thing like that. Neither would Old Man Coyote or anybody else who wears fur or feathers. They might hide and try to catch someone by surprise. That is all right, because each of us is supposed to be on the watch for things of that sort. Oh, dear, what's to be done? It is time I was getting home to the Green Forest. The Black Shadows will soon come creeping out from the Purple Hills, and I must be safe in my hemlock-tree by then. I would be scared to death to be out after dark. Yet those Ducks ought to be warned. Oh, dear, what shall I do?"

Blacky peered over at the Green Forest and then over toward the Purple Hills, behind which jolly, round, red Mr. Sun would go to bed very shortly. He shivered as he thought of the Black Shadows that soon would come swiftly out from the Purple Hills across the Big River and over the

Green Meadows. With them might come Hooty the Owl, and Hooty wouldn't object in the least to a Crow dinner. He wished he was in that hemlock-tree that very minute.

Then Blacky looked at the hunter with his terrible gun and thought of what might happen, what would be almost sure to happen, unless those Ducks were warned. "I'll wait a little while longer," muttered Blacky, and tried to feel brave. But instead, he shivered.

Chapter XXII
Blacky Goes Home Happy

No greater happiness is won
Than through a deed for others done.
Blacky the Crow.

B LACKY sat in the top of a tree near the bank of the Big River and couldn't make up his mind what to do. He wanted to get home to the big, thick hemlock-tree in the Green Forest before dusk, for Blacky is afraid of the dark. That is, he is afraid to be out after dark.

"Go along home," said a voice inside him, "there is hardly time now for you to get there before the Black Shadows arrive. Don't waste any more time here. What may happen to those silly Ducks is no business of yours, and there is nothing you can do, anyway. Go along home."

"Wait a few minutes," said another little voice down inside him. "Don't be a coward. You ought to warn Dusky the Black Duck and his flock that a hunter with a terrible gun is waiting for them. Is it true that it is no business of yours what happens to those Ducks? Think again, Blacky; think again. It is the duty of each one who sees a common danger to warn his neighbors. If something dreadful should happen to Dusky because you were afraid of the dark, you never would be comfortable in your own mind. Stay a little while and keep watch."

Not five minutes later Blacky saw something that made him, oh, so glad he had kept watch. It was a swiftly moving black line just above the water far down the Big River, and it was coming up. He knew what that black line was. He looked over at the hunter hiding behind some bushes close to the edge of the water. The hunter was crouching with his terrible gun in his hands and was peeping over the bushes, watching that black line. He, too, knew what it was. It was a flock of Ducks flying.

Blacky was all ashake again, but this time it wasn't with fear of being caught away from home in the dark; it was with excitement. He knew that those Ducks had become so eager for more of that corn, that delicious yellow corn which every night for a week they had found scattered in the rushes just in front of the place where that hunter was now hiding, that they couldn't wait for the coming of the Black Shadows. They were so sure there was no danger that they were coming in to eat without waiting for the Black Shadows, as they usually did. And Blacky was glad. Perhaps now he could give them warning.

Up the middle of the Big River, flying just above the water, swept the flock with Dusky at its head. How swiftly they flew, those nine big birds! Blacky envied them their swift wings. On past the hidden hunter but far out over the Big River, they swept. For just a minute Blacky thought they were going on up the river and not coming in to eat, after all. Then they turned toward the other shore, swept around in a circle and headed straight in toward that hidden hunter. Blacky glanced at him and saw that he was ready to shoot.

Almost without thinking, Blacky spread his wings and started out from that tree. "Caw, caw, caw, caw, caw!" he shrieked at the top of his lungs. "Caw, caw, caw, caw, caw!" It was his danger cry that everybody on the Green Meadows and in the Green Forest knows.

Instantly Dusky turned and began to climb up, up, up, the other Ducks following him until, as they passed over the hidden hunter, they were so high it was useless for him to shoot. He did put up his gun and aim at them, but he didn't shoot. You see, he didn't want to frighten them so that they would not return. Then the flock turned and started off in the direction from which they had come, and in a few minutes, they were merely a black line disappearing far down the Big River.

Blacky headed straight for the Green Forest, chuckling as he flew. He knew that those Ducks would not return until after dark. He had saved them this time, and he was so happy he didn't even notice the Black Shadows. And the hunter stood up and shook his fist at Blacky the Crow.

Chapter XXIII
BLACKY CALLS FARMER BROWN'S BOY

BLACKY awoke in the best of spirits. Late the afternoon before he had saved Dusky the Black Duck and his flock from a hunter with a terrible gun. He wasn't quite sure whether he was most happy in having saved those Ducks by warning them just in time, or in having spoiled the plans of that hunter. He hates a hunter with a terrible gun, does Blacky. For that matter, so do all the little people of the Green Forest and the Green Meadows.

So Blacky started out for his breakfast in high spirits. After breakfast, he flew over to the Big River to see if Dusky the Black Duck was feeding in the rushes along the shore. Dusky wasn't, and Blacky guessed that he and his flock had been so frightened by that warning that they had kept away from there the night before.

"But they'll come back after a night or so," muttered Blacky, as he alighted in the top of a tree, the same tree from which he had watched the hunter the afternoon before. "They'll come back, and so will that hunter. If he sees me around again, he'll try to shoot me. I've done all I can do. Anyway, Dusky ought to have sense enough to be suspicious of this place after that warning. Hello, who is that? I do believe it is Farmer Brown's boy. I wish he would come over here. If he should find out about that hunter, perhaps he would do something to drive him away. I'll see if I can call him over here."

Blacky began to call in the way he does when he has discovered something and wants others to know about it. "Caw, caw, caaw, caaw, caw, caw, caaw!" screamed Blacky, as if greatly excited.

Now Farmer Brown's boy, having no work to do that morning, had started for a tramp over the Green Meadows, hoping to see some of his little friends in feathers and fur. He heard the excited cawing of Blacky and at once turned in that direction.

"That black rascal has found something over on the shore of the Big River," said Farmer Brown's boy to himself. "I'll go over there to see what it is. There isn't much escapes the sharp eyes of that black busybody. He has led me to a lot of interesting things, one time and another. There he is on the top of that tree over by the Big River."

As Farmer Brown's boy drew near, Blacky flew down and disappeared below the bank. Fanner Brown's boy chuckled. "Whatever it is, it is right down there," he muttered.

He walked forward rapidly but quietly, and presently he reached the edge of the bank. Up flew Blacky cawing wildly and pretending to be scared half to death. Again, Farmer Brown's boy chuckled. "You're just making believe," he declared. "You're trying to make me believe that I have surprised you, when all the time you knew I was coming and have been waiting for me. Now, what have you found over here?"

He looked eagerly along the shore, and at once he saw a row of low bushes close to the edge of the water. He knew what it was instantly. "A Duck blind!" he exclaimed. "A hunter has built a blind over here from which to shoot Ducks. I wonder if he has killed any yet. I hope not."

He went down to the blind, for that is what a Duck hunter's hiding-place is called and looked about. A couple of grains of corn just inside the blind caught his eyes, and his face darkened. "That fellow has been baiting Ducks," thought he. "He has been putting out corn to get them to come here regularly. My, how I hate that sort of thing! It is bad enough to hunt them fairly, but to feed them and then kill them — ugh! I wonder if he has shot any yet."

He looked all about keenly, and his face cleared. He knew that if that hunter had killed any Ducks, there would be tell-tale feathers in the blind, and there were none.

Chapter XXIV
FARMER BROWN'S BOY DOES SOME THINKING

FARMER BROWN'S boy sat on the bank of the Big River in a brown study. That means that he was thinking very hard. Blacky the Crow sat in the top of a tall tree a short distance away and watched him. Blacky was silent now, and there was a knowing look in his shrewd little eyes. In calling Farmer Brown's boy over there, he had done all he could, and he was quite satisfied to leave the matter to Farmer Brown's boy.

"A hunter has made that blind to shoot Black Ducks from," thought Farmer Brown's boy, "and he has been baiting them in here by scattering corn for them. Black Ducks are about the smartest Ducks that fly, but if they have been coming in here every evening and finding corn and no sign of danger, they probably think it perfectly safe here and come straight in without being at all suspicious. Tonight, or some night soon, that hunter will be waiting for them.

"I guess the law that permits hunting Ducks is all right, but there ought to be a law against baiting them in. That isn't hunting. No, Sir, that isn't hunting. If this land were my father's, I would know what to do. I would put up a sign saying that this was private property, and no shooting was allowed. But it isn't my father's land, and that hunter has a perfect right to shoot here. He has just as much right here as I have. I wish I could stop him, but I don't see how I can."

A frown puckered the freckled face of Farmer Brown's boy. You see, he was thinking very hard, and when he does that, he is very apt to frown.

"I suppose," he muttered, "I can tear down his blind. He wouldn't know who did it. But that wouldn't do much good; he would build another. Besides, it wouldn't be right. He has a perfect right to make a blind here, and having made it, it is his and I haven't any right to touch it. I won't do a thing I haven't a right to do. That wouldn't be honest. I've got to think of some other way of saving those Ducks."

The frown on his freckled face grew deeper, and for a long time he sat without moving. Suddenly his face cleared, and he jumped to his feet. He began to chuckle. "I have it!" he exclaimed. "I'll do a little shooting myself!" Then he chuckled again and started for home. Presently he began to whistle, a way he has when he is in good spirits.

Blacky the Crow watched him go, and Blacky was well satisfied. He didn't know what Farmer Brown's boy was planning to do, but he had a feeling that he was planning to do something, and that all would be well. Perhaps Blacky wouldn't have felt so sure could he have understood what Farmer Brown's boy had said about doing a little shooting himself.

As it was, Blacky flew off about his own business, quite satisfied that now all would be well, and he need worry no more about those Ducks. None of the little people of the Green Forest and the Green Meadows knew Farmer Brown's boy better than did Blacky the Crow. None knew better than he that Farmer Brown's boy was their best friend.

"It is all right now," chuckled Blacky. "It is all right now." And as the cheery whistle of Farmer Brown's boy floated back to him on the Merry Little Breezes, he repeated it: "It is all right now."

Chapter XXV
BLACKY GETS A DREADFUL SHOCK

When friends prove false, whom may we trust?
The springs of faith are turned to dust.
Blacky the Crow.

BLACKY the Crow was in the top of his favorite tree over near the Big River early this afternoon. He didn't know what was going to happen, but he felt in his bones that something was, and he meant to be on hand to see. For a long time he sat there, seeing nothing unusual. At last he spied a tiny figure far away across the Green Meadows. Even at that distance he knew who it was; it was Farmer Brown's boy, and he was coming toward the Big River.

"I thought as much," chuckled Blacky. "He is coming over here to drive that hunter away."

The tiny figure grew larger. It was Farmer Brown's boy beyond a doubt. Suddenly Blacky's eyes opened so wide that they looked as if they were in danger of popping out of his head. He had discovered that Farmer Brown's boy was carrying something and that that something was a gun! Yes, Sir, Farmer Brown's boy was carrying a terrible gun! If Blacky could have rubbed his eyes, he would have done so, just to make sure that there was nothing the matter with them.

"A gun!" croaked Blacky. "Farmer Brown's boy with a terrible gun! What does it mean?"

Nearer came Farmer Brown's boy, and Blacky could see that terrible gun plainly now. Suddenly an idea popped into his head. "Perhaps he is going to shoot that hunter!" thought Blacky, and somehow he felt better.

Farmer Brown's boy reached the Big River at a point some distance below the blind built by the hunter. He laid his gun down on the bank and went down to the edge of the water. The rushes grew very thick there, and for a while, Farmer Brown's boy was very busy among them. Blacky from his high perch could watch him, and as he watched, he grew more and more puzzled. It looked very much as if Farmer Brown's boy was building a blind much like that of the hunter's. At last he carried an old log down there, got his gun, and sat down just as the hunter had done in his blind the afternoon before. He was quite hidden there, excepting from a place high up like Blacky's perch.

"I—I—I do believe he is going to try to shoot those Ducks himself," gasped Blacky. "I wouldn't have believed it if anyone had told me. No, Sir, I wouldn't have believed it. I—I— can't believe it now. Farmer Brown's boy hunting with a terrible gun! Yet I've got to believe my own eyes."

A noise up river caught his attention. It was the noise of oars in a boat. There was the hunter, rowing down the Big River. Just as he had done the day before, he came ashore above his blind and walked down to it.

"This is no place for me," muttered Blacky. "He'll remember that I scared those Ducks yesterday, and as likely as not he'll try to shoot me."

Blacky spread his black wings and hurriedly left the treetop, heading for another tree farther back on the Green Meadows where he would be safe, but from which he could not see as well. There he sat until the Black Shadows warned him that it was high time for him to be getting back to the Green Forest.

He had to hurry, for it was later than usual, and he was afraid to be out after dark. Just as he reached the Green Forest, he heard a faint "bang, bang" from over by the Big River, and he knew that it came from the place where Farmer Brown's boy was hiding in the rushes.

"It is true," croaked Blacky. "Farmer Brown's boy has turned hunter." It was such a dreadful shock to Blacky that it was a long time before he could go to sleep.

Chapter XXVI
WHY THE HUNTER GOT NO DUCKS

THE hunter who had come down the Big River in a boat and landed near the place where Dusky the Black Duck and his flock had found nice yellow corn scattered in the rushes night after night saw Blacky the Crow leave the top of a certain tree as he approached.

"It is well for you that you didn't wait for me to get nearer," said the hunter. "You are smart enough to know that you can't play the same trick on me twice. You frightened those Ducks away last night, but if you try it again, you'll be shot as surely as your coat is black."

Then the hunter went to his blind which, you know, was the hiding-place he had made of bushes and rushes, and behind this he sat down with his terrible gun to wait and watch for Dusky the Black Duck and his flock.

Now you remember that farther along the shore of the Big River was

Farmer Brown's boy, hiding in a blind he had made that afternoon. The hunter couldn't see him at all. He didn't have the least idea that anyone else was anywhere near. "With that Crow out of the way, I think I will get some Ducks tonight," thought the hunter and looked at his gun to make sure that it was ready.

Over in the West, jolly, round, red Mr. Sun started to go to bed behind the Purple Hills, and the Black Shadows came creeping out. Far down the Big River, the hunter saw a swiftly moving black line just above the water. "Here they come," he muttered, as he eagerly watched that black line draw nearer.

Twice those big black birds circled around over the Big River opposite where the hunter was crouching behind his blind. It was plain that Dusky, their leader, remembered Blacky's warning the night before. But this time there was no warning. Everything appeared safe. Once more the flock circled and then headed straight for that place where they hoped to find more corn. The hunter crouched lower. They were almost near enough for him to shoot when "bang, bang" went a gun a short distance away.

Instantly Dusky and his flock turned and on swift wings swung off and up the river. If ever there was a disappointed hunter, it was the one crouching in that blind. "Somebody else is hunting, and he spoiled my shot that time," he muttered. "He must have a blind farther down. Probably some other Ducks I didn't see came in to him. I wonder if he got them. Here's hoping that next time those Ducks come in here first."

He once more made himself comfortable and settled down for a long wait. The Black Shadows crept out from the farther bank of the Big River. Jolly, round red Mr. Sun had gone to bed, and the first little star was twinkling high overhead. It was very still and peaceful. From out in the middle of the Big River sounded a low "quack"; Dusky and his flock were swimming in this time. Presently the hunter could see a silver line on the water, and then he made out nine black spots. In a few minutes those Ducks would be where he could shoot them.

"Bang, bang" went that gun below him again. With a roar of wings, Dusky and his flock were in the air and away. That hunter stood up and said things, and they were not nice things. He knew that those Ducks would not come back again that night, and that once more he must go home empty-handed. But first he would find out who that other hunter was and what luck he had had, so he tramped down the shore to where that gun had seemed to be. He found the blind of Farmer Brown's boy, but there was no one there. You see, as soon as he had fired his gun the last time, Farmer Brown's boy had slipped out and away. And as he tramped across the Green Meadows toward home with his gun, he chuckled. "He didn't get those Ducks this time," said Farmer Brown's boy.

Chapter XXVII
THE HUNTER GIVES UP

BLACKY the Crow didn't know what to think. He couldn't make himself believe that Farmer Brown's boy had really turned hunter, yet what else could he believe? Hadn't he with his own eyes seen Farmer Brown's boy with a terrible gun hide in rushes along the Big River and wait for Dusky the Black Duck and his flock to come in? And hadn't he with his own ears heard the "bang, bang" of that very gun?

The very first thing the next morning Blacky had hastened over to the place where Farmer Brown's boy had hidden in the rushes. With sharp eyes, he looked for feathers, that would tell the tale of a Duck killed. But there were no feathers. There wasn't a thing to show that anything so dreadful had happened. Perhaps Farmer Brown's boy had missed when he shot at those Ducks. Blacky shook his head and decided to say nothing to anybody about Farmer Brown's boy and that terrible gun.

You may be sure that early in the afternoon he was perched in the top of his favorite tree over by the Big River. His heart sank, just as on the afternoon before, when he saw Farmer Brown's boy with his terrible gun trudging across the Green Meadows to the Big River. Instead of going to the same hiding place, he made a new one farther down.

Then came the hunter a little earlier than usual. Instead of stopping at his blind, he walked straight to the blind Farmer Brown's boy had first made. Of course, there was no one there. The hunter looked both glad and disappointed. He went back to his own blind and sat down, and while he watched for the coming of the Ducks, he also watched that other blind to see if the unknown hunter of the night before would appear. Of course, he didn't, and when at last the hunter saw the Ducks coming, he was sure that this time he would get some of them.

But the same thing happened as on the night before. Just as those Ducks were almost near enough, a gun went "bang, bang," and away went the Ducks. They didn't come back again, and once more a disappointed hunter went home without any.

The next afternoon he was on hand very early. He was there before Farmer Brown's boy arrived, and when he did come, of course the hunter saw him. He walked down to where Farmer Brown's boy was hiding in the rushes. "Hello!" said he. "Are you the one who was shooting here last night and the night before?"

Farmer Brown's boy grinned. "Yes," said he.

"What luck did you have?" asked the hunter.

"Fine," replied Farmer Brown's boy.

"How many Ducks did you get?" asked the hunter.

Farmer Brown's boy grinned more broadly than before. "None," said he. "I guess I'm not a very good shot."

"Then what did you mean by saying you had fine luck?" demanded the hunter.

"Oh," replied Farmer Brown's boy, "I had the luck to see those Ducks and the fun of shooting," and he grinned again.

The hunter lost patience. He tried to order Farmer Brown's boy away. But the latter said he had as much right there as the hunter had, and the hunter knew that this was so. Finally, he gave up, and muttering angrily, he went back to his blind. Again, the gun of Farmer Brown's boy frightened away the Ducks just as they were coming in.

The next afternoon there was no hunter nor the next, though Farmer Brown's boy was there. The hunter had decided that it was a waste of time to hunt there while Farmer Brown's boy was about.

Chapter XXVIII
BLACKY HAS A TALK WITH DUSKY THE BLACK DUCK

Doubt not a friend, but to the last
Grip hard on faith and hold it fast.

Blacky the Crow.

EVERY morning Blacky the Crow visited the rushes along the shore of the Big River, hoping to find Dusky the Black Duck. He was anxious, was Blacky. He feared that Dusky or some of his flock had been killed, and he wanted to know. You see, he knew that Farmer Brown's boy had been shooting over there. At last early one morning, he found Dusky and his flock in the rushes and wild rice. Eagerly he counted them. There were nine. Not one was missing. Blacky sighed with relief and dropped down on the shore close to where Dusky was taking a nap.

"Hello!" said Blacky.

Dusky awoke with a start. "Hello, yourself," said he.

"I've heard a terrible gun banging over here, and I was afraid you or some of your flock had been shot," said Blacky.

"We haven't lost a feather," declared Dusky. "That gun wasn't fired at us, anyway."

"Then who was it fired at?" demanded Blacky.

"I haven't the least idea," replied Dusky.

"Have you seen any other Ducks about here?" inquired Blacky.

"Not one," was Dusky's prompt reply. "If there had been any, I guess we would have known it."

"Did you know that when that terrible gun was fired there was another terrible gun right over behind those bushes?" asked Blacky.

Dusky shook his head. "No," said he, "but I learned long ago that where there is one terrible gun, there is likely to be more, and so when I heard that one bang, I led my flock away from here in a hurry. We didn't want to take any chances."

"It is a lucky thing you did," replied Blacky. "There was a hunter hiding behind those bushes all the time. I warned you of him once."

"That reminds me that I haven't thanked you," said Dusky. "I knew there was something wrong over here, but I didn't know what. So, it was a hunter. I guess it is a good thing that I heeded your warning."

"I guess it is," retorted Blacky dryly. "Do you come here in daytime instead of night now?"

"No," replied Dusky. "We come in after dark and spend the night here. There is nothing to fear from hunters after dark. We've given up coming here until late in the evening. And since we did that, we haven't heard a gun."

Blacky gossiped a while longer, then flew off to look for his breakfast; and as he flew his heart was light. His shrewd little eyes twinkled.

"I ought to have known Farmer Brown's boy better than even to suspect him," thought he. "I know now why he had that terrible gun. It was to frighten those Ducks away so that the hunter would not have a chance to shoot them. He wasn't shooting at anything. He just fired in the air to scare those Ducks away. I know it just as well as if I had seen him do it. I'll never doubt Farmer Brown's boy again. And I'm glad I didn't say a word to anybody about seeing him with a terrible gun."

Blacky was right. Farmer Brown's boy had taken that way of making sure that the hunter who had first baited those Ducks with yellow corn scattered in the rushes in front of his hiding place should have no chance to kill any of them. While appearing to be an enemy, he really had been a friend of Dusky the Black Duck and his flock.

Chapter XXIX
BLACKY DISCOVERS AN EGG

BLACKY is fond of eggs, as you know. In this he is a great deal like other people, Farmer Brown's boy for instance. But as Blacky cannot keep hens, as Farmer Brown's boy does, he is obliged to steal eggs or else go without. If you come right down to plain, everyday truth, I suppose Blacky isn't so far wrong when he insists that he is no more of a thief than Farmer Brown's boy. Blacky says that the eggs which the hens lay belong to the hens, and that he, Blacky has just as much right to take them as Farmer Brown's boy. He quite overlooks the fact that Farmer Brown's boy feeds the biddies and takes the eggs as pay. Anyway, that is what Farmer Brown's boy says, but I do not know whether or not the biddies understand it that way.

So, Blacky the Crow cannot see why he should not help himself to an egg when he gets the chance. He doesn't get the chance very often to steal eggs from the hens, because usually they lay their eggs in the henhouse, and Blacky is too suspicious to venture inside. The eggs he does get are mostly those of his neighbors in the Green Forest and the Old Orchard. But once in a great while, some foolish hen will make a nest outside the henhouse somewhere, and if Blacky happens to find it, the black scamp watches every minute he can spare from other mischief for a chance to steal an egg.

Now Blacky knows just what a rogue Farmer Brown's boy thinks he is, and for this reason Blacky is very careful about approaching Farmer Brown or any other man until he has made sure that he runs no risk of being shot. Blacky knows quite as well as anyone what a gun looks like. He also knows that without a terrible gun, there is little Farmer Brown or anyone else can do to him. So, when he sees Farmer Brown out in his fields, Blacky often will fly right over him and shout "Caw, caw, caw, ca-a-w!" in the most provoking way, and Fanner Brown's boy insists that he has seen Blacky wink when he was doing it.

But Blacky doesn't do anything of this kind around the buildings of Farmer Brown. You see, he has learned that there are doors and windows in buildings, and out of one of these a terrible gun may bang at any time. Though he has suspected that Farmer Brown's boy would not now try to harm him, Blacky is naturally cautious and takes no chances. So, when he comes spying around Farmer Brown's house and barn, he does it when he is quite sure that no one is about, and he makes no noise about it. First, he sits in a tall tree from which he can watch Farmer Brown's home. When he is quite sure that the way is clear, he flies over to the Old Orchard, and from there he inspects the barnyard, never once making a sound. If he is quite sure that no one is about, he sometimes drops down into the henyard and helps himself to corn, if any happens to be there.

It was on one of these silent visits that Blacky spied something which he couldn't forget. It was a box just inside the henhouse door. In the box was some hay and, in that hay, he was sure that he had seen an egg. In fact, he was sure that he saw two eggs there. He might not have noticed them but for the fact that a hen had jumped down from that box, making a terrible fuss. She didn't seem frightened, but very proud. What under the sun she had to be proud about Blacky couldn't understand, but he didn't stay to find out. The noise she was making made him nervous. He was afraid that it would bring someone to find out what was going on. So, he spread his black wings and flew away as silently as he had come.

As he was flying away, he saw those eggs. You see, as he rose into the air, he managed to pass that open door in such a way that he could glance in. That one glance was enough. You know Blacky's eyes are very sharp. He saw the hay in the box and the two eggs in the hay, and that was enough for him. From that instant Blacky the Crow began to scheme and plan to get one or both of those eggs. It seemed to him that he never, never, had wanted anything quite so much, and he was sure that he would not and could not be happy until he succeeded in getting one.

Chapter XXX
BLACKY SCREWS UP HIS COURAGE

IF out of sight, then out of mind. This is a saying which you often hear. It may be true sometimes, but it is very far from true at other times. Take the case of Blacky. He had had only a glance into that nest just inside the door of Farmer Brown's henhouse, but that glance had been enough to show him two eggs there. Then, as he flew away toward the Green Forest, those eggs were out of sight, of course. But do you think they were out of mind? Not much! No, indeed! In fact, those eggs were very much in Blacky's mind. He couldn't think of anything else. He flew straight to a certain tall pine-tree in a lonely part of the Green Forest. Whenever Blacky wants to think or to plan mischief, he seeks that particular tree, and in the shelter of its broad branches, he keeps out of sight of curious eyes, and there he sits as still as still can be.

"I want one of those eggs," muttered Blacky, as he settled himself in comfort on a certain particular spot on a certain particular branch of that tall pine-tree. Indeed, that particular branch might well be called the "mischief branch," for on it Blacky has thought out and planned most of the mischief he is so famous for. "Yes, sir," he continued, "I want one of those eggs, and what is more, I am going to have one."

He half closed his eyes and tipped his head back and swallowed a couple of times, as if he already tasted one of those eggs.

"There is more in one of those eggs than in a whole nestful of Welcome Robin's eggs. It is a very long time since I have been lucky enough to taste a hen's egg, and now is my chance. I don't like having to go inside that henhouse, even though it is barely inside the door. I'm suspicious of doors. They have a way of closing most unexpectedly. I might see if I cannot get Unc' Billy Possum to bring one of those eggs out for me. But that plan won't do, come to think of it, because I can't trust Unc' Billy. The old sinner is too fond of eggs himself. I would be willing to divide with him, but he would be sure to eat his first, and I fear that it would taste so good that he would eat the other. No. I've got to get one of those eggs myself. It is the only way I can be sure of it.

"The thing to do is to make sure that Farmer Brown's boy and Farmer Brown himself are nowhere about. They ought to be down in the cornfield pretty soon. With them down there, I have only to watch my chance and slip in. It won't take but a second. Just a little courage,

Blacky, just a little courage! Nothing in this world worth having is gained without some risk. The thing to do is to make sure that the risk is as small as possible."

Blacky shook out his feathers and then flew out of the tall pine-tree as silently as he had flown into it. He headed straight toward Farmer Brown's cornfield. When he was near enough to see all over the field, he dropped down to the top of a fence post, and there he waited. He didn't have long to wait. In fact, he had been there but a few minutes when he spied two people coming down the Long Lane toward the cornfield. He looked at them sharply, and then gave a little sigh of satisfaction. They were Farmer Brown and Farmer Brown's boy. Presently they reached the cornfield and turned into it. Then they went to work, and Blacky knew that so far as they were concerned, the way was clear for him to visit the henyard.

He didn't fly straight there. Oh, my, no! Blacky is too clever to do anything like that. He flew toward the Green Forest. When he knew that he was out of sight of those in the cornfield, he turned and flew over to the Old Orchard, and from the top of one of the old apple-trees, he studied the henyard and the barnyard and Farmer Brown's house and the barn, to make absolutely sure that there was no danger near. When he was quite sure, he silently flew down into the henyard as he had done many times before. He pretended to be looking for scattered grains of corn, but all the time he was edging nearer and nearer to the open door of the henhouse. At last he could see the box with the hay in it. He walked right up to the open door and peered inside. There was nothing to be afraid of that he could see. Still, he hesitated. He did hate to go inside that door, even for a minute, and that is all it would take to fly up to that nest and get one of those eggs.

Blacky closed his eyes for just a second, and when he did that, he seemed to see himself eating one of those eggs. "What are you afraid of?" he muttered to himself as he opened his eyes. Then with a hurried look in all directions, he flew up to the edge of the box. There lay the two eggs!

Chapter XXXI
AN EGG THAT WOULDN'T BEHAVE

If you had an egg and it wouldn't behave
Just what would you do with that egg, may I ask?
To make an egg do what it don't want to do
Strikes me like a difficult sort of a task.

ALL of which is pure nonsense. Of course. Who ever heard of an egg either behaving or misbehaving? Nobody. That is, nobody that I know, unless it be Blacky. It is best not to mention eggs in Blacky's presence these days. They are a forbidden topic when he is about. Blacky is apt to be a little resentful at the mere mention of an egg. I don't know as I wholly blame him. How would you feel if you *knew* you knew all there was to know about a thing, and then found out that you didn't know anything at all? Well, that is the way it is with Blacky the Crow.

If anyone had told Blacky that he didn't know all there is to know about eggs, he would have laughed at the idea. Wasn't he, Blacky, hatched from an egg himself? And hadn't he, ever since he was big enough, hunted eggs and stolen eggs and eaten eggs? If he didn't know about eggs, who did? That is the way he would have talked before his visit to Farmer Brown's henhouse. It is since then that it has been unwise to mention eggs when Blacky is about.

When Blacky saw the two eggs in the nest in Farmer Brown's henhouse, how Blacky did wish that he could take both. But he couldn't. One would be all that he could manage. He must take his choice and go away while the going was good. Which should he take?

It often happens in this life that things which seem to be unimportant, mere trifles in themselves, prove to be just the opposite. Now, so far as Blacky could see, it didn't make the least difference which egg he took, excepting that one was a little bigger than the other. As a matter of fact, it made all the difference in the world. One was brown and very good to look at. The other, the larger of the two, was white and also very good to look at. In fact, Blacky thought it the better of the two to look at, for it was very smooth and shiny. So, partly on this account, and partly because it was the largest, Blacky chose the white egg. He seized it in his claws and started to fly with it, but somehow he could not seem to get a good grip on it. He fluttered to the ground just outside the door, and there he got a better grip. Just as old Dandycock the Rooster, with head down and all the feathers on his neck standing out with anger, came charging at him, Blacky rose into the air and started over the Old Orchard toward the Green Forest.

Never had Blacky felt more like cawing at the top of his lungs. You see, he felt that he had been very smart, and I suspect that he also felt that he had been very brave. He would have liked to boast a little. But he didn't. He wisely held his tongue. It would be time enough to do his boasting after he had reached a place of safety and had eaten that egg.

He was halfway across the Old Orchard when he felt that egg beginning to slip. Now at best it isn't easy to carry an egg without breaking it. You know how very careful you have to be. Just imagine how Blacky felt when that egg began to slip. Do what he would, he couldn't get a better grip on it. It slipped a wee bit more. Blacky started down towards the ground. But he wasn't quick enough. Striped Chipmunk, watching Blacky from the old stone wall, saw something white drop from Blacky's claws. He saw Blacky dash after it and clutch at it only to miss it. Then the white thing struck a branch of an old apple tree, bounced off and fell to the ground. Blacky followed it.

Striped Chipmunk stole very softly through the grass to see what Blacky was doing. Blacky was standing close beside a white thing that looked very much like an egg. He was looking at it with the queerest expression.

Now and then he would reach out and rap it sharply with his bill, and then look as if he didn't know what to make of it. He didn't. That egg wasn't behaving right. It should have broken when it hit the branch of the apple tree. Certainly, it should have broken when he struck it that way with his bill. However, was he to eat that egg, if he couldn't break the shell? Blacky didn't know.

STRIPED CHIPMUNK SAW SOMETHING WHITE DROP FROM BLACKY'S CLAWS.

Chapter XXXII
WHAT BLACKY DID WITH THE STOLEN EGG

B LACKY was puzzled. He didn't know what to make of that egg he had stolen from Farmer Brown's henhouse. It wasn't like any egg he ever had seen or even heard of. It was a beautiful-looking egg, and he had been sure that it would taste as good, quite as good as it looked. Even now he wasn't sure that if he could only taste it, it would be all that he had hoped. But how could he taste it, when he couldn't break that shell? He never had heard of such a shell. He doubted if anybody else ever had, either. He had hammered at it with his stout bill until he was afraid that he would break that, instead of the egg. The more he tried to break into it and couldn't, the hungrier he grew, and the more certain that nothing else in all the world could possibly taste so good.

But the Old Orchard was not the place for him to work on that egg. In the first place, it was too near Farmer Brown's house. This made Blacky uneasy. You see, he had something of a guilty conscience. Not that he felt at all a sense of having done wrong. To his way of thinking, if he were smart enough to get that egg, he had just as much right to it as anyone else, particularly Farmer Brown's boy. Yet he wasn't at all sure that Farmer Brown's boy would look at the matter quite that way. In fact, he had a feeling that Farmer Brown's boy would call him a thief if he should be discovered with that egg. Then, too, there were too many sharp eyes in the Old Orchard. He wanted to get away where he could be sure of being alone. Then if he couldn't break that shell, no one would be the wiser. So, he picked up the egg and flew straight over to the Green Forest, and this time he managed to get there without dropping it.

Now you would never suspect Blacky the Crow, he of the sharp wits and crafty ways, of being amused by bright things, would you? But he is. In fact, Blacky is quite like a little child in this matter. Anything that is bright and shiny interests Blacky right away. If he finds anything of this kind, he will take it away to a certain secret place, and there he will admire it and play with it and finally hide it. If I didn't know that it isn't so, because it couldn't possibly be so, I should think that Blacky was some relation to certain small boys I know. Always their pockets are filled with all sorts of useless odds and ends which they have picked up here and there. Blacky has no pockets, so he keeps his treasures of this kind in a secret hiding-place, a sort of treasure storehouse. He visits this secretly every day, uncovers his treasures, and gloats over them and plays with them, then carefully covers them up again.

First, Blacky took this egg over near his home, and there he once more tried and tried and tried to break the shell. But the shell wouldn't break, not even when Blacky quite lost his temper and hammered at it for all he was worth. Then he gave the thing up as a bad matter and flew up to his favorite roost in the top of a tall pine-tree, leaving the egg on the ground. But from where he sat on his favorite roost in the tall pine-tree, he could see that provoking egg, a little spot of shining white. When a Jolly Little Sunbeam found it and rested on it, it was so very bright and shiny that Blacky couldn't keep his eyes off it.

Little by little he forgot that it was an egg. At least, he forgot that he wanted to eat it. He began to find pleasure in just looking at it. It might not satisfy his stomach, but it certainly was very satisfying to his eyes. He forgot to think of it as a thing to eat but began to think of it wholly as a thing to look at and admire. He was glad he hadn't been able to break that shell.

Once more he spread his black wings and flew down to the egg. He cocked his head to one side and looked at it. He cocked his head to the other side and looked at it. He walked all around it, chuckling and saying to himself, "Pretty, pretty, pretty, pretty and all mine, mine, mine, mine! Pretty, pretty, and all mine!"

Then he craftily looked all about to make sure that no one was watching him. Having made quite sure, he rolled the egg over and turned it around and admired it to his heart's content. At last he picked it up and carried it to his treasure-house and covered it over very carefully. And there that china nest-egg, for that is what he had stolen, is still his chief treasure to this day, and Blacky still sometimes wonders what kind of a hen laid such a hard-shelled egg.

Blacky has had very many other adventures, but it would take another book to tell about all of them. That would be hardly fair to some of the other little people who also have had adventures and want them told to you. One of these is a beautiful little fellow who lives in the Green Forest, and so the next book will be Whitefoot the Wood Mouse.

WHITEFOOT
THE WOOD
MOUSE

Chapter I
WHITEFOOT SPENDS A HAPPY WINTER

IN all his short life Whitefoot the Wood Mouse never had spent such a happy winter. Whitefoot is one of those wise little people who never allow unpleasant things of the past to spoil their present happiness, and who never borrow trouble from the future. Whitefoot believes in getting the most from the present. The things which are past are past, and that is all there is to it. There is no use in thinking about them. As for the things of the future, it will be time enough to think about them when they happen.

If you and I had as many things to worry about as does Whitefoot the Wood Mouse, we probably never would be happy at all. But Whitefoot is happy whenever he has a chance to be, and in this he is wiser than most human beings. You see, there is not one of all the little people in the Green Forest who has so many enemies to watch out for as has Whitefoot. There are ever so many who would like nothing better than to dine on plump little Whitefoot. There are Buster Bear and Billy Mink and Shadow the Weasel and Unc' Billy Possum and Hooty the Owl and all the members of the Hawk family, not to mention Blacky the Crow in times when other food is scarce. Reddy and Granny Fox and Old Man Coyote are always looking for him.

So, you see, Whitefoot never knows at what instant he may have to run for his life. That is why he is such a timid little fellow and is always running away at the least little unexpected sound. In spite of all this, he is a happy little chap.

It was early in the winter that Whitefoot found a little hole in a corner of Farmer Brown's sugarhouse and crept inside to see what it was like in there. It didn't take him long to decide that it was the most delightful place he ever had found. He promptly decided to move in and spend the winter. In one end of the sugarhouse was a pile of wood. Down under this, Whitefoot made himself a warm, comfortable nest. It was a regular castle

IT WAS EARLY IN THE WINTER THAT WHITEFOOT FOUND A LITTLE HOLE IN A
CORNER OF FARMER BROWN'S SUGARHOUSE.

to Whitefoot. He moved over to it the store of seeds he had laid up for winter use.

Not one of his enemies ever thought of visiting the sugarhouse in search of Whitefoot, and they wouldn't have been able to get in if they had. When rough Brother North Wind howled outside, and sleet and snow were making other little people shiver, Whitefoot was warm and comfortable. There was all the room he needed or wanted in which to run about and play. He could go outside when he chose to, but he didn't choose to very often. For days at a time, he didn't have a single fright. Yes indeed, Whitefoot spent a happy winter.

Chapter II
WHITEFOOT SEES QUEER THINGS

WHITEFOOT had spent the winter undisturbed in Farmer Brown's sugarhouse. He had almost forgotten the meaning of fear. He had come to look on that sugarhouse as belonging to him. It wasn't until Farmer Brown's boy came over to prepare things for sugaring that Whitefoot got a single real fright. The instant Farmer Brown's boy opened the door, Whitefoot scampered down under the pile of wood to his snug little nest, and there he lay, listening to the strange sounds. At last he could stand it no longer and crept to a place where he could peep out and see what was going on. It didn't take him long to discover that this great two-legged creature was not looking for him, and right away he felt better. After a while, Farmer Brown's boy went away, and Whitefoot had the little sugarhouse to himself again.

But Farmer Brown's boy had carelessly left the door wide open. Whitefoot didn't like that open door. It made him nervous. There was nothing to prevent those who hunt him from walking right in. So, the rest of that night Whitefoot felt uncomfortable and anxious.

He felt still more anxious when next day Farmer Brown's boy returned and became very busy putting things to right. Then Farmer Brown himself came and strange things began to happen. It became as warm as in summer. You see, Farmer Brown had built a fire under the evaporator. Whitefoot's curiosity kept him at a place where he could peep out and watch all that was done. He saw Farmer Brown and Farmer Brown's boy pour pails of sap into a great pan. By and by a delicious odor filled the sugarhouse. It didn't take him a great while to discover that these two-legged creatures were so busy that he had nothing to fear from them, and so he crept out to watch. He saw them draw the golden syrup from one end of the evaporator and fill shining tin cans with it. Day after day, they did the same thing. At night when they had left and all was quiet inside the sugarhouse, Whitefoot stole out and found delicious crumbs where they had eaten their lunch. He tasted that thick golden stuff and found it sweet and good. Later he watched them make sugar and nearly made himself sick that night when they had gone home, for they had left some of that sugar where he could get at it. He didn't understand these queer doings at all. But he was no longer afraid.

Chapter III
FARMER BROWN'S BOY BECOMES ACQUAINTED

IT didn't take Farmer Brown's boy long to discover that Whitefoot the Wood Mouse was living in the little sugarhouse. He caught glimpses of Whitefoot peeping out at him. Now Farmer Brown's boy is wise in the ways of the little people of the Green Forest. Right away he made up his mind to get acquainted with Whitefoot. He knew that not in all the Green Forest is there a more timid little fellow than Whitefoot, and he thought it would be a fine thing to be able to win the confidence of such a shy little chap.

So, at first, Farmer Brown's boy paid no attention whatever to Whitefoot. He took care that Whitefoot shouldn't even know that he had been seen. Every day when he ate his lunch, Farmer Brown's boy scattered a lot of crumbs close to the pile of wood under which Whitefoot had made his home. Then he and Farmer Brown would go out to collect sap. When they returned, not a crumb would be left.

One day Farmer Brown's boy scattered some particularly delicious crumbs. Then, instead of going out, he sat down on a bench and kept perfectly still. Farmer Brown and Bowser the Hound went out. Of course, Whitefoot heard them go out, and right away he poked his little head out from under the pile of wood to see if the way was clear. Farmer Brown's boy sat there right in plain sight, but Whitefoot didn't see him. That was because Farmer Brown's boy didn't move the least bit. Whitefoot ran out and at once began to eat those delicious crumbs. When he had filled his little stomach, he began to carry the remainder back to his storehouse underneath the woodpile. While he was gone on one of these trips, Farmer Brown's boy scattered more crumbs in a line that led right up to his foot. Right there he placed a big piece of bread crust.

Whitefoot was working so hard and so fast to get all those delicious bits of food that he took no notice of anything else until he reached that piece of crust. Then he happened to look up right into the eyes of Farmer Brown's boy. With a frightened little squeak, Whitefoot darted back, and for a long time he was afraid to come out again.

But Farmer Brown's boy didn't move, and at last Whitefoot could stand the temptation no longer. He darted out halfway, scurried back, came out again, and at last ventured right up to the crust. Then he began to drag it back to the woodpile. Still Farmer Brown's boy did not move.

For two or three days the same thing happened. By this time, Whitefoot had lost all fear. He knew that Farmer Brown's boy would not harm him, and it was not long before he ventured to take a bit of food from Farmer Brown's boy's hand. After that, Farmer Brown's boy took care that no crumbs should be scattered on the ground. Whitefoot had to come to him for his food, and always Farmer Brown's boy had something delicious for him.

Chapter IV
WHITEFOOT GROWS ANXIOUS

'Tis sad indeed to trust a friend
Then have that trust abruptly end.
Whitefoot.

I KNOW of nothing that is sadder than to feel that a friend is no longer to be trusted. There came a time when Whitefoot the Wood Mouse almost had this feeling. It was a very, very anxious time for Whitefoot.

You see, Whitefoot and Farmer Brown's boy had become the very best of friends there in the little sugarhouse. They had become such good friends that Whitefoot did not hesitate to take food from the hands of Farmer Brown's boy. Never in all his life had he had so much to eat or such good things to eat. He was getting so fat that his handsome little coat was uncomfortably tight. He ran about fearlessly while Farmer Brown and Farmer Brown's boy were making maple syrup and maple sugar. He had even lost his fear of Bowser the Hound, for Bowser had paid no attention to him whatever.

Now you remember that Whitefoot had made his home way down beneath the great pile of wood in the sugarhouse. Of course, Farmer Brown and Farmer Brown's boy used that wood for the fire to boil the sap to make the syrup and sugar. Whitefoot thought nothing of this until one day he discovered that his little home was no longer as dark as it had been. A little ray of light crept down between the sticks. Presently another little ray of light crept down between the sticks.

It was then that Whitefoot began to grow anxious. It was then he realized that that pile of wood was growing smaller and smaller, and if it kept on growing smaller, by and by there wouldn't be any pile of wood and his little home wouldn't be hidden at all. Of course, Whitefoot didn't understand why that wood was slipping away. In spite of himself he began to grow suspicious. He couldn't think of any reason why that wood should be taken away, unless it was to look for his little home. Farmer Brown's boy was just as kind and friendly as ever, but all the time more and more light crept in, as the wood vanished.

"Oh dear, what does it mean?" cried Whitefoot to himself. "They must be looking for my home, yet they have been so good to me that it is hard to believe they mean any harm. I do hope they will stop taking this wood away. I won't have any hiding-place at all, and then I will have to go outside back to my old home in the hollow stump. I don't want to do that. Oh, dear! Oh, dear! I was so happy and now I am so worried! Why can't happy times last always?"

Chapter V
THE END OF WHITEFOOT'S WORRIES

You never can tell! You never can tell!
Things going wrong will often end well.
Whitefoot.

THE next time you meet him just ask Whitefoot if this isn't so. Things had been going very wrong for Whitefoot. It had begun to look to Whitefoot as if he would no longer have a snug, hidden little home in Farmer Brown's sugarhouse. The pile of wood under which he had made that snug little home was disappearing so fast that it began to look as if in a little while there would be no wood at all.

Whitefoot quite lost his appetite. He no longer came out to take food from Farmer Brown's boy's hand. He stayed right in his snug little home and worried.

Now Farmer Brown's boy had not once thought of the trouble he was making. He wondered what had become of Whitefoot, and in his turn, he began to worry. He was afraid that something had happened to his little friend. He was thinking of this as he fed the sticks of wood to the fire for boiling the sap to make syrup and sugar. Finally, as he pulled away two big sticks, he saw something that made him whistle with surprise. It was

Whitefoot's nest which he had so cleverly hidden way down underneath that pile of wood when he had first moved into the sugarhouse. With a frightened little squeak, Whitefoot ran out, scurried across the little sugarhouse and out though the open door.

Farmer Brown's boy understood. He understood perfectly that little people like Whitefoot want their homes hidden away in the dark. "Poor little chap," said Farmer Brown's boy. "He had a regular castle here and we have destroyed it. He's got the snuggest kind of a little nest here, but he won't come back to it so long as it is right out in plain sight. He probably thinks we have been hunting for this little home of his. Hello! Here's his storehouse! I've often wondered how the little rascal could eat so much, but now I understand. He stored away here more than half of the good things I have given him. I am glad he did. If he hadn't, he might not come back, but I feel sure that tonight, when all is quiet, he will come back to take away all his food. I must do something to keep him here."

Farmer Brown's boy sat down to think things over. Then he got an old box and made a little round hole in one end of it. Very carefully he took up Whitefoot's nest and placed it under the old box in the darkest corner of the sugarhouse. Then he carried all Whitefoot's supplies over there and put them under the box. He went outside and got some branches of hemlock and threw these in a little pile over the box. After this he scattered some crumbs just outside.

Late that night, Whitefoot did come back. The crumbs led him to the old box. He crept inside. There was his snug little home! All in a second Whitefoot understood, and trust and happiness returned.

Chapter VI
A VERY CARELESS JUMP

WHITEFOOT once more was happy. When he found his snug little nest and his store of food under that old box in the darkest corner of Farmer Brown's sugarhouse, he knew that Farmer Brown's boy must have placed them there. It was better than the old place under the woodpile. It was the best place for a home Whitefoot ever had had. It didn't take him long to change his mind about leaving the little sugarhouse. Somehow he seemed to know right down inside that his home would not again be disturbed.

So, he proceeded to rearrange his nest and to put all his supplies of food in one corner of the old box. When everything was placed to suit him, he ventured out, for now that he no longer feared Farmer Brown's boy, he wanted to see all that was going on. He liked to jump up on the bench where Farmer Brown's boy sometimes sat. He would climb up to where Farmer Brown's boy's coat hung and explore the pockets of it. Once he stole Farmer Brown's boy's handkerchief. He wanted it to add to the material his nest was made of. Farmer Brown's boy discovered it just as it was disappearing, and how he laughed as he pulled it away.

So, what with eating and sleeping and playing about, secure in the feeling that no harm could come to him, Whitefoot was happier than ever before in his little life. He knew that Farmer Brown's boy and Farmer Brown and Bowser the Hound were his friends. He knew, too, that so long as they were about, none of his enemies would dare come near. This being so, of course there was nothing to be afraid of. No harm could possibly come to him. At least, that is what Whitefoot thought.

But you know, enemies are not the only dangers to watch out for. Accidents will happen. When they do happen, it is very likely to be when the possibility of them is farthest from your thoughts. Almost always they are due to heedlessness or carelessness. It was heedlessness that got Whitefoot into one of the worst mishaps of his whole life.

He had been running and jumping all around the inside of the little sugarhouse. He loves to run and jump, and he had been having just the best time ever. Finally, Whitefoot ran along the old bench and jumped from the end of it for a box standing on end, which Farmer Brown's boy sometimes used to sit on. It wasn't a very long jump, but somehow Whitefoot misjudged it. He was heedless, and he didn't jump quite far enough. Right beside that box was a tin pail half filled with sap. Instead of landing on the box, Whitefoot landed with a splash in that pail of sap.

Chapter VII
WHITEFOOT GIVES UP HOPE

WHITEFOOT had been in many tight places. Yes, indeed, Whitefoot had been in many tight places. He had had narrow escapes of all kinds. But never had he felt so utterly hopeless as now.

The moment he landed in that sap, Whitefoot began to swim frantically. He isn't a particularly good swimmer, but he could swim well enough to keep afloat for a while. His first thought was to scramble up the side of the tin pail, but when he reached it and tried to fasten his sharp little claws into it in order to climb, he discovered that he couldn't. Sharp as they were, his little claws just slipped, and his struggles to get up only resulted in tiring him out and in plunging him wholly beneath the sap. He came up choking and gasping. Then round and round inside that pail he paddled, stopping every two or three seconds to try to climb up that hateful, smooth, shiny wall.

The more he tried to climb out, the more frightened he became.

He was in a perfect panic of fear. He quite lost his head, did Whitefoot. The harder he struggled, the more tired he became, and the greater was his danger of drowning.

Whitefoot squeaked pitifully. He didn't want to drown. Of course not. He wanted to live. But unless he could get out of that pail very soon, he would drown. He knew it. He knew that he couldn't hold on much longer. He knew that just as soon as he stopped paddling, he would sink. Already he was so tired from his frantic efforts to escape that it seemed to him that he couldn't hold out any longer. But somehow he kept his legs moving, and so kept afloat.

Just why he kept struggling, Whitefoot couldn't have told. It wasn't because he had any hope. He didn't have the least bit of hope. He knew now that he couldn't climb the sides of that pail, and there was no other way of getting out. Still, he kept on paddling. It was the only way to keep from drowning, and though he felt sure that he had got to drown at last, he just wouldn't until he actually had to. And all the time Whitefoot squeaked hopelessly, despairingly, pitifully. He did it without knowing that he did it, just as he kept paddling round and round.

Chapter VIII
THE RESCUE

WHEN Whitefoot made the heedless jump that landed him in a pail half filled with sap, no one else was in the little sugarhouse. Whitefoot was quite alone. You see, Farmer Brown and Farmer Brown's boy were out collecting sap from the trees, and Bowser the Hound was with them.

Farmer Brown's boy was the first to return. He came in just after Whitefoot had given up all hope. He went at once to the fire to put more wood on. As he finished this job, he heard the faintest of little squeaks. It was a very pitiful little squeak. Farmer Brown's boy stood perfectly still and listened. He heard it again. He knew right away that it was the voice of Whitefoot.

"Hello!" exclaimed Farmer Brown's boy. "That sounds as if Whitefoot is in trouble of some kind. I wonder where the little rascal is. I wonder what can have happened to him. I must look into this." Again, Farmer Brown's boy heard that faint little squeak. It was so faint that he couldn't tell where it came from. Hurriedly and anxiously, he looked all over the little sugarhouse, stopping every few seconds to listen for that pitiful little squeak. It seemed to come from nowhere in particular. Also, it was growing fainter.

At last Farmer Brown's boy happened to stand still close to that tin pail half filled with sap. He heard the faint little squeak again and with it a little splash. It was the sound of the little splash that led him to look down. In a flash, he understood what had happened. He saw poor little Whitefoot struggling feebly, and even as he looked Whitefoot's head went under. He was very nearly drowned.

Stooping quickly, Farmer Brown's boy grabbed Whitefoot's long tail and pulled him out. Whitefoot was so nearly drowned that he didn't have strength enough to even kick. A great pity filled the eyes of Farmer Brown's boy as he held Whitefoot's head down and gently shook him. He was trying to shake some of the sap out of Whitefoot. It ran out of Whitefoot's nose and out of his mouth. Whitefoot began to gasp. Then Farmer Brown's boy spread his coat close by the fire, rolled Whitefoot up in his handkerchief and gently placed him on the coat. For some time Whitefoot lay just gasping. But presently his breath came easier, and after a while, he was breathing naturally. But he was too weak and tired to move, so he just lay there while Farmer Brown's boy gently stroked his head and told him how sorry he was.

Little by little Whitefoot recovered his strength. At last he could sit up, and finally he began to move about a little, although he was still wobbly on his legs. Farmer Brown's boy put some bits of food where Whitefoot could get them, and as he ate, Whitefoot's beautiful soft eyes were filled with gratitude.

Chapter IX
TWO TIMID PERSONS MEET

Thus always you will meet life's test —
To do the thing you can do best.
Whitefoot.

JUMPER the Hare sat crouched at the foot of a tree in the Green Forest. Had you happened along there, you would not have seen him. At least, I doubt if you would. If you had seen him, you probably wouldn't have known it. You see, in his white coat, Jumper was so exactly the color of the snow that he looked like nothing more than a little heap of snow.

Just in front of Jumper was a little round hole. He gave it no attention.

It didn't interest him in the least. All through the Green Forest were little holes in the snow. Jumper was so used to them that he seldom noticed them. So, he took no notice of this one until something moved down in that hole. Jumper's eyes opened a little wider and he watched. A sharp little face with very bright eyes filled that little round hole. Jumper moved just the tiniest bit, and in a flash that sharp little face with the bright eyes disappeared.

Jumper sat still and waited. After a long wait, the sharp little face with bright eyes appeared again. "Don't be frightened, Whitefoot," said Jumper softly.

At the first word, the sharp little face disappeared, but in a moment, it was back, and the sharp little eyes were fixed on Jumper suspiciously. After a long stare, the suspicion left them, and out of the little round hole came trim little Whitefoot in a soft brown coat with white waistcoat and with white feet and a long, slim tail. This winter he was not living in Farmer Brown's sugarhouse.

"Gracious, Jumper, how you did scare me!" said he.

Jumper chuckled. "Whitefoot, I believe you are more timid than I am," he replied.

"Why shouldn't I be? I'm ever so much smaller, and I have more enemies," retorted Whitefoot.

"It is true you are smaller, but I am not so sure that you have more enemies," replied Jumper thoughtfully. "It sometimes seems to me that I couldn't have more, especially in winter."

"Name them," commanded Whitefoot.

"Hooty the Great Horned Owl, Yowler the Bob Cat, Old Man Coyote, Reddy Fox, Terror the Goshawk, Shadow the Weasel, Billy Mink." Jumper paused.

"Is that all?" demanded Whitefoot.

"Isn't that enough?" retorted Jumper rather sharply.

"I have all of those and Blacky the Crow and Butcher the Shrike and Sammy Jay in winter, and Buster Bear and Jimmy Skunk and several of the Snake family in summer," replied Whitefoot. "It seems to me sometimes as if I need eyes and ears all over me. Night and day there is always someone hunting for poor little me. And then some folks wonder why I am so timid. If I were not as timid as I am, I wouldn't be alive now; I would have been caught long ago. Folks may laugh at me for being so easily frightened, but I don't care. That is what saves my life a dozen times a day."

Jumper looked interested. "I hadn't thought of that," said he. "I'm a very timid person myself, and sometimes I have been ashamed of being so easily frightened. But come to think of it, I guess you are right; the more timid I am, the longer I am likely to live."

Whitefoot suddenly darted into his hole. Jumper didn't move, but his eyes widened with fear. A great white bird had just alighted on a stump a short distance away. It was Whitey the Snowy Owl, down from the Far North.

"There is another enemy we both forgot," thought Jumper, and tried not to shiver.

Chapter X
THE WHITE WATCHERS

Much may be gained by sitting still
If you but have the strength of will.
Whitefoot.

JUMPER the Hare crouched at the foot of a tree in the Green Forest, and a little way from him on a stump sat Whitey the Snowy Owl. Had you been there to see them, both would have appeared as white as the snow around them unless you had looked very closely. Then you might have seen two narrow black lines back of Jumper's head. They were the tips of his ears, for these remain black. And near the upper part of the white mound which was Whitey, you might have seen two round yellow spots, his eyes.

There they were for all the world like two little heaps of snow. Jumper didn't move so much as a hair. Whitey didn't move so much as a feather. Both were waiting and watching. Jumper didn't move because he knew that Whitey was there. Whitey didn't move because he didn't want anyone to know he was there and didn't know that Jumper was there. Jumper was sitting still because he was afraid. Whitey was sitting still because he was hungry.

So, there they sat, each in plain sight of the other but only one seeing the other. This was because Jumper had been fortunate enough to see Whitey alight on that stump. Jumper had been sitting still when Whitey arrived, and so those fierce yellow eyes had not yet seen him. But had Jumper so much as lifted one of those long ears, Whitey would have seen, and his great claws would have been reaching for Jumper.

Jumper didn't want to sit still. No, indeed! He wanted to run. You know it is on those long legs of his that Jumper depends almost wholly for safety. But there are times for running and times for sitting still, and this was a time for sitting still. He knew that Whitey didn't know that he was anywhere near. But just the same it was hard, very hard to sit there with one he so greatly feared watching so near. It seemed as if those fierce yellow eyes of Whitey must see him. They seemed to look right through him. They made him shake inside.

"I want to run. I want to run. I want to run," Jumper kept saying to himself. Then he would say, "But I mustn't. I mustn't. I mustn't."

And so, Jumper did the hardest thing in the world, — sat still and stared danger in the face. He was sitting still to save his life.

Whitey the Snowy Owl was sitting still to catch a dinner. I know that sounds queer, but it was so. He knew that so long as he sat still, he was not likely to be seen. It was for this purpose that Old Mother Nature had given him that coat of white. In the Far North, which was his real home, everything is white for months and months, and anyone dressed in a dark suit can be seen a long distance. So, Whitey had been given that white coat that he might have a better chance to catch food enough to keep him alive.

And he had learned how to make the best use of it. Yes, indeed, he knew how to make the best use of it. It was by doing just what he was doing now, — sitting perfectly still. Just before he had alighted on that stump, he had seen something move at the entrance to a little round hole in the snow. He was sure of it.

"A Mouse," thought Whitey, and alighted on that stump. "He saw me flying, but he'll forget about it after a while and will come out again. He won't see me then if I don't move. And I won't move until he is far enough from that hole for me to catch him before he can get back to it."

So, the two watchers in white sat without moving for the longest time, one watching for a dinner and the other watching the other watcher.

Chapter XI
JUMPER IS IN DOUBT

When doubtful what course to pursue
'T is sometimes best to nothing do.
Whitefoot.

JUMPER the Hare was beginning to feel easier in his mind. He was no longer shaking inside. In fact, he was beginning to feel quite safe. There he was in plain sight of Whitey the Snowy Owl, sitting motionless on a stump only a short distance away, yet Whitey hadn't seen him. Whitey had looked straight at him many times, but because Jumper had not moved so much as a hair, Whitey had mistaken him for a little heap of snow.

"All I have to do is to keep right on sitting perfectly still, and I'll be as safe as if Whitey were nowhere about. Yes, sir, I will," thought Jumper. "By and by he will become tired and fly away. I do hope he'll do that before Whitefoot comes out again. If Whitefoot should come out, I couldn't warn him because that would draw Whitey's attention to me, and he wouldn't look twice at a Wood Mouse when there was a chance to get a Hare for his dinner.

"This is a queer world. It is so. Old Mother Nature does queer things. Here she has given me a white coat in winter so that I may not be easily seen when there is snow on the ground, and at the same time she has given one of those I fear most a white coat so that he may not be easily seen, either. It certainly is a queer world."

Jumper forgot that Whitey was only a chance visitor from the Far North and that it was only once in a great while that he came down there, while up in the Far North where he belonged, nearly everybody was dressed in white.

Jumper hadn't moved once, but once in a while Whitey turned his great round head for a look all about in every direction. But it was done in such a way that only eyes watching him sharply would have noticed it. Most of the time he kept his fierce yellow eyes fixed on the little hole in the snow in which Whitefoot had disappeared. You know Whitey can see by day quite as well as any other bird.

Jumper, having stopped worrying about himself, began to worry about Whitefoot. He knew that Whitefoot had seen Whitey arrive on that stump and that was why he had dodged back into his hole and since then had not even poked his nose out. But that had been so long ago that by this time Whitefoot must think that Whitey had gone on about his business, and Jumper expected to see Whitefoot appear any moment. What Jumper didn't know was that Whitefoot's bright little eyes had all the time been watching Whitey from another little hole in the snow some distance away. A tunnel led from this little hole to the first little hole.

Suddenly off among the trees, something moved. At least, Jumper thought he saw something move. Yes, there it was, a little black spot moving swiftly this way and that way over the snow. Jumper stared very hard. And then his heart seemed to jump right up in his throat. It did so. He felt as if he would choke. That black spot was the tip end of a tail, the tail of a small, very slim fellow dressed all in white, the only other one in all the Green Forest who dresses all in white. It was Shadow the Weasel! In his white winter coat, he is called Ermine.

He was running this way and that way, back and forth, with his nose to the snow. He was hunting, and Jumper knew that sooner or later Shadow would find him. Safety from Shadow lay in making the best possible use of those long legs of his, but to do that would bring Whitey the Owl swooping after him. What to do Jumper didn't know. And so, he did nothing. It happened to be the wisest thing he could do.

Chapter XII
WHITEY THE OWL SAVES JUMPER

It often happens in the end
An enemy may prove a friend.
Whitefoot.

WAS ever anyone in a worse position than Jumper the Hare? To move would be to give himself away to Whitey the Snowy Owl. If he remained where he was, very likely Shadow the Weasel would find him, and the result would be the same as if he were caught by Whitey the Owl. Neither Whitey nor Shadow knew he was there, but it would be only a few minutes before one of them knew it. At least, that is the way it looked to Jumper.

Whitey wouldn't know it unless he moved, but Shadow the Weasel would find his tracks, and his nose would lead him straight there. Back and forth, back and forth, this way, that way and the other way, just a little distance off, Shadow was running with his nose to the snow. He was hunting — hunting for the scent of someone whom he could kill. In a few minutes he would be sure to find where Jumper had been, and then his nose would lead him straight to that tree at the foot of which Jumper was crouching.

Nearer and nearer came Shadow. He was slim and trim and didn't look at all terrible. Yet there was no one in all the Green Forest more feared by the little people in fur, by Jumper, by Peter Rabbit, by Whitefoot, even by

Chatterer the Red Squirrel.

"Perhaps," thought Jumper, "he won't find my scent after all. Perhaps he'll go in another direction." But all the time Jumper felt in his bones that Shadow would find that scent. "When he does, I'll run," said Jumper to himself. "I'll have at least a chance to dodge Whitey. I am afraid he will catch me, but I'll have a chance. I won't have any chance at all if Shadow finds me."

Suddenly Shadow stopped running and sat up to look about with fierce little eyes, all the time testing the air with his nose. Jumper's heart sank. He knew that Shadow had caught a faint scent of someone. Then Shadow began to run back and forth once more, but more carefully than before. And then he started straight for where Jumper was crouching! Jumper knew then that Shadow had found his trail.

Jumper drew a long breath and settled his long hind feet for a great jump, hoping to so take Whitey the Owl by surprise that he might be able to get away. And as Jumper did this, he looked over to that stump where Whitey had been sitting so long. Whitey was just leaving it on his great silent wings, and his fierce yellow eyes were fixed in the direction of Shadow the Weasel. He had seen that moving black spot which was the tip of Shadow's tail.

Jumper didn't have time to jump before Whitey was swooping down at Shadow. So, Jumper just kept still and watched with eyes almost popping from his head with fear and excitement.

Shadow hadn't seen Whitey until just as Whitey was reaching for him with his great cruel claws. Now if there is anyone who can move more quickly than Shadow the Weasel, I don't know who it is. Whitey's claws closed on nothing but snow; Shadow had dodged. Then began a game, Whitey swooping and Shadow dodging, and all the time they were getting farther and farther from where Jumper was.

The instant it was safe to do so, Jumper took to his long heels and the way he disappeared, lipperty-lipperty-lip, was worth seeing. Whitey the Snowy Owl had saved him from Shadow the Weasel and didn't know it. An enemy had proved to be a friend.

Chapter XIII
WHITEFOOT DECIDES QUICKLY

Your mind made up a certain way
Be swift to act; do not delay.
Whitefoot.

W HEN Whitefoot had discovered Whitey the Snowy Owl, he had dodged down in the little hole in the snow beside which he had been sitting. He had not been badly frightened. But he was somewhat upset. Yes, sir, he was somewhat upset. You see, he had so many enemies to watch out for, and here was another.

"Just as if I didn't have troubles enough without having this white robber to add to them," grumbled Whitefoot. "Why doesn't he stay where he belongs, way up in the Far North? It must be that food is scarce up there. Well, now that I know he is here, he will have to be smarter than I think he is to catch me. I hope Jumper the Hare will have sense enough to keep perfectly still. I've sometimes envied him his long legs, but I guess I am better off than he is, at that. Once he has been seen by an enemy, only those long legs of his can save him, but I have a hundred hiding-places down under the snow. Whitey is watching the hole where I disappeared; he thinks I'll come out there again after a while. I'll fool him."

Whitefoot scampered along through a little tunnel and presently very cautiously peeped out of another little round hole in the snow. Sure enough, there was Whitey the Snowy Owl back to him on a stump, watching the hole down which he had disappeared a few minutes before. Whitefoot grinned. Then he looked over to where he had last seen Jumper. Jumper was still there; it was clear that he hadn't moved, and so Whitey hadn't seen him. Again, Whitefoot grinned. Then he settled himself to watch patiently for Whitey to become tired of watching that hole and fly away.

So, it was that Whitefoot saw all that happened. He saw Whitey suddenly sail out on silent wings from that stump and swoop with great claws reaching for someone. And then he saw who that someone was, — Shadow the Weasel! He saw Shadow dodge in the very nick of time. Then

HE WATCHED WHITEY SWOOP AGAIN AND AGAIN AS SHADOW DODGED THIS WAY AND THAT WAY.

he watched Whitey swoop again and again as Shadow dodged this way and that way. Finally, both disappeared amongst the trees. Then he turned just in time to see Jumper the Hare bounding away with all the speed of his wonderful, long legs.

Fear, the greatest fear he had known for a long time, took possession of Whitefoot. "Shadow the Weasel!" he gasped and had such a thing been possible he certainly would have turned pale. "Whitey won't catch him; Shadow is too quick for him. And when Whitey has given up and flown away, Shadow will come back. He probably had found the tracks of Jumper the Hare and he will come back. I know him; he'll come back. Jumper is safe enough from him now, because he has such a long start, but Shadow will be sure to find one of my holes in the snow. Oh, dear! Oh, dear! What shall I do?"

You see, Shadow the Weasel is the one enemy that can follow Whitefoot into most of his hiding-places.

For a minute or two Whitefoot sat there, shaking with fright. Then he made up his mind. "I'll get away from here before he returns," thought Whitefoot. "I've got to. I've spent a comfortable winter here so far, but there will be no safety for me here any longer. I don't know where to go, but anywhere will be better than here now."

Without waiting another second, Whitefoot scampered away. And how he did hope that his scent would have disappeared by the time Shadow returned. If it hadn't, there would be little hope for him, and he knew it.

Chapter XIV
SHADOWS RETURN

He little gains and has no pride
Who from his purpose turns aside.
Whitefoot.

SHADOW the Weasel believes in persistence. When he sets out to do a thing, he keeps at it until it is done, or he knows for a certainty it cannot be done. He is not easily discouraged. This is one reason he is so feared by the little people he delights to hunt. They know that once he gets on their trail, they will be fortunate indeed if they escape him.

When Whitey the Snowy Owl swooped at him and so nearly caught him, he was not afraid as he dodged this way and that way. Any other of the little people with the exception of his cousin, Billy Mink, would have been frightened half to death. But Shadow was simply angry. He was angry that anyone should try to catch him. He was still more angry because his hunt for Jumper the Hare was interfered with. You see, he had just found Jumper's trail when Whitey swooped at him.

So, Shadow's little eyes grew red with rage as he dodged this way and that and was gradually driven away from the place where he had found the trail of Jumper the Hare. At last he saw a hole in an old log and into this he darted. Whitey couldn't get him there. Whitey knew this and he knew, too, that waiting for Shadow to come out again would be a waste of time. So, Whitey promptly flew away.

Hardly had he disappeared when Shadow popped out of that hole, for he had been peeping out and watching Whitey. Without a moment's pause, he turned straight back for the place where he had found the trail of Jumper the Hare. He had no intention of giving up that hunt just because he had been driven away. Straight to the very spot where Whitey had first swooped at him, he ran, and there once more his keen little nose took up the trail of Jumper. It led him straight to the foot of the tree where Jumper had crouched so long.

But, as you know, Jumper wasn't there then. Shadow ran in a circle and presently he found where Jumper had landed on the snow at the end of that first bound. Shadow snarled. He understood exactly what had happened.

"Jumper was under that tree when that white robber from the Far North tried to catch me, and he took that chance to leave in a hurry. I can tell that by the length of this jump. Probably he is still going. It is useless to follow him because he has too long a start," said Shadow, and he snarled again in rage and disappointment.

Then, for such is his way, he wasted no more time or thought on

Jumper the Hare. Instead, he began to look for other trails. So, it was that he found one of the little holes of Whitefoot the Wood Mouse.

"Ha! So, this is where Whitefoot has been living this winter!" he exclaimed. Once more his eyes glowed red, but this time with eagerness and the joy of the hunt. He plunged down into that little hole in the snow. Down there the scent of Whitefoot was strong. Shadow followed it until it led out of another little hole in the snow. But there he lost it. You see, it was so long since Whitefoot had hurriedly left that the scent on the surface had disappeared.

Shadow ran swiftly this way and that way in a big circle, but he couldn't find Whitefoot's trail again. Snarling with anger and disappointment, he returned to the little hole in the snow and vanished. Then he followed all Whitefoot's little tunnels. He found Whitefoot's nest. He found his store of seeds. But he didn't find Whitefoot.

"He'll come back," muttered Shadow, and curled up in Whitefoot's nest to wait.

Chapter XV
WHITEFOOT'S DREADFUL JOURNEY

Danger may be anywhere,
So I expect it everywhere.
Whitefoot.

WHITEFOOT the Wood Mouse was terribly frightened. Yes, sir, he was terribly frightened. It was a long, long time since he had been as frightened as he now was. He is used to frights, is Whitefoot. He has them every day and every night, but usually they are sudden frights, quickly over and as quickly forgotten.

This fright was different. You see, Whitefoot had caught a glimpse of Shadow the Weasel. And he knew that if Shadow returned, he would be sure to find the little round holes in the snow that led down to Whitefoot's private little tunnels underneath.

The only thing for Whitefoot to do was to get just as far from that place as he could before Shadow should return. And so poor little Whitefoot started out on a journey that was to take him he knew not where. All he could do was to go and go and go until he could find a safe hiding-place.

My, my, but that was a dreadful journey! Every time a twig snapped, Whitefoot's heart seemed to jump right up in his throat. Every time he saw a moving shadow, and the branches of the trees moving in the wind were constantly making moving shadows on the snow, he dodged behind a tree trunk or under a piece of bark or wherever he could find a hiding-place.

You see, Whitefoot has so many enemies always looking for him that he hides whenever he sees anything moving. When at home, he is forever dodging in and out of his hiding-places. So, because everything was strange to him, and because of the great fear of Shadow the Weasel, he suspected everything that moved and every sound he heard. For a long way no one saw him, for no one was about. Yet all that way Whitefoot twisted and dodged and darted from place to place and was just as badly frightened as if there had been enemies all about.

"Oh, dear! Oh, dear me!" he kept saying over and over to himself. "Wherever shall I go? Whatever shall I do? However, shall I get enough to eat? I won't dare go back to get food from my little storehouses, and I shall have to live in a strange place where I won't know where to look for food. I am getting tired. My legs ache. I'm getting hungry. I want my nice, warm, soft bed. Oh, dear! Oh, dear! Oh, dear me!"

But in spite of his frights, Whitefoot kept on. You see, he was more afraid to stop than he was to go on. He just had to get as far from Shadow the Weasel as he could. Being such a little fellow, what would be a short distance for you or me is a long distance for Whitefoot. And so that journey was to him very long indeed. Of course, it seemed longer because of the constant frights which came one right after another. It really was a terrible journey. Yet if he had only known it, there wasn't a thing along the whole way to be afraid of. You know it often happens that people are frightened more by what they don't know than by what they do know.

Chapter XVI
WHITEFOOT CLIMBS A TREE

I'd rather be frightened
With no cause for fear
That fearful of nothing
When danger is near.

Whitefoot.

WHITEFOOT kept on going and going. Every time he thought that he was so tired he must stop, he would think of Shadow the Weasel and then go on again. By and by he became so tired that not even the thought of Shadow the Weasel could make him go much farther. So, he began to look about for a safe hiding-place in which to rest.

Now the home which he had left had been a snug little room beneath the roots of a certain old stump. There he had lived for a long time in the greatest comfort. Little tunnels led to his storehouses and up to the surface of the snow. It had been a splendid place and one in which he had felt perfectly safe until Shadow the Weasel had appeared. Had you seen him playing about there, you would have thought him one of the little people of the ground, like his cousin Danny Meadow Mouse.

But Whitefoot is quite as much at home in trees as on the ground. In fact, he is quite as much at home in trees as is Chatterer the Red Squirrel, and a lot more at home in trees than is Striped Chipmunk, although Striped Chipmunk belongs to the Squirrel family. So, now that he must find a hiding-place, Whitefoot decided that he would feel much safer in a tree than on the ground.

"If only I can find a hollow tree," whimpered Whitefoot. "I will feel ever so much safer in a tree than hiding in or near the ground in a strange place."

So, Whitefoot began to look for a dead tree. You see, he knew that there was more likely to be a hollow in a dead tree than in a living tree. By and by he came to a tall, dead tree. He knew it was a dead tree, because there was no bark on it. But, of course, he couldn't tell whether or not that tree was hollow. I mean he couldn't tell from the ground.

"Oh, dear!" he whimpered again. "Oh, dear! I suppose I will have to climb this, and I am so tired. It ought to be hollow. There ought to be splendid holes in it. It is just the kind of a tree that Drummer the Woodpecker likes to make his house in. I shall be terribly disappointed if I don't find one of his houses somewhere in it, but I wish I hadn't got to climb it to find out. Well, here goes."

He looked anxiously this way. He looked anxiously that way. He looked anxiously the other way. In fact, he looked anxiously every way. But he saw no one and nothing to be afraid of, and so he started up the tree.

He was half-way up when, glancing down, he saw a shadow moving across the snow. Once more Whitefoot's heart seemed to jump right up in his throat. That shadow was the shadow of someone flying. There couldn't be the least bit of doubt about it. Whitefoot flattened himself against the side of the tree and peeked around it. He was just in time to see a gray and black and white bird almost the size of Sammy Jay alighted in the very next tree. He had come along near the ground and then risen sharply into the tree. His bill was black, and there was just a tiny hook on the end of it. Whitefoot knew who it was. It was Butcher the Shrike. Whitefoot shivered.

Chapter XVII
WHITEFOOT FINDS A HOLE JUST IN TIME

Just in time, not just too late,
Will make you master of your fate.
Whitefoot.

WHITEFOOT, half-way up that dead tree, flattened himself against the trunk and, with his heart going pit-a-pat, pit-a-pat with fright, peered around the tree at an enemy he had not seen for so long that he had quite forgotten there was such a one. It was Butcher the Shrike. Often, he is called just Butcher Bird.

He did not look at all terrible. He was not quite as big as Sammy Jay. He had no terrible claws like the Hawks and Owls. There was a tiny hook at the end of his black bill, but it wasn't big enough to look very dreadful. But you cannot always judge a person by looks, and Whitefoot knew that Butcher was one to be feared.

So, his heart went pit-a-pat, pit-a-pat as he wondered if Butcher had seen him. He didn't have to wait long to find out. Butcher flew to a tree back of Whitefoot and then straight at him. Whitefoot dodged around to the other side of the tree. Then began a dreadful game. At least, it was dreadful to Whitefoot. This way and that way around the trunk of that tree he dodged, while Butcher did his best to catch him.

Whitefoot would not have minded this so much, had he not been so tired, and had he known of a hiding-place close at hand. But he *was* tired, very tired, for you remember he had had what was a very long and terrible journey to him. He had felt almost too tired to climb that tree in the first place to see if it had any holes in it higher up. Now he didn't know whether to keep on going up or to go down. Two or three times he dodged around the tree without doing either. Then he decided to go up.

Now Butcher was enjoying this game of dodge. If he should catch Whitefoot, he would have a good dinner. If he didn't catch Whitefoot, he would simply go hungry a little longer. So, you see, there was a very big difference in the feelings of Whitefoot and Butcher. Whitefoot had his life to lose, while Butcher had only a dinner to lose.

Dodging this way and dodging that way, Whitefoot climbed higher and higher. Twice he whisked around that tree trunk barely in time. All the time he was growing more and more tired, and more and more discouraged. Supposing he should find no hole in that tree!

"There must be one. There must be one," he kept saying over and over to himself, to keep his courage up. "I can't keep dodging much longer. If I don't find a hole pretty soon, Butcher will surely catch me. Oh, dear! Oh, dear!"

Just above Whitefoot was a broken branch. Only the stub of it

THEN BEGAN A DREADFUL GAME. AT LEAST, IT WAS DREADFUL TO
WHITEFOOT.

remained. The next time he dodged around the trunk, he found himself just below that stub. Oh, joy! There, close under that stub, was a round hole. Whitefoot didn't hesitate a second. He didn't wait to find out whether or not anyone was in that hole. He didn't even think that there might be someone in there. With a tiny little squeak of relief, he darted in.

He was just in time. He was just in the nick of time. Butcher struck at him and just missed him as he disappeared in that hole. Whitefoot had saved his life and Butcher had missed a dinner.

Chapter XVIII
AN UNPLEASANT SURPRISE

Be careful never to be rude
Enough to thoughtlessly intrude.
Whitefoot.

IF ever anybody in the Great World felt relief and thankfulness, it was Whitefoot when he dodged into that hole in the dead tree just as Butcher the Shrike all but caught him. For a few minutes he did nothing but pant, for he was quite out of breath.

"I was right," he said over and over to himself, "I was right. I was sure there must be a hole in this tree. It is one of the old houses of Drummer the Woodpecker. Now I am safe."

Presently he peeped out. He wanted to see if Butcher was watching outside. He was just in time to see Butcher's gray and black and white coat disappearing among the trees. Butcher was not foolish enough to waste time watching for Whitefoot to come out. Whitefoot sighed happily. For the first time since he had started on his dreadful journey, he felt safe. Nothing else mattered. He was hungry, but he didn't mind that. He was willing to go hungry for the sake of being safe.

Whitefoot watched until Butcher was out of sight. Then he turned to see what that house was like. Right away he discovered that there was a soft, warm bed in it. It was made of leaves, grass, moss, and the lining of bark. It was a very fine bed indeed.

"My, my, my, but I am lucky," said Whitefoot to himself. "I wonder who could have made this fine bed. I certainly shall sleep comfortably here. Goodness knows, I need a rest. If I can find food enough near here, I'll make this my home. I couldn't ask for a better one."

Chuckling happily, Whitefoot began to pull away the top of that bed so as to get to the middle of it. And then he got a surprise. It was an unpleasant surprise. It was a most unpleasant surprise. There was someone in that bed! Yes, sir, there was someone curled up in a little round ball in the middle of that fine bed. It was someone with a coat of the softest, finest fur. Can you guess who it was? It was Timmy the Flying Squirrel.

It seemed to Whitefoot as if his heart flopped right over. You see, at first, he didn't recognize Timmy. Whitefoot is himself so very timid that his thought was to run; to get out of there as quickly as possible. But he had no place to run to, so he hesitated. Never in all his life had Whitefoot had a greater disappointment. He knew now that this splendid house was not for him.

Timmy the Flying Squirrel didn't move. He remained curled up in a soft little ball. He was asleep. Whitefoot remembered that Timmy sleeps during the day and seldom comes out until the Black Shadows come creeping out from the Purple Hills at the close of day. Whitefoot felt easier in his mind then. Timmy was so sound asleep that he knew nothing of his visitor. And so Whitefoot felt safe in staying long enough to get rested. Then he would go out and hunt for another home.

So, down in the middle of that soft, warm bed, Timmy the Flying Squirrel, curled up in a little round ball with his flat tail wrapped around him, slept peacefully, and on top of that soft bed Whitefoot the Wood Mouse rested and wondered what he should do next. Not in all the Green Forest could two more timid little people be found than the two in that old home of Drummer the Woodpecker.

Chapter XIX
WHITEFOOT FINDS A HOME AT LAST

True independence he has known
Whose home has been his very own.
Whitefoot.

CURLED up in his splendid warm bed, Timmy the Flying Squirrel slept peacefully. He didn't know he had a visitor. He didn't know that on top of that same bed lay Whitefoot the Wood Mouse. Whitefoot wasn't asleep. No, indeed! Whitefoot was too worried to sleep. He knew he couldn't stay in that fine house because it belonged to Timmy. He knew that as soon as Timmy awoke, he, Whitefoot, would have to get out. Where should he go? He wished he knew. How he did long for the old home he had left. But when he thought of that, he remembered Shadow the Weasel. It was better to be homeless than to feel that at any minute Shadow the Weasel might appear.

It was getting late in the afternoon. Before long, jolly, round, red Mr. Sun would go to bed behind the Purple Hills, and the Black Shadows would come creeping through the Green Forest, then Timmy the Flying Squirrel would awake. "It won't do for me to be here then," said Whitefoot to himself. "I must find some other place before he wakes. If only I knew this part of the Green Forest, I might know where to go. As it is, I shall have to go hunt for a new home and trust to luck. Did ever a poor little Mouse have so much trouble?"

After a while, Whitefoot felt rested and peeped out of the doorway. No enemy was to be seen anywhere. Whitefoot crept out and climbed a little higher up in the tree. Presently he found another hole. He peeped inside and listened long and carefully. He didn't intend to make the mistake of going into another house where someone might be living.

At last, sure that there was no one in there, he crept in. Then he made a discovery. There were beech nuts in there and there were seeds. It was a storehouse! Whitefoot knew at once that it must be Timmy's storehouse. Right away he realized how very, very hungry he was. Of course, he had no right to any of those seeds or nuts. Certainly not! That is, he wouldn't have had any right had he been a boy or girl. But it is the law of the Green Forest that whatever anyone finds, he may help himself to if he can.

So, Whitefoot began to fill his empty little stomach with some of those seeds. He ate and ate and ate and quite forgot all his troubles. Just as he felt that he hadn't room for another seed, he heard the sound of claws outside on the trunk of the tree. In a flash he knew that Timmy the Flying Squirrel was awake, and that it wouldn't do to be found in there by him. In a jiffy Whitefoot was outside. He was just in time. Timmy was almost up to the entrance.

"Hi, there!" cried Timmy. "What were you doing in my storehouse?"

"I—I—I was looking for a new home," stammered Whitefoot.

"You mean you were stealing some of my food," snapped Timmy suspiciously.

"I—I—I did take a few seeds because I was almost starved. But truly I was looking for a new home," replied Whitefoot.

"What was the matter with your old home?" demanded Timmy.

Then Whitefoot told Timmy all about how he had been obliged to leave his old home because of Shadow the Weasel, of the terrible journey he had had, and how he didn't know where to go or what to do. Timmy listened suspiciously at first, but soon he made up his mind that Whitefoot was telling the truth. The mere mention of Shadow the Weasel made him very sober.

He scratched his nose thoughtfully. "Over in that tall, dead stub you can see from here is an old home of mine," said he. "No one lives in it now. I guess you can live there until you can find a better home. But remember to keep away from my storehouse."

So, it was that Whitefoot found a new home.

Chapter XX
WHITEFOOT MAKES HIMSELF AT HOME

Look not too much on that behind
Lest to the future you be blind.
Whitefoot.

WHITEFOOT didn't wait to be told twice of that empty house. He thanked Timmy and then scampered over to that stub as fast as his legs would take him. Up the stub he climbed, and near the top he found a little round hole. Timmy had said no one was living there now, and so Whitefoot didn't hesitate to pop inside.

There was even a bed in there. It was an old bed, but it was dry and soft. It was quite clear that no one had been in there for a long time. With a little sigh of pure happiness, Whitefoot curled up in that bed for the sleep he so much needed. His stomach was full, and once more he felt safe. The very fact that this was an old house in which no one had lived for a long time made it safer. Whitefoot knew that those who lived in that part of the Green Forest probably knew that no one lived in that old stub, and so no one was likely to visit it.

He was so tired that he slept all night. Whitefoot is one of those who sleeps when he feels sleepy, whether it be by day or night. He prefers the night to be out and about in, because he feels safer then, but he often comes out by day. So, when he awoke in the early morning, he promptly went out for a look about and to get acquainted with his new surroundings.

Just a little way off was the tall, dead tree in which Timmy the Flying Squirrel had his home. Timmy was nowhere to be seen. You see, he had been out most of the night and had gone to bed to sleep through the day. Whitefoot thought longingly of the good things in Timmy's storehouse in that same tree but decided that it would be wisest to keep away from there. So, he scurried about to see what he could find for a breakfast. It didn't take him long to find some pinecones in which a few seeds were still clinging. These would do nicely. Whitefoot ate what he wanted and then carried some of them back to his new home in the tall stub.

Then he went to work to tear to pieces the old bed in there and make it over to suit himself. It was an old bed of Timmy the Flying Squirrel, for you know this was Timmy's old house.

Whitefoot soon had the bed made over to suit him. And when this was done, he felt quite at home. Then he started out to explore all about within a short distance of the old stub. He wanted to know every hole and every possible hiding-place all around, for it is on such knowledge that his life depends.

When at last he returned home, he was very well satisfied. "It is going to be a good place to live," said he to himself. "There are plenty of hiding-places and I am going to be able to find enough to eat. It will be very nice to have Timmy the Flying Squirrel for a neighbor. I am sure he and I will get along together very nicely. I don't believe Shadow the Weasel, even if he should come around here, would bother to climb up this old stub. He probably would expect to find me living down in the ground or close to it, anyway. I certainly am glad that I am such a good climber. Now if Buster Bear doesn't come along in the spring and pull this old stub over, I'll have as fine a home as anyone could ask for."

And then, because happily it is the way with the little people of the Green Forest and the Green Meadows, Whitefoot forgot all about his terrible journey and the dreadful time he had had in finding his new home.

Chapter XXI
WHITEFOOT ENVIES TIMMY

A useless thing is envy;
A foolish thing to boot.
Why should a Fox who has a bark
Want like an Owl to hoot?

WHITEFOOT was beginning to feel quite at home. He would have been wholly contented but for one thing, — he had no well-filled storehouse. This meant that each day he must hunt for his food.

It wasn't that Whitefoot minded hunting for food. He would have done that anyway, even though he had had close at hand a storehouse with plenty in it. But he would have felt easier in his mind. He would have had the comfortable feeling that if the weather turned so bad that he could not easily get out and about, he would not have to go hungry.

But Whitefoot is a happy little fellow and wisely made the best of things. At first, he came out very little by day. He knew that there were many sharp eyes watching for him, and that he was more likely to be seen in the light of day than when the Black Shadows had crept all through the Green Forest.

He would peek out of his doorway and watch for chance visitors in the daytime. Twice he saw Butcher the Shrike alight a short distance from the tree in which Timmy lived. He knew Butcher had not forgotten that he had chased a badly frightened Mouse into a hole in that tree. Once he saw Whitey the Snowy Owl and so knew that Whitey had not yet returned to the Far North. Once Reddy Fox trotted along right past the foot of the old stub in which Whitefoot lived and didn't even suspect that he was anywhere near. Twice he saw Old Man Coyote trotting past, and once Terror the Goshawk alighted on that very stub and sat there for half an hour.

So, Whitefoot formed the habit of doing just what Timmy the Flying Squirrel did; he remained in his house for most of the day and came out when the Black Shadows began to creep in among the trees. Timmy came out about the same time, and they had become the best of friends.

Now Whitefoot is not much given to envying others, but as night after night he watched Timmy a little envy crept into his heart in spite of all he could do. Timmy would nimbly climb to the top of a tree and then jump. Down he would come in a long beautiful glide, for all the world as if he were sliding on the air.

The first time Whitefoot saw him do it, he held his breath. He really didn't know what to make of it. The nearest tree to the one from which Timmy had jumped was so far away that it didn't seem possible anyone without wings could reach it without first going to the ground.

"Oh!" squeaked Whitefoot. "Oh! he'll kill himself! He surely will kill himself! He'll break his neck!" But Timmy did nothing of the kind. He sailed down, down, down and alighted on that distant tree a foot or two from the bottom; and without stopping a second scampered up to the top of that tree and once more jumped. Whitefoot had hard work to believe his own eyes. Timmy seemed to be jumping just for the pleasure of it. As a matter of fact, he was. He was getting his evening exercise.

Whitefoot sighed. "I wish I could jump like that," said he to himself. "I wouldn't ever be afraid of anybody if I could jump like that. I envy Timmy. I do so."

Chapter XXII
TIMMY PROVES TO BE A TRUE NEIGHBOR

He proves himself a neighbor true
Who seeks a kindly deed to do.
Whitefoot.

OCCASIONALLY Timmy the Flying Squirrel came over to visit Whitefoot. If Whitefoot was in his house, he always knew when Timmy arrived. He would hear a soft thump down near the bottom of the tall stub. He would know instantly that thump was made by Timmy striking the foot of the stub after a long jump from the top of a tree. Whitefoot would poke his head out of his doorway and there, sure enough, would be Timmy scrambling up towards him.

Whitefoot had grown to admire Timmy with all his might. It seemed to him that Timmy was the most wonderful of all the people he knew. You see, there was none of the others who could jump as Timmy could. Timmy on his part enjoyed having Whitefoot for a neighbor. Few of the little people of the Green Forest are more timid than Timmy the Flying Squirrel, but here was one beside whom Timmy actually felt bold. It was such a new feeling that Timmy enjoyed it.

So, it was that in the dusk of early evening, just after the Black Shadows had come creeping out from the Purple Hills across the Green Meadows and through the Green Forest, these two little neighbors would start out to hunt for food. Whitefoot never went far from the tall, dead stub in which he was now living. He didn't dare to. He wanted to be where at the first sign of danger he could scamper back there to safety. Timmy would go some distance, but he was seldom gone long. He liked to be where he could watch and talk with Whitefoot. You see, Timmy is very much like other people, — he likes to gossip a little.

One evening Whitefoot had found it hard work to find enough food to fill his stomach. He had kept going a little farther and a little farther from home. Finally, he was farther from it than he had ever been before. Timmy had filled his stomach and from near the top of a tree was watching Whitefoot. Suddenly what seemed like a great Black Shadow floated right over the tree in which Timmy was sitting, and stopped on the top of a tall, dead tree. It was Hooty the Owl, and it was simply good fortune that Timmy happened to see him. Timmy did not move. He knew that he was safe so long as he kept perfectly still. He knew that Hooty didn't know he was there. Unless he moved, those great eyes of Hooty's, wonderful as they were, would not see him.

Timmy looked over to where he had last seen Whitefoot. There he was picking out seeds from a pinecone on the ground. The trunk of a tree was between him and Hooty. But Timmy knew that Whitefoot hadn't seen Hooty, and that any minute he might run out from behind that tree. If he did, Hooty would see him, and silently as a shadow would swoop down and catch him. What was to be done?

"It's no business of mine," said Timmy to himself. "Whitefoot must look out for himself. It is no business of mine at all. Perhaps Hooty will fly away before Whitefoot moves. I don't want anything to happen to Whitefoot, but if something does, it will be his own fault; he should keep better watch."

For a few minutes nothing happened. Then Whitefoot finished the last seed in that cone and started to look for more. Timmy knew that in a moment Hooty would see Whitefoot. What do you think Timmy did? He jumped. Yes, sir, he jumped. Down, down, down, straight past the tree on which sat Hooty the Owl, Timmy sailed. Hooty saw him. Of course. He couldn't help but see him. He spread his great wings and was after Timmy in an instant. Timmy struck near the foot of a tree and without wasting a second darted around to the other side. He was just in time. Hooty was already reaching for him. Up the tree ran Timmy and jumped again. Again, Hooty was too late. And so, Timmy led Hooty the Owl away from Whitefoot the Wood Mouse.

Chapter XXIII
WHITEFOOT SPENDS A DREADFUL NIGHT

Pity those who suffer fright
In the dark and stilly night.
Whitefoot.

ONE night of his life Whitefoot will never forget so long as he lives. Even now it makes him shiver just to think of it. Yes, sir, he shivers even now whenever he thinks of that night. The Black Shadows had come early that evening, so that it was quite dusk when Whitefoot crept out of his snug little bed and climbed up to the round hole which was the doorway of his home. He had just poked his nose out that little round doorway when there was the most terrible sound. It seemed to him as if it was in his very ears, so loud and terrible was it. It frightened him so that he simply let go and tumbled backward down inside his house. Of course, it didn't hurt him any, for he landed on his soft bed.

"Whooo-hoo-hoo, whooo-hoo!" came that terrible sound again, and Whitefoot shook until his little teeth rattled. At least, that is the way it seemed to him. It was the voice of Hooty the Owl, and Whitefoot knew that Hooty was sitting on the top of that very stub. He was, so to speak, on the roof of Whitefoot's house.

Now in all the Green Forest, there is no sound that strikes terror to the hearts of the little people of feathers and fur equal to the hunting call of Hooty the Owl. Hooty knows this. No one knows it better than he does. That is why he uses it. He knows that many of the little people are asleep, safely hidden away. He knows that it would be quite useless for him to simply look for them. He would starve before he could find a dinner in that way. But he knows that anyone wakened from sleep in great fright is sure to move, and if they do this, they are almost equally sure to make some little sound. His ears are so wonderful that they can catch the faintest sound and tell exactly where it comes from. So, he uses that terrible hunting cry to frighten the little people and make them move.

Now Whitefoot knew that he was safe. Hooty couldn't possibly get at him, even should he find out that he was in there. There was nothing to fear, but just the same, Whitefoot shivered and shook and jumped almost out of his skin every time that Hooty hooted. He just couldn't help it.

"He can't get me. I know he can't get me. I'm perfectly safe. I'm just as safe as if he were miles away. There's nothing to be afraid of. It is silly to be afraid. Probably Hooty doesn't even know I am inside here. Even if he does, it doesn't really matter." Whitefoot said these things to himself over and over again. Then Hooty would send out that fierce, terrible hunting call and Whitefoot would jump and shake just as before.

After a while, all was still. Gradually Whitefoot stopped trembling. He guessed that Hooty had flown away. Still, he remained right where he was for a very long time. He didn't intend to foolishly take any chances. So, he waited and waited and waited.

At last he was sure that Hooty had left. Once more he climbed up to his little round doorway, and there he waited some time before poking even his nose outside. Then, just as he had made up his mind to go out, that terrible sound rang out again, and just as before he tumbled heels over head down on his bed.

Whitefoot didn't go out that night at all. It was a moonlight night and just the kind of a night to be out. Instead Whitefoot lay in his little bed and shivered and shook, for all through that long night every once in a while, Hooty the Owl would hoot from the top of that stub.

Chapter XXIV
WHITEFOOT THE WOOD MOUSE IS UNHAPPY

Unhappiness without a cause you never, never find;
It may be in the stomach, or it may be in the mind.
Whitefoot.

WHITEFOOT the Wood Mouse should have been happy, but he wasn't. Winter had gone and sweet Mistress Spring had brought joy to all the Green Forest. Everyone was happy, Whitefoot no less so than his neighbors at first. Up from the Sunny South came the feathered friends and at once began planning new homes. Twitterings and songs filled the air. Joy was everywhere. Food became plentiful, and Whitefoot became sleek and fat. That is, he became as fat as a lively Wood Mouse ever does become. None of his enemies had discovered his new home, and he had little to worry about.

But by and by Whitefoot began to feel less joyous. Day by day he grew more and more unhappy. He no longer took pleasure in his fine home. He began to wander about for no particular reason. He wandered much farther from home than he had ever been in the habit of doing. At times he would sit and listen, but what he was listening for he didn't know.

"There is something the matter with me, and I don't know what it is," said Whitefoot to himself forlornly. "It can't be anything I have eaten. I have nothing to worry about. Yet there is something wrong with me. I'm losing my appetite. Nothing tastes good anymore. I want something, but I don't know what it is I want."

He tried to tell his troubles to his nearest neighbor, Timmy the Flying Squirrel, but Timmy was too busy to listen. When Peter Rabbit happened along, Whitefoot tried to tell him. But Peter himself was too happy and too eager to learn all the news in the Green Forest to listen. No one had any interest in Whitefoot's troubles. Everyone was too busy with his own affairs.

So, day by day Whitefoot the Wood Mouse grew more and more

unhappy, and when the dusk of early evening came creeping through the Green Forest, he sat about and moped instead of running about and playing as he had been in the habit of doing. The beautiful song of Melody the Wood Thrush somehow filled him with sadness instead of with the joy he had always felt before. The very happiness of those about him seemed to make him more unhappy.

Once he almost decided to go hunt for another home, but somehow he couldn't get interested even in this. He did start out, but he had not gone far before he had forgotten all about what he had started for. Always he had loved to run about and climb and jump for the pure pleasure of it, but now he no longer did these things. He was unhappy, was Whitefoot. Yes, sir, he was unhappy; and for no cause at all so far as he could see.

Chapter XXV
WHITEFOOT FINDS OUT WHAT THE MATTER WAS

Pity the lonely, for deep in the heart
Is an ache that no doctor can heal by his art.
Whitefoot.

OF all the little people of the Green Forest, Whitefoot seemed to be the only one who was unhappy. And because he didn't know why he felt so, he became day by day more unhappy. Perhaps I should say that night by night he became more unhappy, for during the brightness of the day he slept most of the time.

"There is something wrong, something wrong," he would say over and over to himself.

"It must be with me, because everybody else is happy, and this is the happiest time of all the year. I wish someone would tell me what ails me. I want to be happy, but somehow I just can't be."

One evening he wandered a little farther from home than usual. He wasn't going anywhere in particular. He had nothing in particular to do. He was just wandering about because somehow he couldn't remain at home. Not far away, Melody the Wood Thrush was pouring out his beautiful evening song. Whitefoot stopped to listen. Somehow it made him more unhappy than ever. Melody stopped singing for a few moments. It was just then that Whitefoot heard a faint sound. It was a gentle drumming. Whitefoot pricked up his ears and listened. There it was again. He knew instantly how that sound was made. It was made by dainty little feet beating very fast on an old log. Whitefoot had drummed that way himself many times. It was soft, but clear, and it lasted only a moment.

Right then something very strange happened to Whitefoot. Yes, sir, something very strange happened to Whitefoot. All in a flash he felt better. At first, he didn't know why. He just did, that was all. Without thinking what he was doing, he began to drum himself. Then he listened. At first, he heard nothing. Then, soft and low, came that drumming sound again. Whitefoot replied to it. All the time he kept feeling better. He ran a little nearer to the place from which that drumming sound had come and then once more drummed. At first, he got no reply.

Then in a few minutes he heard it again, only this time it came from a different place. Whitefoot became quite excited. He knew that that drumming was done by another Wood Mouse, and all in a flash it came over him what had been the matter with him.

"I have been lonely!" exclaimed Whitefoot. "That is all that has been the trouble with me. I have been lonely and didn't know it. I wonder if that other Wood Mouse has felt the same way."

Again, he drummed and again came that soft reply. Once more Whitefoot hurried in the direction of it, and once more he was disappointed when the next reply came from a different place. By now he was getting quite excited. He was bound to find that other Wood Mouse. Every time he heard that drumming, funny little thrills ran all over him. He didn't know why. They just did, that was all. He simply *must* find that other Wood Mouse. He forgot everything else. He didn't even notice where he was going. He would drum, then wait for a reply. As soon as he heard it, he would scamper in the direction of it, and then pause to drum again. Sometimes the reply would be very near, then again it would be so far away that a great fear would fill Whitefoot's heart that the stranger was running away.

Chapter XXVI
LOVE FILLS THE HEART OF WHITEFOOT

Joyous all the winds that blow
To the heart with love aglow.
Whitefoot.

IT was a wonderful game of hide-and-seek that Whitefoot the Wood Mouse was playing in the dusk of early evening. Whitefoot was "it" all the time. That is, he was the one who had to do all the hunting. Just who he was hunting for he didn't know. He knew it was another Wood Mouse, but it was a stranger, and do what he would, he couldn't get so much as a glimpse of this little stranger. He would drum with his feet and after a slight pause, there would be an answering drum. Then Whitefoot would run as fast as he could in that direction only to find no one at all. Then he would drum again, and the reply would come from another direction.

Every moment Whitefoot became more excited. He forgot everything, even danger, in his desire to see that little drummer. Once or twice he actually lost his temper in his disappointment. But this was only for a moment. He was too eager to find that little drummer to be angry very long.

At last there came a time when there was no reply to his drumming. He drummed and listened, then drummed again and listened. Nothing was to be heard. There was no reply. Whitefoot's heart sank.

All the old lonesomeness crept over him again. He didn't know which way to turn to look for that stranger. When he had drummed until he was tired, he sat on the end of an old log, a perfect picture of disappointment. He was so disappointed that he could have cried if it would have done any good.

Just as he had about made up his mind that there was nothing to do but to try to find his way home, his keen little ears caught the faintest rustle of dry leaves. Instantly Whitefoot was alert and watchful. Long ago he had learned to be suspicious of rustling leaves. They might have been rustled by the feet of an enemy stealing up on him. No Wood Mouse who wants to live long is ever heedless of rustling leaves. As still as if he couldn't move, Whitefoot sat staring at the place from which that faint sound had seemed to come. For two or three minutes he heard and saw nothing. Then another leaf rustled a little bit to one side. Whitefoot turned like a flash, his feet gathered under him ready for a long jump for safety.

At first, he saw nothing. Then he became aware of two bright, soft little eyes watching him. He stared at them very hard and then all over him crept those funny thrills he had felt when he had first heard the drumming of the stranger. He knew without being told that those eyes belonged to the little drummer with whom he had been playing hide and seek so long.

Whitefoot held his breath, he was so afraid that those eyes would vanish. Finally, he rather timidly jumped down from the log and started toward those two soft eyes. They vanished. Whitefoot's heart sank. He was tempted to rush forward, but he didn't. He sat still. There was a slight rustle off to the right. A little ray of moonlight made its way down through the branches of the trees just there, and in the middle of the light spot it made sat a timid little person. It seemed to Whitefoot that he was looking at the most beautiful Wood Mouse in all the Great World. Suddenly he felt very shy and timid himself.

"Who—who—who are you?" he stammered.

"I am little Miss Dainty," replied the stranger bashfully.

Right then and there Whitefoot's heart was filled so full of something that it seemed as if it would burst. It was love. All in that instant he knew that he had found the most wonderful thing in all the Great World, which of course is love. He knew that he just couldn't live without little Miss Dainty.

"I AM LITTLE MISS DAINTY," REPLIED THE STRANGER BASHFULLY.

Chapter XXVII
MR. AND MRS. WHITEFOOT

When all is said and all is done
'Tis only love of two makes one.
Whitefoot.

LITTLE Miss Dainty, the most beautiful and wonderful Wood Mouse in all the Great World, according to Whitefoot, was very shy and very timid. It took Whitefoot a long time to make her believe that he really couldn't live without her. At least, she pretended not to believe it. If the truth were known, little Miss Dainty felt just the same way about Whitefoot. But Whitefoot didn't know this, and I am afraid she teased him a great deal before she told him that she loved him just as he loved her.

But at last little Miss Dainty shyly admitted that she loved Whitefoot just as much as he loved her and was willing to become Mrs. Whitefoot. Secretly she thought Whitefoot the most wonderful Wood Mouse in the Great World, but she didn't tell him so. The truth is, she made him feel as if she were doing him a great favor.

As for Whitefoot, he was so happy that he actually tried to sing. Yes, sir, Whitefoot tried to sing, and he really did very well for a Mouse. He was ready and eager to do anything that Mrs. Whitefoot wanted to do. Together they scampered about in the moonlight, hunting for good things to eat, and poking their inquisitive little noses into every little place they could find. Whitefoot forgot that he had ever been sad and lonely. He raced about and did all sorts of funny things from pure joy, but he never once forgot to watch out for danger. In fact, he was more watchful than ever, for now he was watching for Mrs. Whitefoot as well as for himself.

At last Whitefoot rather timidly suggested that they should go see his fine home in a certain hollow stub. Mrs. Whitefoot insisted that they should go to her home. Whitefoot agreed on condition that she would afterwards visit his home. So together they went back to Mrs. Whitefoot's home. Whitefoot pretended that he liked it very much, but in his heart, he thought his own home was very much better, and he felt quite sure that

Mrs. Whitefoot would agree with him once she had seen it.

But Mrs. Whitefoot was very well satisfied with her old home and not at all anxious to leave it. It was in an old hollow stump close to the ground. It was just such a place as Shadow the Weasel would be sure to visit should he happen along that way. It didn't seem at all safe to Whitefoot. In fact, it worried him. Then, too, it was not in such a pleasant place as was his own home. Of course, he didn't say this, but pretended to admire everything.

Two days and nights they spent there. Then Whitefoot suggested that they should visit his home. "Of course, my dear, we will not have to live there unless you want to, but I want you to see it," said he.

Mrs. Whitefoot didn't appear at all anxious to go. She began to make excuses for staying right where they were. You see, she had a great love for that old home. They were sitting just outside the doorway talking about the matter when Whitefoot caught a glimpse of a swiftly moving form not far off. It was Shadow the Weasel. Neither of them breathed. Shadow passed without looking in their direction. When he was out of sight, Mrs. Whitefoot shivered.

"Let's go over to your home right away," she whispered. "I've never seen Shadow about here before, but now that he has been here once, he may come again."

"We'll start at once," replied Whitefoot, and for once he was glad that Shadow the Weasel was about.

Chapter XXVIII
Mrs. Whitefoot Decides on a Home

When Mrs. Mouse makes up her mind
Then Mr. Mouse best get behind.
Whitefoot.

WHITEFOOT the Wood Mouse was very proud of his home. He showed it as he led Mrs. Whitefoot there. He felt sure that she would say at once that that would be the place for them to live. You remember that it was high up in a tall, dead stub and had once been the home of Timmy the Flying Squirrel.

"There, my dear, what do you think of that?" said Whitefoot proudly as they reached the little round doorway.

Mrs. Whitefoot said nothing, but at once went inside. She was gone what seemed a long time to Whitefoot, anxiously waiting outside. You see, Mrs. Whitefoot is a very thorough small person, and she was examining the inside of that house from top to bottom. At last she appeared at the doorway.

"Don't you think this is a splendid house?" asked Whitefoot rather timidly.

"It is very good of its kind," replied Mrs. Whitefoot.

Whitefoot's heart sank. He didn't like the tone in which Mrs. Whitefoot had said that.

"Just what do you mean, my dear?" Whitefoot asked.

"I mean," replied Mrs. Whitefoot, in a most decided way, "that it is a very good house for winter, but it won't do at all for summer. That is, it won't do for me. In the first place, it is so high up that if we should have babies, I would worry all the time for fear the darlings would have a bad fall. Besides, I don't like an inside house for summer. I think, Whitefoot, we must look around and find a new home."

As she spoke, Mrs. Whitefoot was already starting down the stub. Whitefoot followed.

"All right, my dear, all right," said he meekly. "You know best. This seems to me like a very fine home, but of course, if you don't like it, we'll look for another."

Mrs. Whitefoot said nothing but led the way down the tree with Whitefoot meekly following. Then began a patient search all about. Mrs. Whitefoot appeared to know just what she wanted and turned up her nose at several places Whitefoot thought would make fine homes. She hardly glanced at a fine hollow log Whitefoot found. She merely poked her nose in at a splendid hole beneath the roots of an old stump. Whitefoot began to grow tired from running about and climbing stumps and trees and bushes.

He stopped to rest and lost sight of Mrs. Whitefoot. A moment later he heard her calling excitedly. When he found her, she was up in a small tree, sitting on the edge of an old nest a few feet above the ground. It was a nest that had once belonged to Melody the Wood Thrush. Mrs. Whitefoot was sitting on the edge of it, and her bright eyes snapped with excitement and pleasure.

"I've found it!" she cried. "I've found it! It is just what I have been looking for."

"Found what?" Whitefoot asked. "I don't see anything but an old nest of Melody's."

"I've found the home we've been looking for, stupid," retorted Mrs. Whitefoot.

Still Whitefoot stared. "I don't see any house," said he.

Mrs. Whitefoot stamped her feet impatiently. "Right here, stupid," said she. "This old nest will make us the finest and safest home that ever was. No one will ever think of looking for us here. We must get busy at once and fix it up."

Even then Whitefoot didn't understand. Always he had lived either in a hole in the ground, or in a hollow stump or tree. How they were to live in that old nest he couldn't see at all.

Chapter XXIX
MAKING OVER AN OLD HOUSE

A home is always what you make it.
With love there you will ne'er forsake it.
Whitefoot.

WHITEFOOT climbed up to the old nest of Melody the Wood Thrush over the edge of which little Mrs. Whitefoot was looking down at him. It took Whitefoot hardly a moment to get up there, for the nest was only a few feet above the ground in a young tree, and you know Whitefoot is a very good climber.

He found Mrs. Whitefoot very much excited. She was delighted with that old nest, and she showed it. For his part, Whitefoot couldn't see anything but a deserted old house of no use to anyone. To be sure, it had been a very good home in its time. It had been made of tiny twigs, stalks of old weeds, leaves, little fine roots and mud. It was still quite solid and was firmly fixed in a crotch of the young tree. But Whitefoot couldn't see how it could be turned into a home for a Mouse. He said as much.

Little Mrs. Whitefoot became more excited than ever. "You dear old stupid," said she, "whatever is the matter with you? Don't you see that all we need do is to put a roof on, make an entrance on the underside, and make a soft comfortable bed inside to make it a delightful home?"

"I don't see why we don't make a new home altogether," protested Whitefoot. "It seems to me that hollow stub of mine is ever so much better than this. That has good solid walls, and we won't have to do a thing to it."

"I told you once before that it doesn't suit me for summer," replied little Mrs. Whitefoot rather sharply, because she was beginning to lose patience. "It will be all right for winter, but winter is a long way off. It may suit you for summer, but it doesn't suit me, and this place does. So, this is where we are going to live."

"Certainly, my dear. Certainly," replied Whitefoot very meekly. "If you want to live here, here we will live. But I must confess it isn't clear to me yet how we are going to make a decent home out of this old nest."

"Don't you worry about that," replied Mrs. Whitefoot. "You can get the material, and I'll attend to the rest. Let us waste no time about it. I am anxious to get our home finished and to feel a little bit settled. I have already planned just what has got to be done and how we will do it. Now you go look for some nice soft, dry weed stalks and strips of soft bark, and moss and any other soft, tough material that you can find. Just get busy and don't stop to talk."

Of course, Whitefoot did as he was told. He ran down to the ground and began to hunt for the things Mrs. Whitefoot wanted. He was very particular about it. He still didn't think much of her idea of making over that old home of Melody's, but if she *would* do it, he meant that she should have the very best of materials to do it with.

So back and forth from the ground to the old nest in the tree Whitefoot hurried, and presently there was quite a pile of weed stalks and soft grass and strips of bark in the old nest. Mrs. Whitefoot joined Whitefoot in hunting for just the right things, but she spent more time in arranging the material. Over that old nest she made a fine high roof. Down through the lower side, she cut a little round doorway just big enough for them to pass through. Unless you happened to be underneath looking up, you never would have guessed there was an entrance at all. Inside was a snug, round room, and in this she made the softest and most comfortable of beds. As it began to look more and more like a home, Whitefoot himself became as excited and eager as Mrs. Whitefoot had been from the beginning. "It certainly is going to be a fine home," said Whitefoot.

"Didn't I tell you it would be?" retorted Mrs. Whitefoot.

Chapter XXX
THE WHITEFOOTS ENJOY THEIR NEW HOME

No home is ever mean or poor
Where love awaits you at the door.
Whitefoot.

"THERE," said Mrs. Whitefoot, as she worked a strip of white birch bark into the roof of the new home she and Whitefoot had been building out of the old home of Melody the Wood Thrush, "this finishes the roof. I don't think any water will get through it even in the hardest rain."

"It is wonderful," declared Whitefoot admiringly. "Wherever did you learn to build such a house as this?"

"From my mother," replied Mrs. Whitefoot. "I was born in just such a home. It makes the finest kind of a home for Wood Mouse babies."

"You don't think there is danger that the wind will blow it down, do you?" ventured Whitefoot.

"Of course I don't," retorted little Mrs. Whitefoot scornfully. "Hasn't this old nest remained right where it is for over a year? Do you suppose that if I had thought there was the least bit of danger that it would blow down, I would have used it? Do credit me with a little sense, my dear."

"Yes'm, I do," replied Whitefoot meekly. "You are the most sensible person in all the Great World. I wasn't finding fault. You see, I have always lived in a hole in the ground or a hollow stump, or a hole in a tree, and I have not yet become used to a home that moves about and rocks as this one does when the wind blows. But if you say it is all right, why of course it is all right. Probably I will get used to it after a while."

Whitefoot did get used to it. After living in it for a few days, it no longer seemed strange, and he no longer minded its swaying when the wind blew. The fact is, he rather enjoyed it. So, Whitefoot and Mrs. Whitefoot settled down to enjoy their new home. Now and then they added a bit to it here and there.

Somehow Whitefoot felt unusually safe, safer than he had ever felt in any of his other homes. You see, he had seen several feathered folks alight close to it and not give it a second look. He knew that they had seen that home but had mistaken it for what it had once been, the deserted home of one of their own number.

Whitefoot had chuckled. He had chuckled long and heartily. "If they make that mistake," said he to himself, "everybody else is likely to make it. That home of ours is right in plain sight, yet I do believe it is safer than the best hidden home I ever had before. Shadow the Weasel never will think of climbing up this little tree to look at an old nest, and Shadow is the one I am most afraid of."

It was only a day or two later that Buster Bear happened along that way. Now Buster is very fond of tender Wood Mouse. More than once Whitefoot had had a narrow escape from Buster's big claws as they tore open an old stump or dug into the ground after him. He saw Buster glance up at the new home without the slightest interest in those shrewd little eyes of his. Then Buster shuffled on to roll over an old log and lick up the ants he found under it. Again, Whitefoot chuckled. "Yes, sir," said he. "It is the safest home I 've ever had."

So, Whitefoot and little Mrs. Whitefoot were very happy in the home which they had built, and for once in his life, Whitefoot did very little worrying. Life seemed more beautiful than it had ever been before. And he almost forgot that there was such a thing as a hungry enemy.

Chapter XXXI
WHITEFOOT IS HURT

The hurts that hardest are to bear
Come from those for whom we care.
Whitefoot.

WHITEFOOT was hurt. Yes, sir, Whitefoot was hurt. He was very much hurt. It wasn't a bodily hurt; it was an inside hurt. It was a hurt that made his heart ache. And to make it worse, he couldn't understand it at all. One evening he had been met at the little round doorway by little Mrs. Whitefoot.

"You can't come in," said she.

"Why can't I?" demanded Whitefoot, in the greatest surprise.

"Never mind why. You can't, and that is all there is to it," replied Mrs. Whitefoot.

"You mean I can't ever come in anymore?" asked Whitefoot.

"I don't know about that," replied Mrs. Whitefoot, "but you can't come in now, nor for some time. I think the best thing you can do is to go back to your old home in the hollow stub."

Whitefoot stared at little Mrs. Whitefoot quite as if he thought she had gone crazy. Then he lost his temper. "I guess I'll come in if I want to," said he. "This home is quite as much my home as it is yours. You have no right to keep me out of it. Just you get out of my way."

But little Mrs. Whitefoot didn't get out of his way, and do what he would, Whitefoot couldn't get in. You see, she quite filled that little round doorway. Finally, he had to give up trying. Three times he came back and each time he found little Mrs. Whitefoot in the doorway. And each time she drove him away. Finally, for lack of any other place to go to, he returned to his old home in the old stub. Once he had thought this the finest home possible, but now somehow it didn't suit him at all. The truth is he missed little Mrs. Whitefoot, and so what had once been a home was now only a place in which to hide and sleep.

Whitefoot's anger did not last long. It was replaced by that hurt feeling. He felt that he must have done something little Mrs. Whitefoot did not like, but though he thought and thought, he couldn't remember a single thing. Several times he went back to see if Mrs. Whitefoot felt any differently but found she didn't. Finally, she told him rather sharply to go away and stay away. After that, Whitefoot didn't venture over to the new home. He would sometimes sit a short distance away and gaze at it longingly. All the joy had gone out of the beautiful springtime for him. He was quite as unhappy as he had been before he met little Mrs. Whitefoot. You see, he was even more lonely than he had been then. And added to this loneliness was that hurt feeling, which made it ever and ever so much worse. It was very hard to bear.

"If I could understand it, it wouldn't be so bad," he kept saying over and over again to himself, "but I don't understand it. I don't understand why Mrs. Whitefoot doesn't love me anymore."

Chapter XXXII
THE SURPRISE

Surprises sometimes are so great
You're tempted to believe in fate.
Whitefoot.

ONE never-to-be forgotten evening Whitefoot met Mrs. Whitefoot and she invited him to come back to their home. Of course, Whitefoot was delighted.

"Sh-h-h," said little Mrs. Whitefoot, as Whitefoot entered the snug little room of the house they had built in the old nest of Melody the Wood Thrush. Whitefoot hesitated. In the first place, it was dark in there. In the second place, he had the feeling that somehow that little bedroom seemed crowded. It hadn't been that way the last time he was there. Mrs. Whitefoot was right in front of him, and she seemed very much excited about something.

Presently she crowded to one side. "Come here and look," said she.

Whitefoot looked. In the middle of a soft bed of moss was a squirming mass of legs and funny little heads. At first, that was all Whitefoot could make out.

"Don't you think this is the most wonderful surprise that ever was?" whispered little Mrs. Whitefoot. "Aren't they darlings? Aren't you proud of them?"

By this time Whitefoot had made out that that squirming mass of legs and heads was composed of baby Mice. He counted them. There were four. "Whose are they, and what are they doing here?" Whitefoot asked in a queer voice.

"Why, you old stupid, they are yours, — yours and mine," declared little Mrs. Whitefoot. "Did you ever, ever see such beautiful babies? Now I guess you understand why I kept you away from here."

Whitefoot shook his head. "No," said he, "I don't understand at all. I don't see yet what you drove me away for."

"Why, you blessed old dear, there wasn't room for you when those babies came; I had to have all the room there was. It wouldn't have done to have had you running in and out and disturbing them when they were so tiny. I had to be alone with them, and that is why I made you go off and live by yourself. I am so proud of them; I don't know what to do. Aren't you proud, Whitefoot? Aren't you the proudest Wood Mouse in all the Green Forest?"

Of course, Whitefoot should have promptly said that he was, but the truth is, Whitefoot wasn't proud at all. You see, he was so surprised that he hadn't yet had time to feel that they were really his. In fact, just then he felt a wee bit jealous of them. It came over him that they would take all the time and attention of little Mrs. Whitefoot. So, Whitefoot didn't answer that question. He simply sat and stared at those four squirming babies.

Finally, little Mrs. Whitefoot gently pushed him out and followed him. "Of course," said she, "there isn't room for you to stay here now. You will have to sleep in your old home because there isn't room in here for both of us and the babies too."

Whitefoot's heart sank. He had thought that he was to stay and that everything would be just as it had been before. "Can't I come over here anymore?" he asked rather timidly.

"What a foolish question!" cried little Mrs. Whitefoot. "Of course, you can. You will have to help take care of these babies. Just as soon as they are big enough, you will have to help teach them how to hunt for food and how to watch out for danger, and all the things that a wise Wood Mouse knows. Why, they couldn't get along without you. Neither could I," she added softly.

At that Whitefoot felt better. And suddenly there was a queer swelling in his heart. It was the beginning of pride, pride in those wonderful babies.

"You have given me the best surprise that ever was, my dear," said Whitefoot softly. "Now I think I will go and look for some supper."

So, now we will leave Whitefoot and his family. You see, there are two very lively little people of the Green Forest who demand attention and insist on having it. They are Buster Bear's Twins, and this is to be the title of the next book.

BUSTER BEAR'S TWINS

Dedication

TO CHILDHOOD

LITTLE HUMAN FOLK, LITTLE PEOPLE IN
FUR AND FEATHERS AND ALL OTHER
CHILDREN OF OLD MOTHER
NATURE THIS BOOK
IS DEDICATED

Chapter I
MOTHER BEAR'S SECRET

The best kept secret soon or late
Will be found out as sure as fate.

Mother Bear.

HAVE you ever wanted to be in a number of places at the same time? Then you know exactly how Peter Rabbit felt in the beautiful springtime. You see, there was so much going on everywhere all the time that Peter felt sure he was missing something, no matter how much he saw and heard. In that he was quite right.

But you may be sure Peter did his best not to miss any more than he had to. He scampered lipperty-lipperty-lip this way, lipperty-lipperty-lip that way, and lipperty-lipperty-lip the other way, watching, listening, asking questions and making a nuisance of himself generally. For a while, there were so many new arrivals in the Old Orchard and on the Green Meadows, feathered friends returning from the Sunny South and in a great hurry to begin housekeeping, and strangers passing through on their way to the Far North, that Peter hardly gave the Green Forest a thought.

But one moonlight night he happened to think of Paddy the Beaver and that he hadn't seen Paddy since before Paddy's pond froze over early in the winter.

"I must run over and pay him my respects," thought Peter.

"I certainly must. I wonder if he is as glad as the rest of us that Sweet Mistress Spring is here."

No sooner did he think of this than Peter started, lipperty-lipperty-lip, through the Green Forest for the pond of Paddy the Beaver. Now the nearest way was past the great windfall where Mrs. Bear made her home. Peter hadn't thought of this when he started. He didn't think of it until he came in sight of it. The instant he saw that old windfall, he stopped short. He remembered Mrs. Bear and that he had heard that she had a secret. Instantly curiosity took possession of him. He forgot all about Paddy the Beaver.

For some time Peter sat perfectly still, looking and listening. There was no sign of Mrs. Bear. Was she under that windfall in her bedroom taking a nap, or was she off somewhere? Peter wished he knew. It was such a lovely night that he had a feeling Mrs. Bear was out somewhere. A hop at a time, pausing to look and listen between hops, Peter drew nearer to the great windfall. Still there was no sign of Mrs. Bear.

With his heart going pit-a-pat, pit-a-pat, pit-a-pat, Peter drew nearer and nearer to the great windfall, and at last was close to it on the side opposite to Mrs. Bear's entrance. Taking care not to so much as rustle a dry leaf on the ground, Peter stole around the end of the great windfall until he could see the entrance Mrs. Bear always used. No one was in sight. Peter drew a long breath and hopped a little nearer. He felt very brave and bold, but you may be sure that at the same time he was ready to jump and run, as only he can at the least hint of danger.

For a long time Peter sat and stared at that entrance and wished he dared just poke his head inside. If Mrs. Bear really had a secret, it was somewhere inside there. Anyway, that is what old Granny Fox had said. He had almost worked his courage up to the point of taking just one hurried little peek in that entrance when his long ears caught a faint rustling sound under the great windfall.

Peter scurried off to a safe distance, then turned and stared at that entrance. He half expected to see Mrs. Bear's great head come poking out and he was ready to take to his heels. Instead, a very small head and then another close beside it appeared.

Peter was so surprised he nearly fell over backward. Then in a flash it came to him that he knew Mrs. Bear's secret. It was out at last. Yes, sir, it was out at last. Mrs. Bear had a family! Mrs. Bear and Buster Bear had twins!

Chapter II
PETER SCARES THE TWINS

For timid folk no joy is quite
Like giving other folks a fright.

Mother Bear.

IT isn't often that Peter Rabbit has a chance to scare anyone. You know he is such a timid fellow himself that he is the one who usually gets the fright. So, when he does happen to scare someone, it always amuses him. Somehow he always has more respect for himself.

When on that moonlight night he discovered Mrs. Bear's secret, he had the most mixed feelings he ever had known. First came surprise, as he saw those two little heads poked out of Mrs. Bear's entrance. He was sitting up very straight, and the surprise was so great that he all but tumbled over backwards. You see, there was no mistaking those two little heads for any but those of baby Bears! He knew that those were two Bear cubs, Mrs. Bear's babies, the secret she had kept hidden so long under the great windfall.

And his surprise at seeing those two little heads was only a little greater than his surprise at the smallness of them. So, for perhaps two minutes Peter sat motionless, quite overcome with surprise, as he stared at those two funny little heads poked out from the entrance under the great windfall. Then all in a flash he understood the cause of Mrs. Bear's short temper and the reason she drove everybody away from there, and he felt a sudden panic of fright.

"This is no place for me," thought Peter, "and the sooner I get away from here the better." He looked hastily all about. There was no sign of Mrs. Bear. Right then and there curiosity returned in full force.

"I wish those youngsters would come out where I can look at them and just see how big they are," thought Peter. "It seems safe enough here now, and perhaps if I wait a few minutes, they will come out."

So, Peter waited. Sure enough, in a few minutes the two little cubs did come out. Plainly it was their first glimpse of the Green Forest, and Peter almost laughed right out at the look of wonder on their faces as they stared all about in the moonlight. But not even his first surprise was greater than Peter's surprise now as he saw how small they were.

"Why," he exclaimed to himself, "why-ee, they are no bigger than I! I didn't suppose anyone so big as great big Mrs. Bear could have such small children. I wonder how old they are. I wonder how big they were when they were born. I wonder if they will grow fast. I wonder if they will go about with Mrs. Bear. I suppose Buster Bear is their father, and I wonder if he ever comes to see them. They look to me rather wobbly on their legs. I wonder if Mrs. Bear told them they could come out."

And then the imp of mischief whispered to Peter. "I wonder if I can scare them," thought Peter. "It would be great fun to scare a Bear, even if it is nothing but a cub, and to scare two at once would be greater fun."

Peter suddenly thumped the ground very hard with his hind feet. It was so still there in the Green Forest that that thump sounded very loud. The two little cubs gave a startled look towards Peter. As he sat up straight in the moonlight, he looked very big. That is, he did to those two little cubs who never had seen him before.

With funny little whimpers of fright, they turned and fairly tumbled over each other as they scurried back through the entrance under the great windfall. Peter laughed and laughed until his sides ached. He, Peter Rabbit, actually had frightened two Bears and made them run. Now he would have something to boast about.

Chapter III
PETER'S GLEE IS SHORT-LIVED

You'll find it very seldom pays
To play a joke that works both ways.
Mother Bear.

AS two frightened little cubs ran, whimpering and tumbling over each other, for the safety of the bedroom under the great windfall, Peter Rabbit thumped twice more just by way of adding to their fright. It was most unkind of Peter. Of course. He should have been ashamed of trying to frighten babies, and those two cubs were babies and nothing more. They were baby Bears.

But Peter had so often felt little cold chills of fear chasing each other up and down his backbone in the presence of Buster Bear and Mrs. Bear that it tickled him to be able to scare any Bears, big or little. Truth to tell, it gave him a feeling as if somehow he was getting even with Buster and Mrs. Bear. Of course, he wasn't. Certainly not. But he had that feeling, and he didn't once stop to think how cowardly it was to frighten babies, even though they were Bear babies.

After the two cubs had disappeared, he could hear them scrambling along under the great windfall as they hurried for the darkest corner of that dark bedroom where Mother Bear had left them when she went out to look for something to eat. All the way there they whimpered just as if they thought some dreadful enemy was after them. Peter laughed until his sides ached, and the tears came to his eyes.

An angry growl right behind him put a sudden end to Peter's laughter and glee. It was his turn to run headlong and to whimper as he ran. My, what jumps he made! It seemed as if his feet barely touched the ground before he was in the air again. If those little cubs had been scared, Peter was twice as scared. They had run without knowing what they ran from. But Peter knew what he was running from. He was running from an angry mother, and that mother was a Bear. It was enough to make anybody run.

Peter had been so intent on frightening those little cubs and then laughing at them that he had not heard Mother Bear until she had given that angry growl right behind him. Then he hadn't stopped to explain. Peter believes in running first and explaining later. But at the rate he was going now, there wouldn't be any explaining, because by the time he stopped, Mother Bear wouldn't be near enough to hear a word he said.

The fact is Mother Bear didn't follow Peter. She simply growled once or twice in her deepest, most grumbly-rumbly voice just to add a little speed to Peter's long legs, if that were possible. Then as she watched Peter run headlong, she grinned. Just as Peter had laughed at the fright of the little cubs, Mother Bear grinned at Peter's fright.

"I hope that will teach him a lesson," muttered Mrs. Bear, way down in her throat. "I don't want that long-eared bunch of curiosity hanging around here. He got a glimpse of those youngsters of mine, and now my secret will be out. Well, I suppose it would have had to be out soon."

Mrs. Bear turned into the entrance to her bedroom under the windfall, while Peter Rabbit kept on, lipperty-lipperty-lip, lipperty-lipperty-lip, through the Green Forest towards the Green Meadows and the dear Old Briar-patch. He was eager to get there and tell the news of Mrs. Bear's long-kept secret.

Chapter IV
BOXER AND WOOF-WOOF

'Tis sometimes well, it seems to me,
To see, but appear not to see.

Mother Bear.

NOT in all the Green Forest could two livelier or more mischievous little folks be found than Boxer and Woof-Woof. Boxer was just a wee bit bigger than his sister, but he was no smarter, nor was he the least bit quicker. For more than three months they had lived under the great windfall in the Green Forest without even once poking their funny little noses outside. You see, when they were born, they were very small and helpless.

And the first time they had poked their heads out, Peter Rabbit had given them a terrible scare by thumping the ground with his hind feet. Safely back in their bedroom they snuggled together.

"Who do you suppose that terrible fellow was?" whispered Woof-Woof. How that would have pleased Peter could he have heard it!

"I haven't the least idea," replied Boxer. "I guess we are lucky to be safely back here. Did you notice how his ears stood up?"

"We must ask Mother Bear about him," said Woof-Woof. "He was only about our size, and perhaps he isn't so terrible after all. Here she comes now."

"Let's not say anything about it," whispered Boxer hurriedly. "You know she told us not to go outside. We may see him again sometime and then we can ask her."

So, when Mrs. Bear arrived, she found Boxer and Woof-Woof curled up with their arms around each other and looking as innocent as it was possible for baby Bears to look. Mother Bear grinned. She knew just what had happened out there, for she had seen it all. You remember that she had frightened Peter Rabbit even more than he had frightened the cubs. But she wisely decided that she would say nothing about it then.

"These cubs have had their first lesson in life," thought she, as she watched them trying so hard to appear to be asleep. "They disobeyed and as a result they got a great fright. I won't tell them that Peter Rabbit is one of the most harmless fellows in all the Great World. They will remember this fright longer if I don't. These scamps are growing like weeds. They went outside tonight while I was away, and that means that it is time to take them out and show them something of the Great World. If I don't, they will try it again while I am away, and something might happen to them. They are still so small that if Old Man Coyote should happen to find one of them alone, I am afraid the sly old sinner would make an end of that cub."

She poked the two cubs. "You're not asleep," said she. "Don't think you can fool your mother. Tomorrow morning you can go outside and play a little while, providing you will promise not to go more than one jump away from the entrance to this home of ours. There are great dangers in the Green Forest for little Bears."

Of course, Boxer and Woof-Woof promised, and so for several mornings they played just outside the entrance while their mother pretended to take a nap. It was then that Chatterer the Red Squirrel and Sammy Jay and Blacky the Crow had great fun frightening those twin cubs. And they didn't know, nor did the twins, that all the time Mother Bear knew just what was going on and was keeping quiet so that the twins might learn for themselves.

Chapter V
OUT IN THE GREAT WORLD

The Great World calls, and soon or late
Must each obey and rule his fate.
Mother Bear.

NOT in all the Green Forest is there a wiser or better mother than Mrs. Bear. No one knows better than she the dangers of the Great World, or the importance of learning early in life all those things which a Bear who would live to a good old age should know. So, after allowing the twins, Boxer and Woof-Woof, to play around the entrance to their home under the great windfall for a few days, she took them for their first walk in the Green Forest.

"Now," said she, as she prepared to lead the way, "you are to do just as I do. You are to follow right at my heels, and the one who turns aside for anything without my permission will be spanked. Do you understand?"

"Yes'm," replied Boxer and Woof-Woof meekly.

My, my, my, how excited they were as Mother Bear led the way out from under the old windfall! This was to be a great, a wonderful adventure. They tingled all over. They were actually going out to see something of the Great World.

The first thing Mother Bear did was to sit up and carefully test the wind with her nose. Boxer sat up and did exactly the same thing. Woof-Woof sat up and did exactly the same thing. The Merry Little Breezes tickled their noses with many scents. Mother Bear knew what each one was, but of course the twins didn't know any of them. All they knew was that they smelled good.

Mother Bear cocked her ears forward and listened. Boxer cocked his ears forward and listened. Woof-Woof cocked her ears forward and listened. Mother Bear looked this way and looked that way. Boxer looked this way and looked that way. So did Woof-Woof.

"These are the things you must always do whenever you start out in the Great World," explained Mother Bear in her deep, grumbly-rumbly

MY, MY, HOW EXCITED THEY WERE AS MOTHER BEAR LED THE WAY.

voice. "You must learn to know the meaning of every scent that reaches your nose, of every sound that reaches your ears, of everything you see, for only by such knowledge can you keep out of danger. But you must never trust your ears or your eyes only. Your nose is more to be trusted than either ears or eyes or both ears and eyes. But always use all three."

"Yes'm," replied Boxer and Woof-Woof.

Then Mother Bear started off among the great trees, shuffling along and swinging her head from side to side. Right at her heels shuffled Boxer, swinging his head from side to side, and right at his heels shuffled Woof-Woof, swinging her head from side to side. Whatever Mother Bear did the twins did. They did it because Mother Bear did it. They were keeping their promise. And little as they were, they felt very big and important, for now at last they were out in the Great World.

Chatterer the Red Squirrel saw them start out, and he chuckled as he watched those two funny little cubs do exactly as Mother Bear did. He followed along in the treetops, jumping from tree to tree, but taking the greatest care to make no noise. He was fairly aching for a chance to scare those cubs. But as long as Mother Bear was with them, he didn't dare to try.

Mother Bear stopped and sniffed at an old log. Then she went on. Boxer stopped and solemnly sniffed at that old log. Then he went on. Woof-Woof stopped and sniffed at that old log. Then she went on. And so, at last they came to a place where the earth was soft and where grew certain roots of which Mrs. Bear is very fond.

Chapter VI
THE TWINS CLIMB A TREE

Those climb the highest who have dared
To keep on climbing when most scared.
Mother Bear.

WHEN Mother Bear reached the place where grew the roots of which she was so fond, she led the twins, Boxer and Woof-Woof, over to a big tree, stood up and dug her great claws into the bark above her head. Of course, Boxer did the same thing. Mother Bear gave him a push. Boxer was so surprised that without realizing what he was doing, he pulled himself up a little higher, clinging to the tree with the claws of all four feet and hugging the trunk with arms and legs.

"Go right on up," said Mother Bear in her deep, grumbly-rumbly voice. "Go right on up until you reach those branches up there. There is nothing to fear. Those claws were given you for climbing, and it is time for you to learn how to use them. When you get up to those branches, you stay up there until I tell you to come down. If you don't, you will be spanked. Now up with you! Let me see you climb."

Boxer scrambled a little higher. Mother Bear turned and started Woof-Woof up after Boxer. It was a strange experience for the twins. Never before had they been above the ground, and it frightened them. They scrambled a little way then looked down and whimpered. Then they looked up at the branches above them. To Boxer and Woof-Woof those branches seemed a terrible distance up. They seemed way, way up in the sky. Really, they were not very high up at all. But you remember the twins were very little, and this was their first climb.

So, they stopped and whimpered and looked down longingly at the ground. But right under them stood Mother Bear, and there was a look in her eyes that told them she intended to be obeyed. Having her standing right below them gave them courage. So, Boxer scrambled a little higher. Then Woof-Woof, who simply couldn't allow her brother to do anything she didn't do, scrambled a little higher. Boxer started again. Woof-Woof followed. And so, at last they reached the branches. Then and not until then Mother Bear left the foot of the tree and shuffled off to dig for roots.

The instant they got hold of those branches, the twins felt safe. They forgot their fears. Quite unexpectedly they felt very much at home. And of course, they felt very big and bold. For a while, they were content to sit and look down at the wonderful Great World. It seemed to them that from way up there they must be looking at nearly all of the Great World. Of course, they really were looking at only a very small part of the Green

Forest. But it was very, very wonderful to the twins, and they looked and looked and for a long time they didn't say a word.

By and by they noticed Mother Bear digging roots some distance away. "Isn't it funny that Mother Bear has grown so much smaller?" ventured Woof-Woof.

Boxer looked puzzled. Mother Bear certainly did look smaller. Even as he watched, she moved farther away, and the farther she went, the smaller she seemed to be. Boxer held on with one hand and scratched his head with the other. For the first time in his life, he was doing some real thinking. "I don't believe she can be any smaller," said he. "It must be she looks smaller because she is so far away. That old log down there looks smaller than it did when we stopped and sniffed at it. Some of those young trees that looked tall when we passed under them don't look tall at all now. I guess the way a thing looks depends on how near it is!"

Of course, Boxer was quite right in this. He was already beginning to learn, beginning to use those lively wits which Old Mother Nature had put in that funny little head of his.

Chapter VII
A SCARE THAT DIDN'T WORK

Take my advice and pray beware
Of how you try to scare a Bear.
Mother Bear.

CHATTERER the Red Squirrel was indignant. He was very indignant. In fact, Chatterer was angry. You know he is short-tempered, and it doesn't take a great deal to make him lose his temper. He had watched Mrs. Bear and the twins start out from the great windfall and had silently followed, keeping in the treetops as much as possible, and taking the greatest care not to let Mrs. Bear or the twins know that he was about.

Inside he had chuckled to see the twins do exactly what Mother Bear did. When she sat up and they sat up beside her, they looked so funny that he had hard work to keep from laughing right out. He had seen many funny things in the Green Forest, but nothing quite so funny as those two little Bears, hardly bigger than Peter Rabbit, gravely doing just exactly what their mother did.

So, Chatterer followed, all the time hoping for a chance to give those twins a scare. But he didn't want to try it while Mother Bear was around. So, he waited, hoping that she would leave them alone for a few minutes. Finally, Mother Bear set the twins to climbing a tree. It was then that Chatterer became so very indignant. His sharp eyes snapped as he watched the twins scramble up that tree. He hoped they would fall. Yes, sir, Chatterer really hoped those twin cubs would fall.

You see, the trouble was that Chatterer didn't like the idea of those little Bears learning to climb trees. He felt that the trees belonged to the Squirrel family. It was bad enough to have Bobby Coon and Unc' Billy Possum climbing them. Now to have two lively little Bears learning to climb was too much. It was altogether too much.

"They haven't any business in trees," sputtered Chatterer to himself, taking care not to be heard. "They haven't any business in trees. They belong on the ground, not in trees. I won't have them in the trees! I won't! I won't!"

Now of course Chatterer knew, right down in his heart, that those cubs had just as much right in the trees as had he.

The real truth of the matter was that so long as those little cubs remained on the ground, Chatterer feared them not at all. He could be as saucy and impudent to them as he pleased. He could tease them and try to scare them and feel quite safe about it, so long as their mother wasn't about. But if those cubs were going to learn to climb, and he had a feeling that they would make very good climbers, matters might be altogether different.

Chatterer watched the twins and he watched Mother Bear. At last the latter disappeared from sight. Unseen by the twins, Chatterer leaped across to the very tree in which they were sitting, but above them. "I'll give them such a scare that they will either fall down or will scramble down and never will want to climb another tree," muttered Chatterer.

Silently he crept up behind them; then he opened his mouth and yelled at them. "Get down out of this tree!" he yelled. "Get down out of this tree!"

He was so close to those little Bears that his voice seemed to be in their very ears. They recognized it as a voice which had scared them two or three times when they had first come out of the great windfall to play. It was so close and so unexpected that it startled them so that they almost let go their hold. Then Boxer turned and for the first time had a good view of Chatterer. He was looking at a very angry Red Squirrel. But instead of being afraid and starting to scramble down from that tree, as Chatterer had expected him to do, Boxer suddenly started straight for him, and it was plain to see that Boxer was an angry small Bear.

Chapter VIII
TOO LATE CHATTERER IS SORRY

Of yourself to hold command
Keep your temper well in hand.
Mother Bear.

THE best laid plans, even those of the smartest of Red Squirrels, sometimes go wrong. Chatterer's plan had gone wrong, just about as wrong as it could go. Those provoking twins, instead of being scared into falling or scrambling down from that tree, had been made angry and actually were starting after him. Boxer started first and Woof-Woof promptly followed. You know whatever Boxer did, Woof-Woof did.

Now Chatterer hadn't reckoned on any such thing as this happening. Not at all. And like most people who try to scare babies, Chatterer is not at all brave. Most of his bravery is in his tongue. For just an instant he was too surprised to move. Even his tongue was still. Then he turned and ran up that tree as fast as he could.

The twins came scrambling after, and they came surprisingly fast. You see, there were plenty of branches to hold on to, so they had no fear of falling. Chatterer was so scared that he didn't use those usually quick wits of his, and he ran up past the only branch of that tree that reached out near enough to another tree for him to jump across. When he thought of it, it was too late. Yes, sir, it was too late. Boxer was already standing on that very branch.

Chatterer felt then that he was trapped. He couldn't jump across to another tree. He didn't dare try to get down past those twins. He wouldn't think of jumping down to the ground, unless he was actually obliged to, for it was a dreadful jump. All he could do was to climb higher and hope those twins would be afraid to follow him.

But by this time Boxer and Woof-Woof were enjoying the chase. They were enjoying the fun of climbing, and they were enjoying the discovery that they were no longer afraid of this saucy, red-coated scamp, but that he was afraid of them.

"See him run!" cried Boxer. "Come on, Woof-Woof, let's catch him! He is so small and quick that he can get about faster than we can, but we are two and he is only one. Between us we ought to be able to catch him."

Woof-Woof was quite willing, and they climbed on up after Chatterer. Chatterer's tongue was still now. He made no sound. He no longer called names. He no longer made faces. He no longer looked saucy or impudent. He looked exactly what he was, a badly scared Red Squirrel. He was sorry now that he had lost his temper and tried to scare those twins. He was very, very sorry. But it was too late. Being sorry didn't help him any now.

He was in a bad scrape, was Chatterer, and he knew it. Either of those twin Bears was much bigger than he, although they were little more than babies. They had found him out and had already discovered that they had nothing to fear from him and that he was afraid of them. It was plain to see that they were having a good time. They were enjoying the chase. Chatterer looked down at their sharp little claws and more than ever he was sorry he had not let them alone.

By this time Chatterer was clinging to the very top of that tree. If those twins came up there, he would have to make the terrible jump to the ground. He shivered as he looked down. Would those surprising twins, or one of them, be able to get up near enough to reach him?

Chapter IX
THE TWINS HAVE TO GO HOME

Obedience is good to see,
Especially when up a tree.

Mother Bear.

BOXER and Woof-Woof were having the best time of their short lives. Climbing was great fun. Although this was the first time they had climbed a tree, they already felt quite at home up there where the branches grew. It was fun just to climb from branch to branch. It was still greater fun to chase that red-coated little rascal who had tried to scare them out of that tree. You see, this was the first time the twins had found anyone afraid of them, and it made them feel quite important. It made them feel big. They felt twice as big as when they had whimperingly started to climb that tree. So, the twins were having a wonderful time.

But Chatterer the Red Squirrel was having anything but a wonderful time. He was wishing with all his might that he had kept his saucy tongue still; that he had not jumped over into that tree to try to scare those cubs; that he had not followed them in the first place; that they would become dizzy and afraid. He even wished that they would fall. The fact is, Chatterer was so badly frightened that he was capable of wishing almost anything dreadful if it would only give him a chance to escape.

Now if Chatterer had not been so badly frightened, he would have seen that Boxer, the twin who was in the lead, was already hesitating. He had reached a point where the branches were so small that they bent dangerously when he stepped on them. He had climbed as high as it was safe for him to climb, and he knew it. But having set out to catch that red mischief-maker, he couldn't bear to give up. That is, he felt that if he did give up, Chatterer would boast that he had been too smart for the cubs and would make fun of them. And this is just what Chatterer would have done.

So, while Chatterer was wishing with all his might that something would happen to those twins, the twins were wishing for some good excuse for stopping the chase without losing the respect they knew Chatterer now had for them.

Just then a deep, grumbly-rumbly voice came up to them from the foot of the tree. "Come down at once," said the voice. It was the voice of Mother Bear.

"Yes'm," replied Woof-Woof meekly, beginning to climb down.

"I want to catch this fellow who tried to scare us," whined Boxer, pretending that he didn't want to come down.

"You heard what I said," replied Mother Bear, and her voice was more grumbly-rumbly than before. "It is time to go home. Come down this instant."

"Yes'm," replied Boxer, and this time he said it quite as meekly as had his sister Woof-Woof. There was something in the sound of Mother Bear's voice that warned Boxer that it would be unwise to disobey.

So, with a warning to Chatterer that next time he would not get off so easily, Boxer began to climb down after Woof-Woof. When the cubs reached the lowest branches and had only the straight trunk to which to cling, they were once more afraid, and all the way down they whimpered. Somehow it was harder to climb down than up. It often is. But at last they were on the ground. Mother Bear's eyes twinkled with pride, but she took care that the cubs should not see this.

"Obedience," said she, "is the first great lesson in life. It saved you a spanking this time." Then she led the way home.

And as Boxer and Woof-Woof followed, doing exactly as she did, they heard the jeering voice of Chatterer the Red Squirrel.

"Couldn't catch me! Couldn't catch me!" jeered Chatterer.

Chapter X
THE TWINS GET EVEN WITH PETER RABBIT

It isn't nice; it isn't kind;
'Tis not at all the thing to do;
But those who do not take a chance
Of getting even are but few.

Mother Bear.

THIS is sad but true. It is so everywhere in the Great World, and the Great World would be a much better place in which to live if it were not so. It is the desire to get even that makes much of the trouble and the hard feeling and the unhappiness everywhere. But there are times when getting even certainly does give a lot of satisfaction. It was so with the twins, Boxer and Woof-Woof.

You remember that the very first time they ventured out from under the great windfall, Peter Rabbit had given them a great fright by thumping the ground with his hind-feet as only Peter can thump. The twins were so small then and they knew so little of the Great World, in fact nothing at all, that Peter had seemed to them a terrible fellow. They never had forgotten him. Whenever they were outside the great windfall, they watched for him, ready to run at sight of him.

But it was a long time before they saw Peter again, and when they did, they had grown so that they were considerably bigger than he. Besides, they had been out on several trips into the Great World with Mother Bear and had learned many things, for little Bears learn very fast and have the best of memories. At last they saw Peter again. It happened this way:

Peter had stayed away from the Green Forest as long as he could. Then curiosity to see what was going on over there had been too much for him, and he had started over to visit Paddy the Beaver. He took great care to keep away from the great windfall where Mother Bear and the twins lived. As curious as he was about those twins, and much as he wanted to see them again, he was too much afraid of Mrs. Bear and her short temper to take any chances. But he felt that it would be quite safe to visit Paddy the Beaver, for Paddy's pond was some distance from the great windfall.

Now Peter didn't know that Mother Bear was in the habit of taking the twins with her wherever she went. It just happened that this very day she had chosen to go over near the pond of Paddy the Beaver. The twins had played until they were tired and then had curled up for a nap in a sunny spot while their mother went fishing in the Laughing Brook.

When Peter arrived in sight of Paddy's pond, Mother Bear was hidden behind some brush a little way up the Laughing Brook and was sitting quietly waiting for a fish to come within reach. For once Peter was careless. He was so intent looking for Paddy the Beaver that he didn't use his eyes and ears for other things, as he should have. So, he passed within a few feet of the twins without seeing them. Just beyond he sat up to look over the pond for Paddy.

Now the twins slept each with an ear open, as the saying is, and they heard Peter pass. Open flew their eyes, and they saw at once that it was the terrible fellow who had so frightened them once. But somehow he no longer looked terrible. He was smaller than they had thought. In fact, they were now considerably bigger than he. You see, they had been growing very fast. Boxer's eyes twinkled. Perhaps this fellow was like Chatterer the Red Squirrel, bold and terrible only to those who feared him. He nudged Woof-Woof. Very softly they got to their feet and stole up behind Peter.

A twig snapped under Boxer's feet. Peter turned. His eyes seemed to pop right out of his head. With a squeal of fright, Peter jumped and started, lipperty-lipperty-lip, for the nearest pile of brush, and after him raced the twins. They knew now that this terrible fellow was more afraid of them than ever they had been of him, and they meant to get even for the fright he had given them when they were so little. It was great fun.

Chapter XI
PETER IS IN A TIGHT PLACE

When you are in a place that's tight
It is no time to think of fright.

Mother Bear.

BOXER and Woof-Woof were having no end of fun. Having chased Peter Rabbit under a pile of brush, they were now trying to catch him. It was even more fun than it had been to try to catch Chatterer the Red Squirrel in the top of a tree.

But for Peter Rabbit, it was no fun at all. The truth is, Peter was in a tight place, and he knew it. Never had he been more badly frightened. It would have been bad enough had there been only one little Bear. Two little Bears made it more than twice as bad.

In the first place, they were very lively, were those two little Bears. Peter hadn't known that little Bears could be so lively. You see, these were the first he ever had seen. The way in which they ran around that pile of brush showed how very quick on their feet they were. Peter didn't doubt that he could outrun them if he could get a fair start; the trouble was to get that fair start. He wished now that he had trusted to his long legs instead of seeking shelter under that pile of brush. He had done that in the suddenness of his fright, when the little Bears had surprised him. It is Peter's nature to seek a hiding-place in time of danger, and usually this is the wisest thing for him to do.

"I see him!" cried Boxer, poking his funny little head under the brush on one side. "I'll crawl under and drive him out to you, Woof-Woof!"

On the other side of the brush pile Woof-Woof danced up and down excitedly. "I'll get him! I'll get him!" she cried. "Drive him out, Boxer! Drive him out!"

"Ouch!" cried Boxer, as a sharp stick scratched his face. "He's crawling towards the end, Woof-Woof! Watch out!"

"Which end?" cried Woof-Woof, running from one end to the other and back again.

BOXER CLIMBED UP ON THE PILE OF BRUSH AND JUMPED UP AND DOWN.

"Ouch! Wow! I'm stuck!" came the voice of Boxer. A minute later he backed out. "No use; I can't get under there," he panted. "I'll jump on top and see if I can't scare him out that way."

So, Boxer climbed up on the pile of brush and jumped up and down, while Woof-Woof ran back and forth around the edge of the pile of brush, stopping to peep under at every opening.

"I see him! I see him, Boxer!" she cried, and began to wriggle in under the brush as Boxer had done.

But she didn't go far. She soon found that Peter could get through places where she couldn't. Besides, it seemed as if sharp sticks were reaching for her from every direction. Twice she squealed as she scratched her face on them. "How do you like it," called Boxer, grinning at the sound of those squeals.

Woof-Woof backed out and brushed bits of bark from her coat, for she was much neater than her brother. "I tell you what," said she, "let's pull this pile of brush all apart. Then we'll get him."

So, the twins set to work, one on one side and one on the other, to pull that pile of brush apart. Yes, Peter Rabbit certainly was in a tight place.

Chapter XII
PETER TAKES A CHANCE

Who never takes a chance confesses
That he a coward's heart possesses.
Mother Bear.

THOSE twin cubs were very much like some boys and girls. They were like them in that they were wholly thoughtless. They were having a splendid time as they tried to catch Peter Rabbit. They hadn't had so much fun for days. Not once did it pop into their funny little heads that Peter was suffering because of their fun. No, sir, they didn't once think of that.

But Peter was suffering. Peter was suffering from fright, and that kind of suffering often is worse than suffering from pain. He was sure that those cubs meant to kill him and eat him. As a matter of fact, such an idea hadn't entered the heads of the twins. You see, they were still too young to eat meat. All they were thinking of was the fun of catching Peter and getting even with him for the scare he had once given them.

Peter didn't know this. Many people had tried to catch him, and every one of them had wanted him for a dinner. So, Peter was sure that this was why Boxer and Woof-Woof were trying so hard to catch him. As he dodged about under that pile of brush, his heart was in his mouth most of the time. At least, that is the way it seemed to him. But this was nothing to the way he felt when those cubs began to pull apart that pile of brush. Then for a minute despair took possession of Peter.

But it was only for a minute. Peter had been in many tight places before, and he had learned that giving up to despair is no way to get out of tight places.

"If I stay here, they will get me," thought Peter. "If I take a chance and run, they may get me, in which case I will be no worse off. But they may not get me; so, I think I'll take the chance."

He listened to those excited little cubs working with might and main to pull that pile of brush apart. One was on one side, and one was on the other. He might get out at either end between them and get a start before they saw him. He started to creep towards one end, but snapped a dead twig, and the quick ears of Boxer heard it. "He's coming out!" squealed Boxer and ran around to that end.

Peter crept back to the middle. In a minute or so Boxer was back, pulling apart that brush. Then an old saying of his mother's popped into Peter's head. He had heard her say it many times when he was little and first venturing out into the Great World.

"When you must take a chance, always do the thing no one expects you to do," was what his mother had said over and over again.

"Those cubs expect me to run out at one end or the other," thought Peter. "They don't expect me to run out where either is at work. To do that will take them by surprise. It is my best chance. Yes, sir, it is my best chance."

Peter crept toward the edge where Boxer was at work tearing that brush apart. Once more his heart seemed to be in his mouth, and it was going pit-a-pat, pit-a-pat. Watching his chance, he darted out under Boxer's very nose.

Chapter XIII
A GREAT MIX-UP OF LITTLE BEARS

If I blame you and you blame me
'Tis clear we're bound to disagree.
Mother Bear.

WHEN Peter darted out under the very nose of Boxer, the little Bear was so surprised that for a couple of seconds he didn't do a thing. This was what Peter had counted on. It gave him a fair start. Then with a squeal Boxer started after him.

"He's out! He's out! Come on, Woof-Woof! We'll catch him now!" cried Boxer, and he was so excited that he stumbled over his own feet as he started after Peter.

When Peter came out from under that pile of brush, he turned to the left and started around the end of it, lipperty-lipperty-lip, as fast as he could go. Again, Peter was doing the unexpected. He knew that Woof-Woof was on the other side of that pile of brush, and he knew that she knew that he knew she was there. Of course, she wouldn't expect him to run around where she was. That would be the last thing in the world she would expect.

So, this is just what Peter did do. Around the end of that pile of brush, lipperty-lipperty-lip, raced Peter, with Boxer at his heels. Just as expected he met Woof-Woof running as fast as she could. Peter dodged as only Peter can. Woof-Woof was running so fast she couldn't stop instantly. Boxer was running so fast he couldn't stop.

Perhaps you can guess what happened. Those two little Bears ran into each other so hard that both were knocked over! Yes, sir, that is just what happened. Then both those little Bears lost their little tempers. They forgot all about Peter Rabbit. Each blamed the other. They scrambled to their feet. Quick as a flash Boxer reached out and boxed his sister side of the head. "Why don't you look where you are going?" he snapped.

Woof-Woof was quite as quick as Boxer. Slap went one of her paws against the side of Boxer's face. "Do some looking out yourself!" she sputtered.

They stood up and danced around each other, cuffing and slapping and saying unkind things. They glared at each other with little eyes red with anger. Boxer suddenly threw his arms around Woof-Woof and upset her. Then they rolled over and over on the ground, striking, scratching, and trying to bite. First one would be on top, then the other. Over and over, they tumbled, so fast that had you been there you would have seen such a mix-up of little Bears that you wouldn't have been able to tell one from the other.

It was dreadful for those twins to fight. But they had lost their tempers and there they were. You would never have guessed that they were brother and sister. After a while, they were so out of breath that they had to stop.

"What are we fighting for?" asked Boxer, looking a little shame-faced as he rubbed one ear.

"I don't know," confessed Woof-Woof, rubbing her nose.

"I-I-guess I lost my temper because you ran into me," said Boxer.

"I didn't. You ran into me," declared Woof-Woof.

"No such thing!" growled Boxer, his eyes beginning to grow red again. "You ran into me."

Woof-Woofs little eyes began to snap, and I am afraid that there would have been another dreadful scene had not the memory of Peter Rabbit popped into Boxer's head just then.

"Where's that long-legged fellow we were after?" he cried. "It was all his fault."

The cubs scrambled to their feet and looked this way and that way, but Peter Rabbit was nowhere to be seen.

Chapter XIV
TWO FOOLISH-FEELING LITTLE BEARS

Who lets his temper get away
Is bound to find it doesn't pay.
Mother Bear.

IF ever there were two foolish-feeling little Bears, the twins of Buster
Bear were those two. And they looked just as foolish as they felt. While
they had been fighting, Peter Rabbit had made the most of his chance and
the best use of his legs and had disappeared. Where he had gone neither
Boxer nor Woof-Woof had the least idea.

They looked this way. They looked that way. They peered under the
pile of brush. They even tore it all apart. There was no sign of Peter. As a
matter of fact, Peter was far away, headed straight for the dear Old Briar-
patch; and Peter was chuckling. The instant those cubs began to fight, all
fear had left Peter. He knew then that he had nothing more to fear from them.

"People who lose their tempers lose their wits with them," chuckled
Peter. "I couldn't have done that better if I had planned it. My, how those
cubs have grown! I think I'll keep away from that part of the Green Forest.
Yes, sir, I'll keep away from there." And in that decision Peter showed
that he wasn't yet too old to learn a lesson and gain wisdom therefrom.

At last the twins gave up looking for Peter. "I-I-I hope I didn't hurt
you," said Boxer meekly, as he saw Woof-Woof rub her nose again. "I
didn't mean to."

"Yes, you did," retorted Woof-Woof. "You did mean to hurt me. I
know, because I know you felt just as I did, and I meant to hurt you. I-I-I
hope I didn't."

"Not much," replied Boxer sheepishly as he felt of one ear.

"I guess we are even. That fellow we didn't catch probably is laughing
at us and will tell everybody he meets what silly little Bears we are. I guess
it doesn't pay to fight."

"That depends," said a deep, grumbly-rumbly voice. The twins turned to find Mother Bear looking at them. "It never pays to fight excepting for your rights, but the one who will not fight for his rights never will get far in the Great World. Neither will the one who is always ready to fight over nothing. Now what have you been fighting about?"

Feeling more and more foolish every minute, the twins told Mother Bear all about Peter Rabbit, how they had tried to catch him, and how they had lost their tempers when they bumped into each other.

Mother Bear's eyes twinkled, but she took care that the twins should not see that twinkle.

"You ought to be spanked, both of you," said she sternly; "and the next time I know of you fighting, you will be spanked. I won't spank you this time, because I hope you have learned a lesson. When two people fight over a thing, someone else is likely to get it. People who lose their tempers usually lose more, just as you lost your chance to catch Peter Rabbit. Now all the Green Forest will laugh at you, and Peter Rabbit will boast that he was smarter than two Bears."

"We'll get even with him yet," muttered Boxer.

"No, you won't," declared Mother Bear. "Peter Rabbit will never give you a chance."

And this is exactly what Peter Rabbit had resolved himself.

Chapter XV
THE TWINS MEET THEIR FATHER

Beware the stranger with a smile
Lest it but hide a trickster's guile.

Mother Bear.

BOXER and Woof-Woof had begun to wonder if they and their mother were the only Bears in the Green Forest. So far, they had seen no other. Then one day as they were playing about near the Laughing Brook, while Mother Bear was busy a little way off tearing open an old stump after ants, Woof-Woof discovered a footprint. She showed it to Boxer. Then the two little cubs sat up and stared at each other and their little eyes were very round with wonder.

"Mother Bear didn't make that footprint," whispered Boxer as if he were afraid of being overheard. "Who do you suppose did?"

Woof-Woof moved a little nearer to Boxer. "I haven't any idea," she whispered back, and hurriedly glanced all around. "It wasn't Mother Bear, for there is one of her footprints right over there, and it is different. There must be a great big stranger around here."

The twins drew very close together and stood up that they might better stare in every direction. They were a little frightened at the thought that a big stranger might be near. Then they remembered that Mother Bear was only a little way off, and at once they felt better. They saw no stranger. Everything about them seemed just as it should be. They cocked their little ears to listen. All they heard was the sound of Mother Bear's great claws tearing open that old stump, the cawing of Blacky the Crow far in the distance, the gurgle of the Laughing Brook, and the whispering of the Merry Little Breezes in the treetops.

Now not even Peter Rabbit has more curiosity than has a little Bear. Presently Boxer dropped down to all fours and approached that footprint. Already he had learned that his ears were better than his eyes and his nose was better than his ears. His eyes had told him nothing. His ears had told him nothing. Now he would try his nose.

He sniffed at that footprint and the hair along his shoulders rose a little. His nose told him that that footprint was made by a Bear he never had seen. There wasn't any question about it. It told him that the stranger had passed this way only a short time before. A great desire to see that stranger took possession of Boxer. Curiosity was stronger than fear.

"Let's follow his tracks; perhaps we can see him," whispered Boxer to Woof-Woof, and started along with his nose to the ground.

Now whatever one twin did, the other did. So, Woof-Woof followed her brother. One behind the other, their noses to the ground, the twins stole through the Green Forest. Every once in a while Boxer sat up to look and listen. When he did this, Woof-Woof did the same thing. It was very exciting. It was so exciting that they quite forgot Mother Bear and that they had been told not to go away. So, they got farther and farther from where Mother Bear was at work.

And then, without any warning at all, a great Bear stepped out from behind a fallen tree. He wore a black coat, and he was just about the size of Mother Bear. Of course, you know who it was. It was Buster Bear. For the first time in their short lives, the twins saw their father and he saw them. But the twins didn't know that he was their father, and he didn't know that they were his children. Things like that happen in the Green Forest.

Chapter XVI
THE TWINS TAKE TO A TREE

Run while you may, nor hesitate
Lest you should prove to be too late.
Mother Bear.

MOTHER Bear is a very wise mother. One of the first things she taught the twins was that safety is the first and most important thing. Then she taught them that it is better to run away from possible danger than to wait to make sure of the danger.

"No harm comes of running away," said she, "but if you wait, you may discover your danger too late to run. It is better to run away a hundred times without cause than to be too late once in time of real danger."

So, when the twins suddenly came face to face with Buster Bear for the first time, they did just the right thing. For a second or two they stared at him in frightened surprise, then they turned and ran.

Do you think it queer that the twins didn't know their own father? And do you think it even more queer that Buster Bear didn't know his own children? Just remember that they had never seen him, and he had never seen them before. For more than three months after they were born, they hadn't been out from under that great windfall in the Green Forest. When they did come out, Buster Bear had been in another part of the Green Forest. Mother Bear had warned him to keep away from that windfall, and Buster had obeyed. So, Boxer and Woof-Woof had known nothing about their father and Buster had known nothing about the twins.

Now when Buster saw those cubs, not knowing they were his own, he was filled with sudden anger. He didn't want any more Bears in the Green Forest. He wanted the Green Forest just for himself and Mrs. Bear. Those young Bears were likely to make a great deal of trouble. Anyway, they would need a lot of food, and this would mean that it would be just so much harder for him to get enough to satisfy his own big appetite. So, after the first surprised stare, Buster growled. It was a grumbly-rumbly growl deep down in his throat. The twins heard it as they started to run, and it was the most awful sound they ever had heard.

Straight to the nearest tall tree ran the twins, and up they scrambled. Chatterer the Red Squirrel could hardly have gone up that tree faster. Somehow they felt safer in a tree than on the ground. Buster Bear walked over to the foot of the tree and looked up at the cubs. They were fat, were those cubs. They were very fat.

"They look good enough to eat," thought Buster, as he stood up at the foot of the tree, looking up at Boxer and Woof-Woof. "They would make me a very good dinner. They have no business here, anyway. I've been living on roots and such things so long that a little fresh meat would taste good. If I go up after them, I can do two things at once, rid the Green Forest of a pair of troublesome youngsters who are bound to make trouble, and get a good dinner. I believe I'll do it."

Of course, this was very dreadful, but you know Buster didn't know that those cubs were his own. They meant no more to him than did Peter Rabbit, and you know he wouldn't have hesitated an instant to gobble up Peter if he had had the chance.

Buster looked all around to make sure that no one saw him. Then he dug his great claws into that tree and started to climb up.

Chapter XVII
MOTHER COMES TO THE RESCUE

In all the world, below, above,
The greatest thing is mother love.

Mother Bear.

THE love of a mother is wonderful beyond all things. There is nothing to compare with it. There is nothing it will not attempt to do. There is no danger it will not face. There is no sacrifice it will not make. It is the most beautiful, the most perfect of all things.

Boxer and Woof-Woof had thought that in climbing a tall tree they were making themselves safe. It had not entered their funny little heads that great big Buster Bear would climb that tree. So, you can imagine how terribly frightened they were when Buster started up that tree after them. They scrambled up and up until they were just as high as they could get. There they clung with feet and hands, the worst scared little folks in all the Green Forest.

Now little Bears are much like little boys and girls in very many ways, and one of these is their faith in mother. Another is that when they are frightened or in trouble, they cry and yell for mother.

That is just what Boxer and Woof-Woof did now. The instant they saw Buster, they began to whimper and cry softly, and they kept it up as they scrambled up the trunk of that tree. But when they saw Buster Bear climbing up after them, they simply opened their months and bawled.

"Mamma! Mamma-a-a!" yelled Boxer, at the top of his lungs.

"Oh-o-o, mamma-a-a!" screamed Woof-Woof.

Now fortunately for the twins, Mother Bear was not so far away that she couldn't hear them. By the sound of their voices, she knew that this was no ordinary trouble they were in. Terror was in the sound of those voices. Those twins were in danger. There was no doubt about it. That danger might be danger for her as well, but she didn't give that a thought. She plunged straight in the direction from which those cries were coming, and she didn't stop to pick her way. She crashed straight through brush and branches in her way, jumped over logs, and broke down young trees.

At the sound of the first crash made by Mother Bear as she started for those cubs, Buster Bear stopped climbing. He turned his head and looked anxiously in that direction, his little ears cocked to catch every sound. At the second crash, Buster Bear decided that that was no place for him. He didn't stop to climb down. He simply let go and dropped. Yes, sir, that is what he did. He let go and dropped.

It was quite a way to the ground, but the ground was where Buster Bear wanted to be, and he wanted to be there right away. He wanted to be there before whoever was coming could reach that tree. And the quickest way of getting there was to drop. A few bruises and a shaking up were nothing to Buster Bear just then.

The grunt he gave when he hit the ground even the twins heard way up in the top of the tree. It made them stop bawling for a minute to wonder if Buster had been killed. But Buster hadn't been killed. Goodness, no! In an instant he was on his feet and running away so fast that even Lightfoot the Deer would have had to do his best to keep up with him. And over his shoulder Buster Bear was throwing frightened glances.

He was not out of sight when Mother Bear burst out from among the trees. She saw him instantly. With a roar of rage, she started after Buster. Buster had seemed to be moving fast, but it was nothing compared to the way he moved when he heard that roar.

Chapter XVIII
THE TWINS ARE COMFORTED

There is no comfort quite like that
Contained in mother's loving pat.
Mother Bear.

THE instant they saw Mother Bear, the twins stopped bawling. Nothing could harm them now. They knew it. Mother would take care of them. Of that there wasn't a shadow of a doubt in the minds of Boxer and Woof-Woof. Hanging on with every claw of hands and feet, they leaned out as far as they could to see what would happen to that great black Bear who had frightened them so.

But nothing happened to Buster Bear for the very good reason that he didn't wait for anything to happen. Buster was doing no waiting at all. In fact, he was moving so fast and at the same time trying to watch behind him that he didn't even pick his path. He bumped into trees and stumbled over logs in a way that to say the least was not at all dignified. But Buster was in too much of a hurry to think of dignity. There was something about the looks of Mother Bear as she tore after him that made him feel sure that he would find it much pleasanter in another part of the Green Forest, and he was in a hurry to get there.

Mother Bear didn't follow him far, only just far enough to make sure that he intended to keep right on going. Then, growling dreadful threats, she hurried back to the tree in which the cubs were. Boxer and Woof-Woof were already scrambling down as fast as they could, whimpering a little, for though they felt wholly safe now, they were not yet over their fright. She reached the foot of the tree just as they reached the ground.

She sat up and the twins rushed to her and snuggled as close to her as they could get. Mother Bear put a big arm around each and patted them gently. It was surprising how gentle great big Mother Bear could be.

"Wha-wha-what would that awful fellow have done to us?" asked Woof-Woof, crowding still closer to Mother Bear.

"Eaten you," growled Mother Bear, and little cold shivers ran all over Woof-Woof and Boxer.

"I hate him!" declared Boxer.

"So do I!" cried Woof-Woof. "I think he is dreadful, and I hope we'll never, never, never, see him again!"

"But you will," replied Mother Bear. "I don't think you'll see him again right away, for he knows it isn't wise for him to hang around here when I am about. But by and by, when you are bigger, you will see him often. The fact is, he is your father."

"What!" screamed the twins, quite horrified. "That dreadful fellow our father!"

"Just so," growled Mrs. Bear. "Just so. And he isn't dreadful at all. You mustn't speak of your father that way."

"But if it isn't dreadful for a father to want to eat his own children, I guess I don't know what dreadful means," declared Boxer in a most decided tone. "I call it dreadful, and I hate him. I do so."

"Softly, Boxer. Softly," chided Mother Bear. "You see, he didn't know you were his children. He knows it now, but until he saw me coming to your rescue, he didn't know it. He never had seen you before. You were simply two tempting-looking little strangers who, if I do say it, look good enough to eat." She squeezed them and patted them fondly. "His name," she added, "is Buster Bear."

Chapter XIX
THE CUBS TALK IT OVER

Things seem good or things seem bad
According to the view you've had.
Mother Bear.

THAT is why people so often cannot agree. Each sees a thing from a different point of view and so it looks different. Just take the case of Buster Bear and the twins. When Boxer and Woof-Woof looked down at Buster Bear climbing the tree after them, he seemed a terrible fellow. But when they saw him running from Mother Bear, he didn't seem so very terrible after all.

Of course, it was a great surprise to the cubs to learn that Buster Bear was their father. They couldn't think or talk of anything else the rest of that day.

"Did you notice what a beautiful black coat he had?" asked Boxer, glancing at his own little black coat with pride.

"I like brown better myself," sniffed Woof-Woof, whose coat was brown like their mother's.

"He really is very big and handsome," continued Boxer.

"And a coward," sniffed Woof-Woof. "You noticed how he ran from Mother Bear."

"That was because he discovered his mistake about us. Of course, he wouldn't fight then," Boxer said in defense.

"I don't care, I think he is a poor sort of a father, and I'm not a bit proud of him," persisted Woof-Woof.

"I hope I grow up to be as big and handsome as he is. I'm glad my coat is black," Boxer declared.

"Huh!" sniffed Woof-Woof. "A black coat may cover a black heart. We are lucky not to be inside that black coat of his right now."

This was true, and Boxer knew it. He wisely attempted no reply. "Where do you suppose he lives?" he ventured.

"I haven't the least idea, but I hope it isn't near here. I don't want to see him again ever," retorted Woof-Woof.

"But he is your own father," protested Boxer.

"I don't care. If all fathers are like him, I don't think much of fathers," sputtered Woof-Woof.

Mother Bear came up just in time to hear this. "Tut, tut, tut," said she. "I won't have you talking that way about your father. By and by you will know him better and learn to respect him. He is the handsomest Bear I have ever seen, and some day you will be proud that he is your father."

"I like mothers best," confided Woof-Woof, snuggling up to Mother Bear. Mother Bear's face suddenly grew very stern. "I want to know," said she, "how he happened to find you up that tree."

"We-we met him, and he chased us up that tree," explained Boxer.

"And how did you happen to meet him?" persisted Mother Bear. "That tree was a long way from where I left you at play and charged you to stay."

The cubs hung their heads.

"We-we-we found his tracks and followed them," stammered Boxer in a low voice.

"And got a fright, which was no more than you deserved," declared

Mother Bear. "You ought to be spanked, both of you, for your disobedience. Now you see what comes of not minding. I hope the fright you have had will be a lesson you never will forget. And don't let me hear you say another word against your father."

"No'm," replied the twins meekly.

Chapter XX
THE TWINS GET THEIR FIRST BATH

You cannot learn to swim on land,
So waste no time in trying.
And if you keep from getting wet
You'll never need a drying.
Mother Bear.

WONDERFUL days were these for the twins, Boxer and Woof-Woof. Every day there was something new to see or hear or taste or smell or feel. And then there had to be tucked away in each funny little head where it could not be forgotten the memory of exactly how each of these new things looked or sounded or tasted or smelled or felt. Mother Bear was very particular about this. So, though the twins didn't know it, they were really going to school all the time that they thought they were simply having good times and wonderful adventures.

One day Mother Bear led them over to the pond of Paddy the Beaver. How the cubs did stare when they got their first glimpse of that pond. The Laughing Brook was the only water they were acquainted with, and in that part of the Green Forest, it was narrow, and the pools were very small. They had not supposed there was so much water in all the Great World as now lay before them in the pond of Paddy the Beaver.

Mother Bear led the way straight to one end of the dam which Paddy had built to make that pond. She started across that dam. The twins followed. Every few steps they stopped to wonder at that pond. The Merry Little Breezes of Old Mother West Wind were dancing across the middle of it and making little ripples that sparkled as the Jolly Little Sunbeams kissed them.

Close to the dam the water was smooth, for the Merry Little Breezes had not come in there. Boxer and Woof-Woof looked down. Perhaps you can guess how they felt when they saw two little Bears of just their size staring back at them. The twins were so surprised that they backed away hastily. The stranger cubs did exactly the same thing. This gave Boxer and Woof-Woof confidence. They moved forward to the very edge of the dam, and there they sat up.

When they did this, they lost sight of the other little Bears. They didn't know what to make of it. Then Boxer happened to look down in the water. There were the stranger cubs sitting up and doing exactly as he and Woof-Woof did. Stranger still, one of them was dressed in black and one in brown, and the latter looked so exactly like his sister that Boxer turned to look at her, to make sure that she was beside him there on the edge of the dam.

Boxer dropped down on all fours. The little stranger in black did the same thing. It provoked Boxer. Like a flash he struck at that stranger. Quick as he was, the stranger was as quick. Boxer saw a stout little paw exactly like his own coming toward him. He dodged, and as he did so his own swiftly moving little paw struck - nothing but water. It so surprised Boxer that he lost his balance, and in he tumbled with a splash.

Now Woof-Woof had been so intent on the little stranger in brown that she had paid no attention to Boxer. Woof-Woof was rather better-natured than her small brother. She had no desire to quarrel with these strangers. Slowly, very slowly, she stretched her head toward the little stranger in brown. The latter did just the same thing. They were just about to touch noses when Boxer fell in. The splash startled Woof-Woof so that she lost her balance, and in she went headfirst with a splash quite equal to that of Boxer.

If ever there were two frightened little Bears, they were the twins. It was the first time they ever had been in the water all over. They tried to

IT WAS THE FIRST TIME THEY EVER HAD BEEN IN THE WATER ALL OVER.

run, but there was nothing for their feet to touch. This frightened them still more, and they made their legs go faster. Then they discovered that they were moving through the water; they were swimming! They were getting their first bath and their first swimming lesson at the same time.

Chapter XXI
THE TWINS ARE STILL PUZZLED

To have true faith is to believe
E'en when appearances deceive.

Mother Bear.

IT wouldn't be quite truthful to say that the twins enjoyed that first bath and swim. They didn't. In the first place, they had gone in all over without the least intention of doing so. In fact, they had tumbled in. This had frightened them. They had opened their mouths to yell and had swallowed more water than was at all pleasant. Some of it had gone down the wrong way, and this had choked them. No, the twins didn't enjoy that first bath and swim at all.

They climbed out on the dam of Paddy the Beaver and shook themselves, making the water fly from their coats in a shower. Mother Bear had started back at the sound of the splashes they had made when they fell in, but seeing them safe, she grinned and went on about her own affairs.

"This has saved me some trouble," muttered she. "I probably would have had hard work to get them into the water without throwing them in. Now they will not be afraid of it. An accident sometimes proves a blessing."

Meanwhile the twins had shaken themselves as nearly dry as they could and were now sitting down side by side, gravely staring at the water. There was something very mysterious about that water. They felt that somehow it had played them a trick; that it was its fault that they had fallen in.

Suddenly Boxer remembered the two little stranger Bears. What had become of them? In the excitement, he had forgotten all about them. He remembered that it was while striking at one of them he had fallen in. That little Bear had struck at him at the same time. Boxer couldn't recall being hit or striking anything but that water. Then he had tumbled in.

But had he tumbled in? Hadn't he been pulled in? Hadn't that other little Bear grabbed him and pulled him in? The instant that idea popped into his head, Boxer was sure that that was how it all came about. He glared as much as such a little Bear could glare all around in search of that other little Bear, but no other little Bear but his sister Woof-Woof was to be seen. She was solemnly gazing at the water.

Now of course the splashing of the twins had made a lot of ripples on the surface of the water, and these destroyed all reflections. But by now the water had become calm again. Woof-Woof happened to look down into it almost at her feet. A little brown Bear looked back at her. It was the same little brown Bear with whom she had tried to touch noses just before she fell into the water.

Woof-Woof poked Boxer and pointed down at the water. Boxer looked. There was that same provoking little black Bear. Boxer lifted his lips and snarled. The other little Bear lifted his lips in exactly the same way, but Boxer heard no sound save his own snarl. Boxer opened his mouth and showed all his teeth. The other little Bear opened his mouth and showed all his teeth. Whatever Boxer did, the other little Bear did. And it was just the same with Woof-Woof and the little brown Bear.

Boxer was tempted to strike at that little Bear as he had before, but just as he was about to do it, he remembered what happened before. This caused him to back away hastily. He wouldn't give that other fellow a chance to pull him in again. When he backed away, the other little Bear did the same thing. In a few steps he disappeared. Boxer cautiously stole forward. The other little Bear came to meet him.

If ever there were two puzzled little Bears, they were Boxer and Woof-Woof, as they tried to get acquainted with their own reflections in the pond of Paddy the Beaver.

Chapter XXII
BOXER GETS A SPANKING

Who fails to spank should have a care;
The well spanked cub, the well trained Bear.
Mother Bear.

WHEREVER Mother Bear went the twins went. In the first place, they were so full of life and mischief that Mother Bear didn't dare leave them for any length of time. Then, too, it was good for them to be with her, for thus they learned many things that they could not have learned otherwise.

But there were times when Mother Bear found Boxer and Woof-Woof very much in the way. Such times she was likely to send them up a tree and tell them to remain there until her return. She always felt that they were quite safe so long as they were up in a tree, where there was no real mischief they could get into.

It happened that one morning Mrs. Bear sent them up a tall pine tree with strict orders to stay there until her return. "Don't you dare come down from that tree until I tell you you may," said she in her deep, grumbly-rumbly voice, as the twins scrambled up the tree.

"No'm," replied Woof-Woof meekly. But Boxer didn't say a word.

No sooner was their mother out of sight than Boxer proposed that they go down on the ground to play. "She won't be back for some time," said he.

"By the time she does return, we will be back up here and she will never know anything about it. Come on, Woof-Woof."

Woof-Woof shook her head. "I'm going to stay right here," said she, "and you'd better do the same thing, Boxer. If you get caught, you'll get a spanking."

"Pooh! Who cares for a spanking!" exclaimed Boxer. "Besides, I'm not going to get one. There isn't any sense in making us stay up in this tree. We can't have any fun up here. Come on down and play hide-and-seek."

But Woof-Woof wouldn't do it. "You're afraid!" declared Boxer.

"I'm not afraid!" retorted Woof-Woof indignantly. "You heard what Mother Bear said and you better mind. You may be sorry if you don't."

"Fraidy! Fraidy!" jeered Boxer, as he slid down the trunk of the tree.

Now Boxer hadn't intended to go more than a few feet from the foot of that tree. He wanted to be near enough to scramble up again at the first hint of Mother Bear's approach. But there was nothing to do down there, and without Woof-Woof to play with, he found it very dull.

Little Bears are very restless and uneasy. Boxer walked round and round that tree because he could think of nothing else to do. By and by a Merry Little Breeze happened along and tickled his nose with a strange smell. The Merry Little Breezes were always doing that. Boxer used to wonder if he ever would learn all the smells of the Green Forest.

Not having anything else to do just then, Boxer decided that he would follow up that smell and find out where and what it came from. Off he started, his inquisitive little nose sniffing the air. After a little that smell grew fainter and fainter, and finally there wasn't any. You see, the Merry Little Breezes were carrying it in quite another direction.

Boxer turned to go back. He thought he was going straight toward that tree where Mother Bear had left him. But he wasn't, and by and by he discovered that he was lost. Then he began to run, and as he ran, he whimpered. Suddenly out from behind a tree stepped Mother Bear. Boxer was so glad to see her he quite forgot that he had disobeyed.

But Mother Bear didn't forget, "What are you doing here?" she demanded. Boxer hung his head and didn't say a word.

"A cub who disobeys must be punished," said Mother Bear, and she promptly gave Boxer the first real spanking he ever had received. How he did wish he had stayed up in that tree with Woof-Woof.

Chapter XXIII
BOXER IS SULKY

The world can do quite well without
The sulky folks and those who pout.
Mother Bear.

SULKY folks are not pleasant to have around. They should be put away by themselves and kept there until they are through being sulky. Now ordinarily little Bears are not sulky. It isn't their nature to be sulky. But Boxer, the disobedient little cub, was sulky. He was very sulky indeed. And it was all because of his twin sister, Woof-Woof.

It had been bad enough to be spanked for his disobedience, but Boxer had felt that he deserved this. He had bawled lustily and then he had whimpered softly all the way back to that tree in which Woof-Woof had obediently remained. Until he reached the foot of that tree and looked up at Woof-Woof, there had been no sulkiness in Boxer.

But when he saw Woof-Woof grinning down at him as if she were glad of all his trouble, Boxer suddenly felt that he was the most abused little Bear in all the Great World.

"Don't you wish you hadn't tried to be so smart?" whispered Woof-Woof, when at Mother Bear's command she had joined Boxer on the ground. "I heard you bawling. I guess next time you'll be good like me."

This was too much for Boxer, and he struck at Woof-Woof.

Instantly he felt the sting of Mother Bear's big paw. It made him squeal. Woof-Woof grinned at him again, but she took care that Mother Bear shouldn't see that grin. Woof-Woof actually seemed to enjoy seeing Boxer in trouble. Little folks and some big ones often are that way.

So, because with Mother Bear there he had no chance to show his spite to Woof-Woof, Boxer sulked. He wanted to be by himself just to pity himself. Instead of walking close at the heels of Mother Bear as usual, he allowed Woof-Woof to take that place, and he tagged on behind just as far back as he dared to. Once in a while Woof-Woof would turn her head and make a face at him. Boxer pretended not to see this.

When they stopped to rest, Boxer curled up by himself and pretended to have a nap, while all the time he was just sulking. When after a while Woof-Woof tried to make friends with him, he would have nothing to do with her. Boxer was actually having a good time being miserable. People can get that way sometimes.

Finally, Mother Bear lost patience and sent him in under the great windfall to the bedroom where he was born. "Stay in there until you get over being sulky," said she. "Don't put foot outside until you can be pleasant."

So, Boxer crept under the great windfall to the bedroom where he had spent his babyhood. There he curled up and was sulkier than ever. He said to himself that he hated Mother Bear and he hated his sister, Woof-Woof. He didn't do anything of the kind. He loved both dearly. But he tried to make himself believe that he hated them. People in the sulks are very fond of doing things like that.

So, while Woof-Woof went over to the Laughing Brook with Mother Bear, under the great windfall, Boxer lay and sulked and tried to think of some way of getting even with Mother Bear and Woof-Woof.

Chapter XXIV
BOXER STARTS OUT TO GET EVEN

Wait a minute; count the cost.
Wasted time is time that's lost.
Mother Bear.

BOXER lay curled up in a corner of the bedroom under the great windfall, and there he sulked and sulked and sulked and tried to make himself believe he was the worst treated little Bear in all the Great World. But sulking all alone isn't any fun at all. No one can truly enjoy being sulky, with no one to see it. So, in spite of himself Boxer was soon wondering what Woof-Woof and Mother Bear were doing. He had seen them start off toward the Laughing Brook and though he wouldn't own up to it, even to himself, he wished that he was with them. He dearly loved to play along the Laughing Brook.

When he could stand it no longer, Boxer stole out to the entrance and poked his head out from under the great windfall. There he stood for the longest time looking, listening, smelling. Everything looked just as usual. There were no strange sounds. The Merry Little Breezes brought him no new smells. There were no signs of Mother Bear and Woof-Woof. He didn't know whether they had gone up the Laughing Brook or down the Laughing Brook. He tried to pretend that he didn't care where they were or what they were doing.

But he didn't succeed. You know it isn't often you can really and truly fool yourself. You may fool other people, but not yourself. So, after a while, Boxer gave up trying to pretend he didn't care. And then sulkiness gave way to temper, bad temper.

"I-I-I'll go way, way off in the Great World and never come back. Then I guess Mother Bear and Woof-Woof will be sorry and wish they had been good to me," muttered Boxer.

He stood up for an instant to look and listen. Then that silly little Bear scampered off as fast as he could go, without paying any attention at all to his direction. His one thought was to get as far as possible from the great windfall before Mother Bear should return. He would show Mother Bear that he was too big to be spanked and sent to bed. He would show Woof-Woof that he could take care of himself and didn't need to tag along after Mother Bear.

So, Boxer ran and ran until his little legs grew tired. The only use he made of his eyes was to keep looking behind him to see if Mother Bear was after him. Not once did he use them to take note of the way in which he was going. So, it was that when at last he stopped, because his legs ached and he was out of breath, Boxer was as completely lost as a little Bear could be. He didn't know it then, but he was. He was to find it out later.

"Now," said Boxer, talking to himself as he rested, "I guess Mother Bear will be sorry she spanked me. And I guess Woof-Woof will wish she hadn't laughed at me and made fun of me. Maybe they'll be so sorry they'll cry. If they come to look for me, I'll hide where they won't ever find me. Then they'll be sorrier than ever, and I'll be even with them. I won't go home until I am as big as my father, Buster Bear. Then I guess they'll treat me nice."

So, Boxer rested and planned the wonderful things he would do out in the Great World and was glad he had run away from home. You see, it was very pleasant there in the Green Forest, and after all, if he really wanted to, he could go back home. That is what he thought, anyway. You see, he hadn't the least idea yet that he was lost.

Chapter XXV
CHATTERER HAS FUN WITH BOXER

Who does not fear to take a chance
Will make the most of circumstance.
Mother Bear.

THAT is Chatterer all over. In all the Green Forest there is no one who appears to enjoy mischief so thoroughly as does Chatterer the Red Squirrel. And there is no one more ready to take a chance when it offers.

It happened that Chatterer discovered Boxer, the runaway little Bear, as he rested and planned what he would do out in the Great World. Chatterer kept quiet until he was sure that Boxer was alone; that Mother Bear and Woof-Woof were nowhere near. When he was sure of this, Chatterer guessed just what had happened. He guessed that Boxer had run away. You know Chatterer is one of the sharpest and shrewdest of all the little people in the Green Forest.

Chatterer grinned. "I believe," said he to himself, "that that silly little Bear has run away and is lost. If he isn't lost, he ought to be, and I'll see to it that he is. Yes, Sir, I'll see to it that he is properly lost. This is my chance to get even for the fright he and his sister gave me when they chased me up a tree."

Chatterer once more looked everywhere to make sure no one else was about. Then he lightly jumped over into the tree under which Boxer was sitting. He took care to make no sound. He crept out on a limb directly over Boxer and then he dropped a pinecone.

The pinecone hit Boxer right on the end of his nose, and because his nose is rather tender, it hurt. It made the tears come. Then, too, it was so unexpected it startled Boxer. "Ouch!" he cried, as he sprang to one side and looked up to see where that cone had come from.

When he saw Chatterer grinning down at him, Boxer grew very angry. That was the same fellow he once had so nearly caught in a treetop. This time he would catch him. Down came another cone on Boxer's head.

"Can't catch me! Can't catch me!" taunted Chatterer, in the most provoking way.

Boxer growled and started up that tree. "Can't catch a flea! Can't catch me!" cried Chatterer gleefully, as he looked down at Boxer and made faces at him.

He waited until Boxer was halfway up that tree then lightly ran out to the end of a branch and leaped across to a branch of the next tree. From there he called Boxer all sorts of names and made fun of him until the little Bear was so angry he hardly knew what he was doing. Of course, he couldn't jump across as Chatterer had. He was too big to run out on a branch that way, even had he dared try it. So, there was nothing to do but to scramble down that tree and climb the next one.

Boxer started down. When he reached the ground, he found Chatterer also on the ground. "Can't catch a flea! Can't catch me!" shouted Chatterer more provokingly than ever.

"I can catch any Red Squirrel that lives," growled Boxer and jumped at Chatterer. Chatterer dodged and ran, Boxer after him. Around trees and stumps, this way, that way and the other way, over logs, behind piles of brush Chatterer led Boxer, until the latter was so out of breath he had to stop.

Chatterer chuckled. "I guess that now he is quite properly lost," said he to himself, as he ran up a tree and dropped another cone on Boxer. "I guess I've turned him around so many times he hasn't any idea where home is or anything else, for that matter. I haven't had so much fun for a long time."

He dropped another cone on Boxer and then started off through the treetops, leaving Boxer all alone.

Chapter XXVI
ALONE AND LOST IN THE GREAT WORLD

He truly brave is who can be
No whit less brave with none to see.
Mother Bear.

SOMEHOW it is easier to be brave when there are others about to see how brave you are. It is a great deal easier. To be brave when you are all alone is quite another matter. That is real bravery. And to be alone and lost and brave is the greatest bravery.

When Chatterer the Red Squirrel raced away through the treetops, leaving Boxer alone to recover his breath and rest his weary little legs, he left a little Bear as completely lost as ever a little Bear had been since the beginning of the Great World. Boxer didn't know it then. He was too busy getting his breath and thinking how good it was to rest to think of anything else.

But after a while, Boxer felt quite himself again, and once more his anger at Chatterer the Red Squirrel began to rise. Boxer looked all about for Chatterer. There was no sign of him. Boxer swelled up with a feeling of importance.

"That fellow must be hiding. I guess I've given him a scare he won't forget in a hurry," boasted Boxer. How that would have tickled Chatterer had he heard it.

Now that Chatterer had disappeared, Boxer began to wonder what he should do next. It suddenly came to him that he was in a strange place. None of the trees or stumps about there was familiar. There wasn't a single familiar thing to be seen anywhere. A queer feeling of uneasiness crept over Boxer. He couldn't sit still. No, Sir, he couldn't sit still. He didn't know why, but he couldn't. So, Boxer started on aimlessly. He had nothing in particular to do and nowhere in particular to go.

Presently he noticed the first of the Black Shadows creeping through the Green Forest. Somehow those Black Shadows made him think of home. Probably Mother Bear and Woof-Woof were back there by this time. He wondered if they had missed him and would start looking for him. If he didn't see them, how would he ever know whether or not they looked for him? How would he ever know if he really did get even with them by making them anxious? Why not go back near the great windfall and watch?

"Of course, I won't go home," muttered Boxer to himself, as he shuffled along. "I've left home for good. I'll just go back and hide near there where I can watch and see all that happens. It will be great fun to watch Mother Bear and Woof-Woof hunt for me. I guess I'll hurry a little," he added, as he noticed how the creeping Black Shadows had increased. So, Boxer began to run.

"I didn't think home was so far," he panted at last, looking fearfully over his shoulder at the Black Shadows. "Ha, there is the great windfall!" he added joyously, as he spied a pile of fallen trees in the distance.

He approached it carefully, stopping often to look and listen, for you know he didn't want to be seen by Mother Bear or Woof-Woof. At least, he thought he didn't want to be seen by them, though way down inside that was just what he did want.

He heard no one and saw no one. Presently he was close to that windfall. A great longing for home swept over him. He no longer wanted to get even with anybody. All he wanted was home and mother. Perhaps

Mother Bear and Woof-Woof hadn't returned yet and he could slip in. Then they would never know. Boxer slipped around the old windfall to where he thought the entrance was. There wasn't any! It wasn't the right windfall! Boxer knew right then and there that he was lost, that he was a lone, lost little Bear out in the Great World. He sat down and began to cry.

Chapter XXVII
A Dreadful Night for a Little Bear

A lot of people, great and small,
Are like a frightened little Bear —
Where danger there is none at all
They somehow get a dreadful scare.

Mother Bear.

MORE and more Black Shadows crept through the Green Forest and all around Boxer, the lone, lost little Bear, as he sat crying and wishing with all his might that he never, never had thought of running away. He wanted to be back in the great windfall which had been his home. He wanted Mother Bear. "Boo, hoo, hoo," sobbed the little Bear, "I would just as soon have a spanking. I wouldn't mind it at all if only I had my Mother. Boo, hoo, hoo."

Now there are many keen ears in the Green Forest after dark, and no one can cry there and not be heard. Hooty the Owl was the first to hear those sobs, and on wings that made no sound at all he flew to see what was the matter. Perched on top of a tall stump just back of Boxer, it didn't take Hooty long to understand that this little Bear was lost.

"He needs a lesson," thought Hooty. "He needs a lesson. He must have run away from home. There is nothing around here for him to fear, but it will be a good thing for him to think here is. Here goes to give him a scare he won't forget in a hurry."

Hooty drew a long breath and then hooted as only he can. It was so sudden, so loud and so fierce, that it was enough to frighten even one accustomed to it. Boxer, who never had heard that call close at hand before, was so frightened he lost his balance and fell over on his back, his legs waving helplessly. But he didn't stay on his back. I should say not! In a twinkling he was on his feet and running pell-mell.

Again, rang out Hooty's terrible hunting call, and Boxer was sure that it was right at his heels. As a matter of fact, Hooty had not moved from the tall stump. Headlong Boxer raced through the woods. And because it was quite dark and because he was trying to look behind him, instead of watching where he was going, he pitched heels over head down the bank of the Laughing Brook, splash into a little pool where Billy Mink was fishing. The tumble and the wetting frightened the little Bear more than ever, and Billy Mink's angry snarl didn't make him feel any better. Without so much as a glance at Billy Mink, he scrambled to his feet and up the bank, sure that a new and terrible enemy was at his heels.

More heedlessly than ever he raced through the Green Forest and just by chance entered the thicket where Mrs. Lightfoot the Deer had a certain wonderful secret. Mrs. Lightfoot jumped, making a crash of brush.

"Oh-oo," moaned Boxer, dodging to one side and continuing headlong. When he could run no more, he crept under a pile of brush and there he spent the rest of the night, the most dreadful night he ever had known or was likely ever to know again. Old Man Coyote happened along and yelled as only he can, and unless you know what it is, that sound is quite dreadful. Boxer never had heard it close at hand before, and he didn't recognize it. He was sure that only a great and terrible creature could make such a dreadful noise, and he shook with fear for an hour after.

So, all night long the little Bear heard strange sounds and imagined dreadful things and couldn't get a wink of sleep. And all the time not once was any real danger near him. There wasn't a single thing to be afraid of.

HE PITCHED HEELS OVER HEAD DOWN THE BANK OF THE LAUGHING BROOK.

Chapter XXVIII
BOXER GETS HIS OWN BREAKFAST

True independence he has earned
Who for himself to do has learned.

Mother Bear.

IT seemed to Boxer, the lost little Bear, that that dreadful night would last forever; that it never would end. Of course, it didn't last any longer than a night at that season of the year usually does, and it wasn't dreadful at all. The truth is, it was an unusually fine night, and everybody but Boxer and anxious Mother Bear thought so.

Perhaps you can guess just how glad Boxer was to see the Jolly Little Sunbeams chase the Black Shadows out of the Green Forest the next morning. He still felt frightened and very, very lonesome, but things looked very different by daylight, and he felt very much braver and bolder.

First of all, he took a nap. All night he had been awake, for he had been too frightened to sleep. That nap did him a world of good. When he awoke, he felt quite like another Bear. And the first thing he thought of was breakfast.

Now always before Mother Bear had furnished Boxer with his breakfast and with all his other meals. But there was no Mother Bear to do it this morning, and his stomach was very empty. If anything were to be put in it, he was the one who would have to put it there.

Just thinking of breakfast made Boxer hungrier than ever. He couldn't lie still. He must have something to eat, and he must have it soon. He crawled out from under the pile of brush, shook himself, and tried to decide where to go in search of a breakfast. But being lost, of course he had no idea which way to turn.

"I guess it doesn't make much difference," grumbled Boxer. "Whichever way I go, I guess I'll find something to eat if I keep going long enough."

So, Boxer started out. And because he had something on his mind, something to do, he forgot that he was lonesome, and he forgot to be afraid. He just couldn't think of anything but breakfast. Now while he never had had to get food for himself before, Boxer had watched Mother Bear getting food and felt that he knew just how to go about it.

He found a thoroughly rotted old stump and pulled it apart. It happened that he found nothing there to eat. But a few minutes later he forgot all about this disappointment as he pulled over a small log and saw ants scurrying in every direction. He promptly swept them into his mouth with his tongue and smacked his lips at the taste of them. He didn't leave that place until not another ant was to be seen.

By and by he dug out certain tender little roots and ate them. How he knew where to dig for them, he couldn't have told himself. He just knew, that was all. Something inside him prompted him to stop and dig, and he did so.

Once he chased a Wood Mouse into a hole and wasted a lot of time trying to dig him out. But it was exciting and a lot of fun, so he didn't mind much, even when he had to give up. He caught three or four beetles and near the Laughing Brook surprised a young frog. Altogether he made a very good breakfast. And because he got it all himself, with no help from anyone, he enjoyed it more than any breakfast he could remember. And suddenly he felt quite a person of the Great World and quite equal to taking care of himself. He forgot that he had cried for his mother only the night before. The Great World wasn't such a bad place after all.

Chapter XXIX
BOXER HAS A PAINFUL LESSON

Don't judge a stranger by his looks,
Lest they may prove to be deceiving.
The stupid-looking may be smart
In ways you'll find beyond believing.

Mother Bear.

HAVING succeeded in getting his own breakfast, and a very good one at that, Boxer felt quite set up, as the saying is. He felt chesty. That is to say, he felt big, self-important, independent. For a little cub who had cried most of the night from loneliness and fear, Boxer showed a surprising change. The light of day, a full stomach, and the feeling that he was able to take care of himself had made a new Bear of that little cub. Anyway, he felt so and thought so.

"I'm not afraid of anybody or anything," boasted the foolish little Bear to himself, as he wandered along through the Green Forest. "I'm glad I left home. I'm glad I am out in the Great World. I guess I know about all there is to know. Anyway, I guess I know all there is any need of knowing."

As he said this, Boxer stood up and swelled himself out and looked so funny that Prickly Porky the Porcupine, who happened along just then, just had to chuckle down inside, and this is something that Prickly Porky seldom does.

"That little rascal must have run away from his mother, and he thinks he is smart and knows all there is to know. I don't believe that even Mother Bear could tell him anything just now. She would be wasting her breath. He needs a lesson or two in practical experience. I believe I'll give him one just for his own good," thought Prickly Porky.

There was something almost like a twinkle in Prickly Porky's usually dull eyes as he slowly waddled straight toward Boxer. Boxer heard the rustle of Prickly Porky's tail dragging through the leaves and turned to see who was coming. What he saw was, of course, the stupidest-looking fellow in all the Green Forest.

It was the first time Boxer had seen Prickly Porky, and he had no idea who he was. Boxer stood up and stared in the rudest and most impolite manner. He wasn't afraid. This fellow was no bigger than he, and he was too stupid-looking and too slow to be dangerous.

Boxer was standing in a narrow little path, and Prickly Porky was coming up this little path straight toward him. One of them would have to step aside for the other. It didn't enter Boxer's head that he should be that one. As Prickly Porky drew near, Boxer growled a warning. It was the best imitation of Mother Bear's deep, grumbly-rumbly growl that Boxer could manage. It was hard work for Prickly Porky to keep from laughing right out when he heard it.

But he acted just as if he didn't hear it. He kept right on. Then he pretended to see Boxer for the first time. "Step aside, little cub, step aside and let me pass," said he.

To be called "little cub" just when he was feeling so important, and grown-up was more than Boxer could stand. His little eyes grew red with anger.

"Step aside yourself," he growled. "Step aside yourself, if you don't want to get hurt."

Prickly Porky didn't step aside. He kept right on coming. He didn't hurry, and he didn't appear to be in the least afraid. It was plain that he expected Boxer to get out of his way. Boxer drew back his lips and showed all his little white teeth. Then he slowly reached out one paw and prepared to strike Prickly Porky on the side of the head if he came any nearer.

Chapter XXX
BOXER IS SADDER BUT MUCH WISER

Experience is not a preacher,
But has no equal as a teacher.
Mother Bear.

SAMMY JAY happened along in the Green Forest just in time to see the meeting between Boxer and Prickly Porky the Porcupine. He saw at once that this was the first time Boxer had seen Prickly Porky, and that he had no idea who this fellow in the path was.

"If that little Bear has any sense at all, he'll be polite and get out of Prickly Porky's way," muttered Sammy. "But I'm afraid he hasn't any sense. He looks to me all puffed up, as if he thinks he knows all there is to know. He'll find out he doesn't in just about a minute if he stays there. Hi, there! Don't do that! Don't hit him!"

This last was screamed at Boxer, who had stretched out a paw as if to strike Prickly Porky as soon as he was near enough. But the warning came too late. Prickly Porky had kept right on coming along that little path, and just as Sammy Jay screamed, Boxer struck.

"Wow!" yelled Boxer, dancing about and holding up one paw, the paw with which he had struck at Prickly Porky, and on his face was such a look of amazement that Sammy Jay laughed so that he nearly tumbled from his perch.

"Wow, Wow!" yelled Boxer, still dancing about and shaking that paw.

"Pull it out. Pull it out at once, before it gets in deeper," commanded Sammy Jay, when he could stop laughing long enough.

"Pull what out?" asked Boxer rather sullenly, for he didn't like being laughed at. No one does when in trouble.

"That little spear that is sticking in your paw," replied Sammy. "If you don't, you'll have a terribly sore paw."

Boxer looked at his paw. Sure enough, there was one of Prickly Porky's little spears. He took hold of it with his teeth and started to pull. Then he let go and shook his paw. "Wow! that hurts!" he cried, the tears in his eyes.

"Of course, it hurts," replied Sammy Jay. "And if you don't do as I tell you and pull it out now, it will hurt a great deal more. That paw will get so sore you can't use it. It is a lucky thing for you, young fellow, that you were in too much of a hurry and struck too soon. If you had waited a second longer, you would have filled your paw with those little spears. What were you thinking of, anyway? Don't you know that no one ever interferes with Prickly Porky? It never pays to. Even Buster Bear, big as he is, is polite to Prickly Porky."

Boxer sat down and looked at his paw carefully. That little spear, or quill, was right in the tenderest part. It must be pulled out. Sammy Jay was right about that. Boxer shut his teeth on that little spear and jerked back his head quick and hard. Out came the little spear. Boxer whimpered a little as he licked the place where the little spear had been. After he had licked it a minute or two, that paw felt better.

Meanwhile Prickly Porky had paid no attention whatever to the little Bear. He had slowly waddled on up the little path, quite as if no one were about. He was attending strictly to his own business. But inside he was chuckling.

"That scamp got off easy," he muttered. "It would have been a good thing for him if he had had a few more of those little spears to pull out. I guess that in the future he will take care to leave me alone. There is nothing like teaching the young to respect their elders."

Chapter XXXI
BOXER MEETS A POLITE LITTLE FELLOW

Because another is polite
Pray do not think he cannot fight.
Mother Bear.

THE memories of little folks are short, so far as their troubles are concerned. Hardly was Boxer, the runaway little Bear, out of sight of Prickly Porky the Porcupine than his eyes, ears and nose were so busy trying to discover new things that he hardly thought of his recent trouble. To be sure that paw from which he had pulled one of Prickly Porky's little spears was sore, but not enough so to worry him much. And there were so many other things to think about that he couldn't waste time on troubles that were over.

So, the little Bear wandered this way and that way, as something new caught his eyes or some strange sound demanded to be looked into. He was having a wonderful time, for he felt that he was indeed out in the Great World, and it was a wonderful and beautiful place. If he thought of his twin sister, Woof-Woof, at all, it was to pity her tagging along at Mother Bear's heels and doing only those things which Mother Bear said she could.

By and by something white moving about near an old stump caught his attention. At once he hurried over to satisfy his curiosity. When he got near enough, he discovered a little fellow dressed in black-and-white. He had a big plumy tail, and he was very busy minding his own business. He hardly glanced at Boxer.

Boxer stared at him for a few minutes. "Hello," he ventured finally.

"Good morning. It is a fine morning, isn't it?" said the little stranger politely.

"What are you doing?" demanded the little Bear rudely.

"Just minding my own business," replied the little stranger pleasantly. "Where is your mother?"

"I don't know, and I don't care. I've left home," said Boxer, trying to look big and important.

"You don't say!" exclaimed the little stranger. "Aren't you rather small to be starting out alone in the Great World?"

Now Boxer was so much bigger than this little stranger in black-and-white, and the little stranger was so very polite, that already Boxer felt that the little stranger must be afraid of him. All Boxer's previous feeling of bigness and importance came back to him. He wanted to show off. He wanted this little stranger to respect him. To have that stranger suggest that he was rather small to be out alone in the Great World hurt Boxer's pride. In fact, it made him angry.

"If I were as small as you, perhaps I would feel that way," retorted Boxer rudely.

"I didn't use the right word. I should have said young instead of small," explained the stranger mildly. "Of course, I am small compared with you, but I am fully grown and have been out in the Great World a long time, while you are very young and just starting out. I wonder if your mother knows where you are."

"It is none of your business whether my mother knows or not," retorted Boxer more rudely than before, for he was growing more and more angry.

"Certainly not. I haven't said it was," replied the stranger, still speaking politely. "I am not in the least interested. Besides, I know anyway. I know that she doesn't know. I know that you have run away, and I know that you have some bitter lessons to learn before you will be fitted to live by yourself in the Great World. If you will just step aside, I will be much obliged. There is a big piece of bark just back of you under which there may be some fat beetles."

Chapter XXXII
Boxer Wishes He Hadn't

This is, you'll find, the law of fate:
Regrets are always just too late.

Mother Bear.

SAMMY JAY had followed Boxer, for he felt sure that things were bound to happen wherever that little Bear was. So, Sammy saw his meeting with Jimmy Skunk. He saw how polite Jimmy was and how very impolite the little Bear was.

Sammy understood perfectly. He knew that probably Boxer knew nothing at all about Jimmy Skunk and never had heard of that little bag of scent carried by Jimmy and dreaded by all of Jimmy's neighbors. He knew that the little Bear was rude, simply because he was so much bigger than Jimmy Skunk that he could see no reason for being polite, especially as Jimmy had asked him to do something he didn't want to do.

When Jimmy Skunk began to lose patience, Sammy Jay thought it was time for him to give Boxer a little advice. "Don't be silly! Do as Jimmy Skunk tell you to, or you will be the sorriest little Bear that ever lived!" screamed Sammy, as he saw Jimmy's great plume of a tail begin to go up, which is Jimmy's signal of danger.

But Boxer, foolish little Bear that he was, couldn't see anything to fear from one so much smaller than he. So, he paid no attention to Jimmy's request that he step aside. Instead, he laughed in the most impudent way.

"Run! Run!" screamed Sammy Jay.

Boxer didn't move. Jimmy Skunk stamped angrily with his front feet. Then something happened. Yes, sir, something happened. It was so sudden and so unexpected that Boxer didn't know exactly what had happened, but he was very much aware that it *had* happened. Something was in his eyes and made them smart and for a few minutes blinded him. Something was choking him; it seemed to him he could hardly breathe. And there was the most awful odor he ever had smelled.

Boxer rolled over and over and over on the ground. He was trying to get away from that awful odor. But he couldn't. He couldn't, for the very good reason that he carried it along with him. You see, Jimmy Skunk had punished that silly little Bear by throwing on him a little of that powerful scent he always carries with him to use in time of danger or when provoked.

"What did I tell you? What did I tell you?" screamed Sammy Jay. "I guess you won't interfere with Jimmy Skunk again in a hurry. It serves you right. It serves you just right. But it is hard on the people who live about here. Yes, sir, it is hard on them to have all the sweetness of the Green Forest spoiled by that scent of Jimmy Skunk's. I can't stand it myself, so I'll be moving along. It serves you right, you silly little Bear. It serves you right." With this Sammy Jay flew away.

Boxer knew then that Jimmy Skunk had been the cause of this new and dreadful trouble he was in, and great respect mingled with fear took possession of him. And oh, how Boxer wished that he hadn't been impolite! How he wished he hadn't refused to do as Jimmy Skunk had politely asked him to!

"I wish I hadn't! I wish I hadn't! I wish I hadn't!" sobbed Boxer over and over, as he tried to get away from that dreadful smell and couldn't.

Chapter XXXIII
WOOF-WOOF TURNS UP HER NOSE

I pray you be not one of those
Who boast the scornful turned-up nose.
Mother Bear.

NOW all the time that Boxer had been losing himself more and more and getting into more and more trouble, Mother Bear had been worrying about him, and she and his twin sister, Woof-Woof, had been everywhere but the right place looking for him.

You remember that Mother Bear and Woof-Woof had been away from home when Boxer decided to run away. When they returned, Boxer had been gone so long that Mother Bear's nose failed to find enough of his scent to follow. So, when she started to look for him, she started in the wrong direction. Of course, she had to take Woof-Woof with her, and because Woof-Woof got tired after a while, Mother Bear couldn't hunt as thoroughly as she would have done had she been alone.

At first, Woof-Woof felt very badly indeed at the loss of her little twin brother. Down in her heart she admired him for his boldness in running away, but when she thought of all the dreadful things that might happen to him out in the Great World, she became very sorrowful. This was at first. After she had tramped and tramped and tramped behind Mother Bear, tramped until her feet ached, she became cross. She blamed Boxer, and quite rightly, for those aching feet. The more they ached, the crosser she became, until she tried to make herself believe that she didn't care what happened to that heedless brother.

"I don't care if I never see him again," she grumbled. "I don't care what happens to him. Whatever happens will serve him right. I wish Mother Bear would remember that my legs are not as long as hers. I'm tired. I want to rest. I want to rest, I do. I want to rest. Ouch! My feet are getting sore."

Now such news as Jimmy Skunk's punishment of Boxer travels fast through the Green Forest, and it wasn't long before the story of it reached Mrs. Bear's ears. She growled dreadful threats of what she would do if she met Jimmy Skunk, though she knew very well that she would politely step aside if she did meet him, and then she started for the place where Boxer had been given his lessons in politeness by Jimmy Skunk.

There was no doubt about the place when they reached it. "Phew!" cried Woof-Woof, holding her nose.

Mother Bear merely grunted and started off faster than before. Woof-Woof had to run to keep up with her. Mother Bear had that smell to guide her now. She knew that all she had to do now to find her runaway son was to follow up that smell.

So, it was that just as the Black Shadows were beginning to creep through the Green Forest, and poor little Boxer, a very lonely, miserable and frightened little Bear, was beginning to dread another night, he heard a crashing in the brush, and out came Mother Bear and Woof-Woof. With a glad squeal of joy, Boxer started to run toward them. But a growl, such an ugly growl, from Mother Bear stopped him.

"Don't you come near us," said she. "You can follow us, but don't you dare come a step nearer than you are now. It would serve you right if we had nothing more to do with you, but after all, you are rather small to be wandering about alone. Besides, there is no knowing what more disgrace you would get us into. Now come along."

Boxer looked at Woof-Woof for some sign of sympathy. But Woof-Woof held her head very high and turned up her nose at him. "Phew!" said she.

Chapter XXXIV
ALL IS WELL AT LAST

If you are taught not to forget
Your punishment you'll ne'er regret.
Mother Bear.

MRS. BEAR is one of those mothers who believe in punishment. She believes that the cub who is never punished for wrong-doing is almost sure to grow up to be of little or no use in the Great World, provided he lives to grow up at all. She doubts if he will live to grow up at all. So, her cubs are promptly punished when they disobey or do wrong, and they are punished in a way to make them remember.

Now when Boxer, the lost little cub who had had such a dreadful time, saw Mother Bear and his sister Woof-Woof, he thought all his troubles were at an end. Perhaps you can guess what his feelings were when he was stopped short by a growl from Mother Bear. He wanted — oh, how he wanted — to rush up to her and snuggle against her and feel her big paws gently patting him.

But there was to be none of that. It was plain that Mother Bear meant exactly what she said when she told him to come no nearer. And when he looked to his twin sister, Woof-Woof, she turned up her nose and it was quite clear that she wanted nothing to do with him.

Poor little Boxer. He didn't understand it at all at first. You see, in the joy of being found, he had forgotten that he still carried that dreadful scent with which Jimmy Skunk had punished him, and so no one, not even his mother or sister, would want him very near. When Woof-Woof cried "Phew!" as she turned up her nose, he remembered. He hung his head and meekly shuffled along after his mother and sister, taking care to get no nearer to them. He didn't dare to, for every few steps Mother Bear would swing her head around and grumble a warning.

And this was just the beginning of Boxer's punishment. Day after day he tagged along, far behind, but always keeping his mother and sister in sight. You may be sure he took care to do that. He had had quite enough of seeing the Great World alone. Not for anything would he be lost again. But it was hard, very hard, to have only what was left when Mother Bear found a feast. What he didn't know was that Mother Bear always took care that there should be a fair share left. At such times Woof-Woof took great joy in smacking her lips while Boxer sat up watching from a distance.

When they slept, Boxer had to curl up by himself. At first, this was the hardest of all. But little by little he got used to it. He didn't know and Woof-Woof didn't know, but Mother Bear did, that this was good for him; it was making him more and more sure of himself. And tagging along behind as he did every day was doing the same thing. He was always looking for something that Mother Bear and Woof-Woof might have missed. And so, he learned to use his eyes and his nose, and his ears better than Woof-Woof did, for she depended more on Mother Bear, being right at her heels.

As the days passed, Boxer's coat became more and more free from that dreadful scent. Boxer had become so used to it that he didn't notice it at all, so he wasn't conscious when it began to grow less. At last it got so that it was hardly to be noticed excepting on rainy or very damp days. For a long time after Mother Bear had permitted him to resume his place with Woof-Woof, she drove him away on such days.

So, at last Boxer's punishment ended. Mother Bear gave him a good talking to and said that she hoped this would be a lesson he never would forget. "Yes'm, it will," he had replied very meekly, and he knew it would. Then he took his place once more, save that now, instead of following at Mother Bear's heels, he allowed Woof-Woof to do that, and he followed her. Though Woof-Woof didn't suspect it, he preferred it so.

So, Buster Bear's twins grew and grew until everyone said that they were the finest young Bears ever seen in the Green Forest.

Billy Mink says that these cubs have received attention enough and that there are other people who should be considered. Perhaps Billy is right, though I suspect he is thinking of himself. Anyway, this ends the Green Forest series, and the next book will be the first in the Smiling Pool series. The title will be Billy Mink.

THE END

About Thornton W. Burgess

Thornton W. Burgess, an American author, naturalist and conservationist, was born on January 17, 1874, in Sandwich, Cape Cod, Massachusetts. Shortly after his birth, his father passed away and Burgess was raised by his mother. With no father in his life, the young Burgess worked on numerous different jobs to support his mother; and the circumstance that would enormously impact his writings came when he worked for Mr. Chipman, who lived in a wildlife habitat of woodland and wetland. This habitat later became the setting of many of his stories in which he refers to as Smiling Pool and the Old Briar Patch.

Burgess's passion was writing. In 1893, after attending a business college in Boston for several months, he left to move to Springfield, Massachusetts and became an editorial assistant at Phelps Publishing Company. He bought a home in Hampden, Massachusetts in 1925 and lived there for the rest of his life. However, he frequently returned to Sandwich as he always considered Sandwich to be his spiritual home.

In 1910. Burgess published his debut novel, *Old Mother West Wind*. In this book, readers meet many of popular characters found in later books and stories including Peter Rabbit, and his friends, Grandfather Frog, Reddy Fox, Jimmy Skunk, along with Sammy Jay, Bobby Raccoon, Joe Otter, Billy Mink, Jerry Muskrat, Spotty the Turtle and of course, Old Mother West Wind and many others.

For the next five decades, with his endless love for the nature and the wildlife, Burgess wrote more than 15,000 short stories for newspaper column *Bedtime Stories*, and 170 books. His works have been published around the world in many languages such as French, German, Italian, Spanish, and obscure language Gaelic.

Burgess wrote the novels alongside his friend and chief illustrator, Harrison Cady of Rockport Massachusetts and New York. Cady gave the familiar form of animal characters that are recognizable today.

In 1960, Burgess published his final book, an autobiography entitled

Now I Remember, Autobiography of an Amateur Naturalist, depicting memories of his early life in Sandwich as well as his career highlights. That same year, he published his 15,000th newspaper column.

Burgess was also involved in conservation endeavors and worked on several projects over his lifetime including:

- *The Green Meadow Club* for land conservation programs,
- Helped pass laws protecting migrant wildlife,
- *The Bedtime Stories Club* for wildlife protection programs,
- *Happy Jack Squirrel Saving Club* for War Savings Stamps & Bonds,
- *The Radio Nature League* broadcast from WBZA Springfield, MA.

Burgess died on June 5, 1965, at the age of 91. For more than one century, his fascinating stories of the animal world that he created have captivated many children and their parents. These stories illustrated his love for the natural world; and have sparked the same kind of passion in his readers.

Books by Thornton W. Burgess

BEDTIME STORY-BOOKS
The Adventures of

1. Reddy Fox
2. Johnny Chuck
3. Peter Cottontail
4. Unc' Billy Possum
5. Mr. Mocker
6. Jerry Muskrat
7. Danny Meadow Mouse
8. Grandfather Frog
9. Chatterer, the Red Squirrel
10. Sammy Jay
11. Buster Bear
12. Old Mr. Toad
13. Prickly Porky
14. Old Man Coyote
15. Paddy the Beaver
16. Poor Mrs. Quack
17. Bobby Coon
18. Jimmy Skunk
19. Bob White
20. Ol' Mistah Buzzard

MOTHER WEST WIND SERIES
1. Old Mother West Wind
2. Mother West Wind's Children
3. Mother West Wind's Animal Friends
4. Mother West Wind's Neighbors
5. Mother West Wind "Why" Stories
6. Mother West Wind "How" Stories
7. Mother West Wind "When" Stories
8. Mother West Wind "Where" Stories

GREEN MEADOW SERIES
1. Happy Jack
2. Mrs. Peter Rabbit
3. Bowser the Hound
4. Old Granny Fox

GREEN FOREST SERIES
1. Lightfoot the Deer
2. Blacky the Crow
3. Whitefoot the Wood Mouse
4. Buster Bear's Twins

WISHING-STONE SERIES
1. Tommy and the Wishing-stone
2. Tommy's Wishes Come True
3. Tommy's Change of Heart

SMILING POOL SERIES
1. Billy Mink
2. Little Joe Otter
3. Jerry Muskrat at Home
4. Longlegs the Heron

The Burgess Bird Book for Children

The Burgess Animal Book for Children

The Burgess Flower Book for Children